PRAISE FOR
The Lifeguards

"A book that is at once riveting and relevant as it unpeels the various meanings of motherhood, family, and loyalty. I tore through it." —Miranda Cowley Heller, #1 *New York Times* bestselling author of *The Paper Palace*

"At once a love letter to my favorite city and a tense interrogation of the bonds of motherhood, The Lifeguards places three very different women in the pressure cooker of one Austin summer and watches the sparks ignite. I love a carefully crafted mystery where all the tricky pieces fit just so. . . . A masterclass." —Chandler Baker, *New York Times* bestselling author of *The Husbands*

"The Lifeguards combines dark intrigue with complex family dynamics and witty social observation. It's a highly charged, compelling page-turner that kept me guessing till the end. Sun, secrets, tequila, and twists—what's not to like?!" —Sophie Kinsella, #1 *New York Times* bestselling author of *The Party Crasher*

"A polyphonic story . . . Ward, with her keen eye for detail and a terrific sense of exactly when to deliver a punchline, knows her characters well. . . . She allows her characters to be petty and myopic, to make the wrong choices again and again, to fail badly, then dust themselves off and try again. Her people are resilient, with a deep longing to do better—particularly for their children."

—*The New York Times Book Review*

"Shake up a margarita and light a citronella; you'll be in this one for awhile." —*Good Housekeeping*

"Ward expertly weaves together each woman's point of view as well as commentary from entertaining neighborhood listservs, secret text messages, and police reports for one of the first true beach reads of the year."

—*E! ONLINE*

"[A]s a commentary on privileged, suburban America, Ward packs a mean punch, delivering crystalline observations with a hearty side of wit and tongue-in-cheek humor."

—*Bookreporter*

"This thriller will keep you turning pages and longing for your own dip in Barton Springs." —*Austin Monthly*

"Insanely addictive, deliciously propulsive, and wholly unpredictable . . . will take your breath away. Big Little Lies meets Mare of Easttown in this masterful, explosive suspense novel set against the backdrop of sun-drenched Austin. A tense and taut thriller brimming with secrets, complex, twisty female friendships, and whiplash plot twists, this is the perfect summer read best devoured with a strong margarita."

—May Cobb, author of *The Hunting Wives*

"Amanda Eyre Ward brings all the thrills of Big Little Lies to the privileged, sun-dappled private patios of Austin's 'rich mom' set. The result is a juicy and irresistible roller coaster of a read."   —Allyson Lynn, author of *Bread*

"Arresting . . . Like a cool lake on a hot day, this story hits the spot."   —*Publishers Weekly*

PRAISE FOR
The Jetsetters

A *New York Times* bestseller
A *New York Times* Editors' Choice
Reese's Book Club x Hello Sunshine Pick
Named One of the Best Beach Reads of 2020 by *PARADE,*
O: The Oprah Magazine, and *Good Housekeeping*

"Are you ready to set sail on a literary adventure? I love the sense of adventure in this story—it's about a disconnected family that reunites on a cruise ship traveling through Europe. If you're packing for Spring Break, be sure to include a copy of this fun read."

—Reese Witherspoon
(Reese's Book Club x Hello Sunshine Pick)

"Dysfunctional family goes away together on a Mediterranean cruise: What's not to love? This novel fell squarely in my wheelhouse and I was delighted anew in every port. *The Jetsetters* is fun, sexy, and engrossing."

—Elin Hilderbrand, #1 *New York Times*
bestselling author of *Summer of '69*

"At the heart of [Amanda Eyre] Ward's comic story of family estrangement and long-buried trauma is the adage 'There's no such thing as a free ride'—but her novel's ultimate destination is both surprising and transporting."

—*The New York Times Book Review* (Editors' Choice)

"Ward reveals that she has a way with humor. . . . The author's eye for forced fun is exquisite. . . . There is a real poignancy in this novel, as wounded characters struggle to regain childhood loyalties. Ward nails how family expeditions are ruined and saved, over and over again, by fleeting moments of connection, and the consensus to survive without killing one another."

—Judy Blundell, *The New York Times Book Review*

"The exuberant activity aboard the *Splendido Marveloso* is no match for the fireworks set off as the lies explode. . . . Full of wicked humor and delicious destination details."

—*People* (Book of the Week)

"The exact kind of hilarious, drama-filled read that will keep you hooked this summer."   —*O: The Oprah Magazine*

"Trust us: Every family will see something of theirs in this one."   —*Good Housekeeping*

"[Amanda] Eyre Ward's genuine, hilarious writing rotates between each characters' perspective over the course of a weeklong European cruise, producing a story of deep-seated familial discord and desire that falls apart as spectacularly as it wills itself back together. If you're in the market for an escape, look no further."   —*Esquire*

BY AMANDA EYRE WARD

The Lifeguards
The Jetsetters
The Sober Lush (with Jardine Libaire)
The Nearness of You
The Same Sky
Close Your Eyes
Love Stories in This Town
Forgive Me
How to Be Lost
Sleep Toward Heaven

The Lifeguards

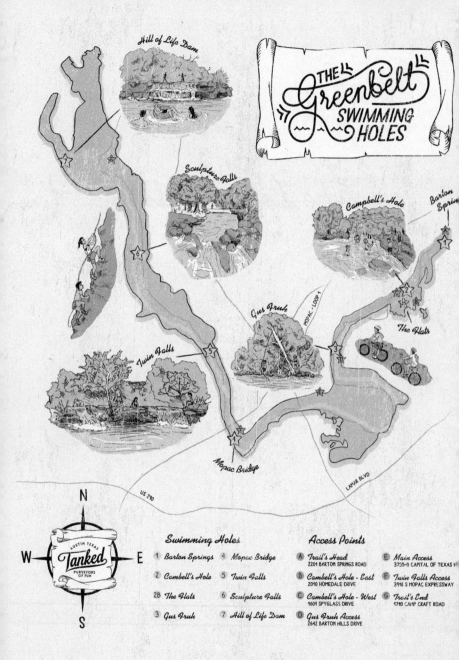

Hill of Life Dam

Sculpture Falls

Campbell's Hole

Barton Springs

Gus Fruh

The Flats

Twin Falls

MOPAC - LOOP 1

Mopac Bridge

US 290

LAMAR BLVD

THE Greenbelt SWIMMING HOLES

N
W · E
S

AUSTIN TEXAS
Tanked
PURVEYORS OF FUN

Swimming Holes

1 Barton Springs
2 Cambell's Hole
2B The Flats
3 Gus Fruh
4 Mopac Bridge
5 Twin Falls
6 Sculpture Falls
7 Hill of Life Dam

Access Points

A Trail's Head
2201 BARTON SPRINGS ROAD

B Cambell's Hole - East
2010 HOMEDALE DRIVE

C Cambell's Hole - West
1601 SPYGLASS DRIVE

D Gus Fruh Access
2642 BARTON HILLS DRIVE

E Main Access
3755-B CAPITAL OF TEXAS H

F Twin Falls Access
3918 S MOPAC EXPRESSWAY

G Trail's End
1710 CAMP CRAFT ROAD

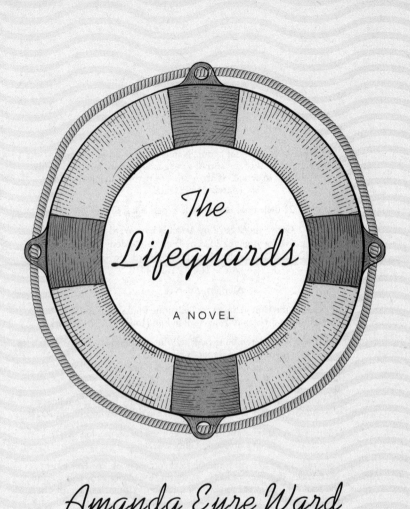

The
Lifeguards

A NOVEL

Amanda Eyre Ward

BALLANTINE BOOKS

NEW YORK

2023 Ballantine Books Trade Paperback Edition

Copyright © 2022 by Amanda Eyre Ward
Book club guide copyright © 2023 by Penguin Random House LLC
Excerpt from *The Peacocks* by Amanda Eyre Ward copyright © 2023 by Amanda Eyre Ward

ISBN 978-0-593-15946-0
Ebook ISBN 978-0-593-15945-3

Printed in the United States of America on acid-free paper

randomhousebooks.com
randomhousebookclub.com

9 8 7 6 5 4 3 2 1

ScoutAutomatedPrintCode

Book design by Debbie Glasserman

FOR TWENTY YEARS
From Blue Lakes to Kauai
For Michelle

Prologue

IT WAS SO STRANGE to be *the older woman*. I'd always been the little one, the kid sister, the vixen. Sly and quick, that was me—a star gymnast, wild. In high school, I was the queen. I'd graduated, and as planned, escaped. But Austin, Texas, had been less triumphant than I'd anticipated. Community college parties were crowded and strange. Nobody knew me, and without my big brothers, I was lost. Everyone at home was so proud of me that I couldn't go back. I'd even given my favorite teddy bear to my baby brother, Arlo. He'd promised to keep Beary safe when I was gone. Some nights, I wished I had Beary to snuggle, even thought I was allegedly grown up.

I was nothing in the big city. My professors talked too fast. My job at the Barton Hills 7-Eleven left me prey to late-night predators: drunk kids, every flavor of unsettling adult.

I was failing two classes when I met him. He had the glitter, and I wanted it back.

I wore makeup even though we were meeting at the Barton Springs Pool. I shaved, made sure I smelled like flowers. My heart beat fast, so good, I drove above the speed limit. In

my bag, I had a towel, sunglasses, and a paperback novel—
Carrie by Stephen King. It was the book I was reading—I'd
thought about subbing in something to impress him, but
why? Neither of us wanted to talk.

The parking lot was packed but I found a space. It was so
hot the air felt thick; I walked toward the park entrance as if
through butter. My sundress stuck to my skin. I paid the entrance fee and stamped my own hand with ink. The kid in the
ticket booth was the same age as my date.

I found a shady spot under a tree and unrolled my pink
towel. I gazed at the pool, which I knew was freezing cold,
fed by an underground spring. I lifted my dress, knowing my
bikini would bring covert glances. I hadn't kept up my punishing gymnastics training for nothing. I couldn't help it: I
brought my arms over my head and stretched, the sun warm-
ing my skin.

I saw him across the shimmering water. He was leaning on
the lifeguard stand with no shirt on, his chest tanned. He was
off duty but still wore his uniform. I wanted to kiss that chest,
to taste him. I saw the girl in the guard chair trying to get his
attention. When I had been his age—not so long ago—I'd
been careless. Like him, I had not understood my power.

I walked to the edge. Pecan trees towered overhead, reaching into a brilliant Texas sky. I willed him to see me. His eyes
moved across the pool. He removed his sunglasses. I imagined
he was smiling, though it was too far to tell.

He raised an arm and waved. In response, I dove, a flawless
arc. The water was shockingly cold and I began to swim
toward the other side, toward him. My lungs filled with hot
summer air. My muscles firing, perfection. After a few strokes,
I paused and lifted my head.

As I'd wanted, as I'd hoped for, he was swimming right
for me.

The
First Night
of Summer

2019

Liza

OUR BOYS WERE *LIFEGUARDS*, we told ourselves, and were surely safe. Weren't they safe? They knew CPR, had shown us their fanny packs filled with Band-Aids and plastic breathing tubes. Xavier, Bobcat, and Charlie (my son) had taken the course together, weekend mornings at Barton Springs. We'd dropped them off at dawn, the Texas sun just starting to climb above the horizon, making the surface of the spring-fed swimming hole flash red and orange. We'd said we'd walk Lady Bird Lake together, or we'd stand-up paddleboard or grab coffee. Instead, we smiled as we dropped the boys, went home to the adult lives we'd begun to create again, now that our children were fifteen. I was ghostwriting a cookbook; Annette was working at Hola, Amigos Daycare; and Whitney had become an Austin real estate titan.

Now that we no longer had endless summer days with elementary schoolers underfoot, it was harder to connect. But our friendship was unbreakable, as safe as the neighborhood where we'd raised our sweet little kids.

Or so we thought.

By the end of the summer, one of us would be gone.

"WHERE *ARE* THEY?" I said, glancing at my watch. (I liked wearing a thin gold watch I'd bought at an antiques store. Sometimes, I told people it had been my mother's, conjuring an "old money" family that didn't exist. Oh, how I loved the idea of a mother who'd wear such an elegant timepiece on a slim wrist! My actual mother, in contrast, had a tattoo of a snake on her hand.)

It was 11:00 P.M., which was definitely too late.

"Riding their bikes around the neighborhood, they said," said Annette. Her son, Bobcat, was rail-thin and six-three, a reluctant ninth-grade basketball star. Despite Bobcat insisting he just wanted to build computers in his room, Annette's husband forced their son to keep playing. During the last game of the season, an opponent elbowed Bobcat—hard—in the soft place underneath his rib cage. It was awful to see Bobcat's face crumple in pain . . . but he only glanced toward the stands at his father . . . and didn't make a sound.

When my son, Charlie, went over his mountain-bike handles on a trail and cut his forehead, I felt his pain viscerally. I could scarcely watch him pedal away, even now that he wore the most expensive safety equipment available: a two-hundred-dollar full-face helmet, padded bike shorts, neck brace, wrist, elbow, and knee pads, and a back protector made of VPD, whatever that was. Despite Charlie's complaints, I'd bought all the items at Dick's Sporting Goods on layaway. (The sign above the gear was a siren call: YOU CAN BUY THE FEELING OF SAFETY!) Sure, the other kids made fun of him with his braces and helmets, but I'd rather my son be embarrassed than dead.

It was possible, as Charlie had suggested gently, that I had anxiety issues. Maybe, as he'd said, I should "use our money to talk to someone." But you couldn't see a therapist on layaway, now could you? I'd handle my brain when I'd somehow gotten Charlie to college without any major bodily damage. Splurging on things that made me feel more secure was working for me, so I ignored Charlie's complaints and insinuations and loved him hard and bought him safety equipment.

Annette went to every game wearing Austin High colors from head to toe. She had platinum blond hair and bronze skin, wide brown eyes. She carefully sculpted her thick eyebrows into perfect arches, accented her high cheekbones and naturally plump lips with drugstore makeup, and wore expensive jewelry at all times. When Louis (who had been too short to play basketball himself) led cheers for Bobcat from the stands and stomped his feet on the bleachers, tried to start "the wave" and was largely ignored, Annette stood by his side. We all loved Louis, his childlike enthusiasm, but Annette knew, as we all did, that Bobcat played only to please his father but really came alive when explaining the best graphics card for his latest home-built PC.

Louis wanted his son to be the athlete he'd dreamed of becoming himself—he couldn't fathom a person with physical gifts not wanting to use them. I thought it was just a matter of time before Bobcat either became who he was meant to be or stopped trying. Did Annette defend her son behind closed doors? Or was marriage about acquiescence, silencing yourself in the name of marital harmony?

I wouldn't know. I was a single mom, the struggling one in a sea of serene, wealthy wives. Everyone I knew had the money for psychiatrists, aestheticians, Peloton machines, and massages. I didn't own my house. I worried about our electricity bill. I was so nervous that my friends would drop me—*nobody* wanted a single woman at their barbecue.

Sometimes, I drove by neighborhood parties I hadn't been invited to. Not on purpose! I just happened to be going for a swim at Barton Springs, or grabbing a bottle of Sauv Blanc at the Barton Hills Food Mart. On the way home, I'd swing past a friend's house to see the street jammed with cars, the yard filled with people I would have thought would have included me.

Would have included *us*—me and Charlie. If Charlie was with me, we wouldn't mention the fête. If I was alone, I would swallow my sadness. I told myself, as I lay awake in my queen-sized bed littered with cookbooks and recipe notes, that I was glad I could toss and turn without bothering anyone, could eat a bowl of cereal at three in the morning if I wanted to. Or a sandwich. At three in the morning. Hooray!

But on this night, I wasn't alone. I was cozy in the circle of my two best friends, Whitney and Annette, celebrating the end of the school year. The boys would start their first full days as summer lifeguards in the morning.

We had been through so much together in the fifteen years since our children's births. Annette and Whitney both really did seem to love me, which meant everything. I was so scared of losing their warmth.

I watched TV shows and movies about "BFFs," puzzled over women seeming utterly relaxed with each other. Around my best friends, I was very careful. I needed them too much, I knew. I made gift bags for them "just because." I was on high alert, the ultimate people pleaser, shape-shifting into whatever Whitney and Annette wanted: a good listener, someone to praise their choices, free at the spur of the moment for a glass or three of wine. I ignored what I needed to be the perfect friend, terrified they would ditch me.

Among them, I was safe inside the "rich mom" circle. If I messed up and was cast out, I'd just be a woman who couldn't quite afford the neighborhood, and Charlie would feel like I had as a kid: miserable, desperate to escape. He would leave me if the world I made for him wasn't good enough to want to stay. I knew on some level that this chain of causation was overly dramatic, but on the other hand, the securities of wealth were absolutely real. Our rental home fed to schools with resources and college counselors. We had a Neighborhood Watch.

"The boys are fine, Lizey," said Whitney, using her affectionate nickname for me. She was five-two with thick black hair that always fell in a shining curtain as if she'd *just* left a salon chair.

Whitney knew I was a worrier; she passed me the bottle of Chardonnay. We were sipping out of Whitney and Jules's stemless glasses. The glasses were expensive and fashionable, but I liked a stem, myself. Not that I'd ever say so. "You're fine, Lizey," said Whitney. My best friend knew me well: her words made my stomach ease.

I'd met Whitney sixteen years before, when I'd been pregnant with Charlie. I'd arrived in Austin with a few hundred dollars in my wallet, and Whitney had been on floor duty when I'd walked into Zilker Park Realty. She had a friend (Whitney *always* had a friend) whose elderly mother had just moved into a nursing home and was considering renting out her Barton Hills bungalow. As soon as I walked into the twelve-hundred-square-foot house (the kitchen cabinets and refrigerator a perfect 1970s avocado green), I knew that 1308 Oak Glen was where my new life would begin.

The bungalow was probably worth three quarters of a million now, a "teardown." Whitney and Jules had bought it awhile back, becoming my landlords. It was a bit odd how it went down, to be honest: One day Whitney just mentioned that I should write the rent check to *her* from now on. They hadn't raised my rent—not yet—and I was hardly in a position to negotiate, but I'd been a bit confused, even upset, at first. Why hadn't they told me they were buying my home? I never could have bought it myself, but it would have been nice to have been asked, to have been given a chance to bid.

Although I told everyone I was a food writer, I had myriad side hustles to keep us afloat. I was careful, lest any Barton Hills neighbors see me working a menial job. I walked dogs in Round Rock and took on "Tasks" for TaskRabbit. A folder on my desk labeled "Recipe Ideas" was actually a checklist of odd jobs to follow up on each day. Every minute Charlie wasn't home, I was trying to make some money.

It was possible people thought I had "family money" keeping us afloat.

It was possible I allowed—even encouraged—people to make this assumption.

I did not have "family money."

I didn't even have a family.

(Except Charlie. My shining, wonderful Charlie.)

In the end, I'd decided to write the monthly check to Whitney and stop thinking about the whole situation. I wanted to believe Whitney had my best interests at heart. So I made myself believe it.

I adored every inch of our bungalow, even the wall-to-wall shag and vintage appliances. Sometimes, I woke in the middle of the night worrying about Whitney selling and evicting us. But she'd never do that, I told myself, and I usually fell back asleep. At her birthday party the month before, Whitney had drunk a lot of champagne and cornered me by her peonies. "How would you feel," she asked me, slurring a bit, "about a five—or ten—year lease on Oak Glen? How about rent-to-own?" I had shrieked and hugged her, telling her it was my absolute dream come true.

It *was* my absolute dream come true.

But she hadn't mentioned it since.

Our neighborhood, which had been middle-class when I'd moved here, was no longer a place a food writer (or an artist of any kind) could possibly afford. It was built on the edge of the Barton Creek Greenbelt, an eight-mile swath of almost eight hundred acres. From various streets and the land behind the Episcopal church we went to on holidays (joining Whitney and her family—I wanted Charlie to have *some* organized religion and I had none of my own), we could access the trails of sheer limestone cliff walls, dense lush vegetation, and popular swimming holes. You never knew who you'd find on the greenbelt—we'd coined the acronym "WDA" to mean "Weird Dude Alert," so when we were hiking or swimming, we could let the kids know to steer clear without offending anyone. There were so many weird dudes, from stoner University of Texas students, to men walking pit bulls on chains and carrying boom boxes, to homeless campers. There were secret waterfalls and rumored caves. It was a wonderland.

By the time Charlie was born, I had become the sort of mother I'd fervently wished for. (A 180-degree opposite of my actual mom, an aging Cape Cod party girl.) I loved being Liza Bailey, a writer with a bold bob haircut, my bangs cut straight across. I wore Revlon All Night Fuchsia lipstick from the South Lamar Walgreens.

Whitney was generous, hilarious, rich but not spoiled. She'd been a ballet dancer until a hip injury forced her into retirement; her posture was a marvel. She told me where to shop, where to get my hair cut; she introduced me to a chef who needed help writing his first cookbook. As Whitney's star rose, so did mine.

I'd thought I would need a rich husband to pave my path, but a rich best friend was even better.

I wondered sometimes why Whitney had chosen me. I

wanted to believe it was because I was *authentic*, an honest person and a real friend. Sometimes, I feared it was because I was malleable, more loyal than someone who didn't need her so desperately. But Whitney, too, was vulnerable. Like me, she'd had a sad childhood, and was trying in real time to figure out how happiness was supposed to look.

It was easier to figure out the details of adulthood: where to own a house, what to wear. How joy should *feel* was a complete mystery to me. All I ever felt, to be honest, was scared.

By the time Charlie was old enough to ask, I told him his father had died of a heart attack while skiing, a complete fabrication. I even saw the event in my imagination: Patrick, in Vuarnet sunglasses and some fancy ski outfit, falling into fresh snow at a luxury Colorado resort.

I'd never been skiing.

Whitney had kept my secrets.

"YOU'RE FINE, LIZEY," REPEATED Whitney. She tended to repeat herself when she was tipsy.

"I know," I said. Whitney leaned over to hug me, and it felt so wonderful, I almost cried. I had stopped dating years ago. It was too confusing, a distraction. There might be time for my heart later, when Charlie was in college. A deep part of me hoped so.

Annette, oblivious, refilled her glass. She didn't know the real story of Charlie's father, because by the time I met her in prenatal yoga, I'd stopped telling it. She knew me as a quirky single mom, a stylish artist in cat-eye glasses: Whitney had gifted me the expensive frames on my thirty-first birthday and got me a new pair every year from Optique.

I CHECKED MY WATCH again—11:05. I stood, and went out front to have a Marlboro Light. (My smoking was another secret I kept from my son—I'd been addicted since childhood. I placed the blame squarely on my mom, a pack-a-day smoker herself, who taught me how to buy her cigarettes from the Falmouth gas mart when I was a kid, gave me a cig in payment starting when I was twelve.)

As I pushed open the screen door, the heat hit me like a hair dryer aimed at my face. It had been over 90 degrees for a week, and even at night, the temperatures hovered in the eighties. I had just lit my forbidden cigarette when the boys showed up, wheeling into Whitney's driveway and throwing their bikes to the ground. "Mom," said Charlie. He dropped an armful of his protective gear as he moved toward me.

"Charlie, you need to *wear* the pads, not carry them," I admonished, dropping my cigarette into Whitney's terracotta planter before he could see it.

Charlie looked frightened in the dim light of the Brownsons' front porch. His best friends flanked him, boys I'd known since they were toddlers. We'd called them "the Three Musketeers," as we sipped wine or margaritas (which we called "mom margs") on the deck and watched them run around my scrappy yard brandishing wooden swords: red-haired Charlie, blond Xavier, Bobcat with his jet-black hair (so unlike his mother's platinum tresses).

All three boys breathed heavily, their skin flushed from biking in the heat. "Mom," said my son. When I replay this moment later, I can see his eyes searching for mine, seeking a connection. If I could go back in time and change anything, it would be this: I wish I had seen that Charlie was drowning, that he needed me to ask him for the truth. But no—I was buzzed from wine and distracted. I could have said, "You can tell me anything." I could have said, "I'm here."

Instead, worried about Whitney's new carpeting, I said, "Take off your shoes before you come inside. They're covered with mud."

Whitney's son, Xavier, had his hands on his knees. He lifted his head and said, "The greenbelt."

In my boozy haze, I associated the words with weekend afternoons, sunlight through leaves, my son ahead of me on a muddy trail. Magnolia trees and bug spray and take-out sandwiches from ThunderCloud Subs.

"Mom," said Charlie. "There's someone on the greenbelt."

"Someone on the greenbelt?" I repeated. For a moment, I didn't understand—it seemed impossible to darken my leafy visions with violence and danger.

"We didn't do it," said Annette's son, Bobcat. I could still remember Bobcat as a three-year-old in diapers clinging to my leg when it was my turn to pick up the kids at Hola, Amigos Daycare. He'd asked Santa for a bobcat when he was little, and the name had stuck.

"We need to call 911," said Xavier. He pushed his too-long hair off his face. Although he was no longer a child, his blond curls were the same ones he'd had at age five, before Whitney finally, belatedly, got him a haircut. Even now, she let him go to Bird's Barbershop only once a year, a bit too attached to his curls if you asked me. (No one asked me.) His twin sister, Roma, wore her straight hair long and swingy.

"Should we call 911, Mom?" said Charlie.

"It's OK," I said, struggling to catch up. "It's all going to be OK."

"Liza," said Xavier, "we need to call 911. Like, now."

"We just *found* her," said Bobcat insistently. "We didn't do anything," he said.

"OK, honey," I said, opening my arms. And Bobcat collapsed against me.

"We just found her," he said, his voice cracking.

I felt strong for a moment, giant Bobcat clutching me like a little kid again. I knew it was pathetic, but I loved being needed. Xavier began to cry.

We tumbled into Whitney's glass-and-steel house, perfectly chilled air rushing over us in waves. "It's the boys!" cried Annette, rising from what I was pretty sure was a real Eames chair. (But I'd never ask . . . asking, I'd learned from watching Whitney, was *gauche*. My family had spoken freely about money: who had it, who didn't, who'd bought a new TV. Being around Whitney and her wealthy clients had shown me another way. Money was conveyed via signifiers: the Eames chair, Rag & Bone sandals, a tattered ski pass from Telluride you "forgot" to remove from your rumpled Patagonia jacket.)

"The boys!" said Whitney, unfurling her yoga-toned body, clad in a silky jumpsuit.

Annette was animated from the wine, pink cheeked. Her blond hair was natural—she had Northern European relatives—but she highlighted her hair to make it even more fabulous. She saw Bobcat's expression and said, "Robert?"

"I didn't do anything!" said Bobcat. Of all the boys, he seemed the most worked up. I knew his father had threatened to send him to live with his grandparents in Midland, Texas, after he'd refused to go on a "father-son hunting weekend" because he wanted to wait in line at Best Buy to score a computer chip that was in short supply. "I just want him to grow up like I did—outdoors!" Louis had said.

I did sympathize with Louis, who was utterly perplexed by his son. He wanted Bobcat to be a person he could understand and help succeed. I had to remind myself to be thankful that Charlie and I connected easily, honestly. It wasn't like that for everyone.

"What's going on?" said Whitney.

"Something happened on the greenbelt," I said.

"We found . . . someone," said Xavier.

"What does that mean?" said Whitney, splaying out her hands as if she were pushing something down. "Who is he? Where is he? I don't understand."

"It's a woman," said Charlie.

"She might be dead," said Xavier, his gaze jumping between his mother and his friends.

"Oh my God!" said Annette. She picked up her phone. "Who do I call? Oh my God!"

Whitney ran to wake Jules, who entered the living room in rumpled silk pajamas. He was a tall British man with a shoulder-length mane that made him seem distinguished. "OK, OK," he said, trying to force himself awake.

As they'd built their real estate empire, Jules had begun referring to himself as "The Lion," as in "Call Whitney and the Lion—for all your real estate needs!" I think he wanted clients to think it was an old prep school nickname, when in reality he'd come home one day and said, "Honey, how about I go by *The Lion* from now on?" Whitney had called me and we had laughed for ten minutes. What a dork! But he was a savvy businessman—the name had stuck.

"What's happened?" he said. He looked disheveled, his face showing panic despite the Botox Whitney had confided that they had both received the week before during a realtor open house that featured "Botox and Bubbles."

"The kids found . . . somebody on the greenbelt," I said. For a moment, I felt a flash of fear—this night, this event, would be my downfall. Somehow the horror—*the kids found somebody on the greenbelt*—would discolor our friendship, making me unwelcome in Whitney's beautiful home.

"Where's Roma?" said Jules.

"In her room? I don't know!" cried Whitney.

"Did you touch the body?" asked Jules.

The boys were silent, looking at each other, deciding something, it seemed.

"Answer me," said Jules.

His son lifted his chin. "We gave her mouth-to-mouth," said Xavier. "We tried to save her. That's what we've been trained to do."

"We tried chest compressions, too," said Charlie. "But they didn't work!"

"It's not our fault," said Bobcat. His tone was low and pained.

"Oh my God," said Jules.

"I'm calling 911," said Annette. "Did you call 911?"

Again, the boys seemed uneasy. "We didn't know what to do," said Charlie.

"Our phones didn't work down there!" said Bobcat, shaking his hands anxiously.

"We didn't call anyone," said Xavier, his voice breathless, bordering on hysterical. "We just came home!"

"Come out back. All of you. Leave your phones," said Jules.

Something in his tone made us obey. I was relieved to follow his lead. Even as an adult, I sometimes wondered, "Who's in charge of this situation?" before realizing it might have to be me.

In the far corner of the Brownsons' yard, fireflies flaring against a black sky, the boys talked and we listened. The Texas heat pressed on us, a living thing.

What choice did we have? We promised we believed them.

The
Second Day
of Summer

2019

-1-

Salvatore

AT APPROXIMATELY 6:45 A.M., Allie informed her father, Austin Police Detective Salvatore Revello, that she did *not*, in fact, want to be a cat for Dress Up Day but, instead, Dora the Explorer. "Or," she said, crossing her arms across her skinny chest, "I'll be the Incredible Hulk. But definitely not *a cat*."

Where had a seven-year-old learned to speak with such contempt? And what the hell was wrong with Allie's cat costume, which Salvatore had ordered on Amazon Prime the night before, the cost totaling thirty-eight dollars after paying for the two-hour delivery fee and tipping the hapless millennial who'd shown up at his door at 11:00 P.M.? His goddamn wife, Jacquie, had always made their costumes. *By hand.*

"Allie, you're being immature," noted Allie's brother, Joe. Joe was twelve. He'd wanted to be his favorite basketball player, Steph Curry, for Dress Up Day at summer camp, because Joe was a crafty little demon and knew he could request the Chinese New Year Warriors jersey, call it a "costume," and get some cred at middle school, even among the preppy little cretins who wore Vineyard Vines and Supreme T-shirts that cost seventy-five dollars apiece.

Joe trolled eBay, Craigslist, and the thrift stores near their ranch house in a sprawling development of identical beige homes called Whisper Valley. He was on an endless quest for shoes and clothing that could make him seem rich. When he'd won an Alexa smart speaker at the school Wellness Fair and Salvatore had told him he could not plug in the spying device (oh my God, the things he'd learned about people from their Alexa smart speakers), Joe had sold it on eBay within hours and bought a pair of gently used Adidas Human Race NMDs just a few sizes too big for him.

Salvatore was proud of his kid.

"That's true," said Salvatore, smiling at Allie. "You *are* being immature."

Allie's defiant expression crumpled, and Salvatore hated himself. She was so fragile now—they all were. He had to remember that.

"What about Taylor Swift?" said Joe.

"How would I be Taylor Swift?" said Allie, glaring at the Cuteshower Girl Cat costume, which had come in a plastic case and included chintzy-looking ears on a headband and a sad strip of "tail."

"Can she use Mom's makeup?" said Joe. Allie's face lit up.

IT HAD BEEN A long night securing a crime scene on East Riverside. Salvatore could have handed off the investigation, but he was careful not to use the "single father" card unless he absolutely needed to. His boss had been pushing him to take time off ever since Jacquie's death, but Salvatore knew that he couldn't slow for an instant. The sheer adrenaline his work provided—the blood, the bodies, the hysteria, the interrogations, the late nights compiling evidence, the stories only he could untangle—his job was a hypodermic needle of the purest relief. As long as he could work, could keep from sinking into the anguish that yawned under him, pulling at him, seeping into his weird, swampy dreams . . . if he could focus on nailing perps, he would be OK.

Thanks to his next-door neighbor, Peach, an elderly woman always happy enough (or lonely enough) to come sleep in the guest room when he needed to burn the midnight oil, Salvatore was able to arrive at the crime scene at the same time as Katrina, the medical examiner.

When he arrived, he tried to slide into the place where he could silence all the noise around him and really *see*. He tried to get into this tunnel before even entering a crime scene, standing very still, his mind laser-focused, asking himself, *What is wrong here?*

Clothes too hastily strewn, a necklace in a kitchen, bloodstain patterns, a child's stuffed toy where it should not be, a broken window. Each item out of place was an essential clue, a way to unlock the mystery of what had happened to bring Salvatore and his team to the scene. In the tunnel, Salvatore could try to interpret how a night had gone wrong, how an ordinary evening had led to one less soul alive.

His team surveyed and photographed the street where the body was found and Katrina determined the time of death, signing off so she could arrange transport to the morgue for autopsy. Near dawn, Salvatore collapsed into bed, only to be woken up an hour or two later by Allie shrieking about Dress Up Day.

Salvatore rubbed his face. He knew that opening his wife's makeup drawer was something he'd get reprimanded for at family therapy on Wednesday. Ditto for saying nothing (even getting choked up) when Joe went into Jacquie's closet and pulled out the neon-pink T-shirt she'd used for yoga class, slipping it over Allie's head and cinching it at the waist with the gold belt Jacquie had worn to '80s Night at the kids' elementary school.

(And afterward, they had made love, Jacquie in only that belt, her hair in a side ponytail . . . but he would not think about Jacquie. Even remembering good things was hellish.)

"I look awesome," whispered Allie, admiring herself in Jacquie's full-length mirror.

Joe had already fetched rhinestone clip-ons that had once belonged to Jacquie's mom, Valerie, who was still alive and judgmental in Tarrytown, New York.

(Valerie called every Sunday, telling him he should move to Tarrytown, making him feel like a failure, incapable of raising his own kids . . . but he would not think about Valerie.)

"Daddy, look!" cried Allie, who somehow knew how to apply eye shadow and lipstick. She spritzed herself with Jacquie's Burberry perfume—unbearable, smelling it, and also wonderful, so wonderful. He'd stopped into Macy's once after beers with his friends and had thrown down his Visa for the $102 giant-sized eau de parfum.

(He breathed through his mouth. He would not think about Jacquie, how she'd loved to spray Burberry and then step through the cloud of perfume.)

Joe cued up "Welcome to New York" on the iPhone he'd fished from the recycle bin at the Slaughter Lane Target. He and his sister danced to Taylor Swift, singing aloud to a song beloved by their mother, a brilliant and serious woman from New York who had also happened to adore teen pop.

Had.

Who had.

"OK, let's get a move on," said Salvatore. He'd been dressed since dawn, uniform pressed, tattooed arms covered (Austin Police Department shield on his right bicep; "Jacquie Forever" on his left—oh, the irony), face shaven and dark hair clean and combed. His gruff voice did not break. He did not fall to the ground and give in to the tumble of unbearable and beautiful emotions that rushed over him watching his daughter dance to her dead mother's favorite song.

"I said, get in the car!" said Salvatore, too loudly. The strain it took to stay functional came out as anger, he knew. The kids looked stricken, Joe cutting the music and Allie looking down as she passed him, grabbing her light-up Keds to put on en route to school.

Salvatore felt ashamed as he drove up Lamar Boulevard, past Target, Valero, and the sketchy 7-Eleven that served as a destination for both the rich white people who lived in the Barton Hills neighborhood just beyond (kombucha, $5.99) and the poorer saps who stopped for gas or breakfast on their way to manual labor, often in Barton Hills yards or neighborhood construction sites (two hot dogs for a dollar). From the backseat, Salvatore heard his son speak to his sister in a low voice. "Your kicks are just like the ones in the video."

"Which video?" said Allie, tapping the toes of her sneakers together to make them light up.

"I can't remember. Maybe 'Bad Blood'? Or 'You Belong with Me'?"

"I love those songs," whispered Allie.

"I know," Joe answered.

Salvatore looked into the rearview mirror. The sadness on his kids' faces almost made him sob, so he averted his eyes.

If you look away, it will go away. Salvatore's own mother had taught him that.

At a stoplight, Salvatore cued up "You Belong with Me" on

his phone. If he was caught texting while driving, it would be some scandal, but he didn't care. He rolled down the windows and turned up the volume, hit play.

At the first notes, Allie brightened. She scrunched her eyes closed, began twitching her head back and forth, imitating a teen at Austin City Limits music festival. (The busiest weekend of the year for Salvatore and every other cop on the beat, not to mention Uber drivers, restaurant owners, and oh my God the bars.) Allie opened her lipsticked mouth and Salvatore could hear her voice, sweet and pure. She knew every word. Who didn't?

Rolling up Lamar, turning on Mary, all the way to Zilker Elementary (they'd won the lottery and transferred in . . . and signed up for the full-summer day camp), Salvatore and his children sang their fucking hearts out about high heels and sneakers and bleachers.

He kept the music going as he rolled into the drop-off lane. The summer camp director (also the school librarian), Ms. Contrera, was directing traffic, and she met his eyes and grinned, surprised. She lifted her fists and swayed a bit to the beat. The fifth-grade safety patrol kids danced. A girl dressed as Harry Potter opened the car door and Allie climbed out in her mom's T-shirt, greeted by her whole school rocking out.

"I'm Taylor Swift!" cried Allie. "I'm Taylor Swift for Dress Up Day!"

"Of course you are," said Ms. Contrera. "I can tell." Allie ran into the school, her hand-me-down backpack hanging from her shoulders. There was no time to relish a tiny, fleeting victory—Ms. Contrera waved him on.

"Can you switch it to Ty Dolla $ign?" asked Joe from the backseat, his persona transforming into a taciturn, middle school hoodlum within seconds.

"Absolutely not," said Salvatore.

Joe giggled. Twelve! Joe could make his voice a man's or let loose that little-kid giggle. Salvatore had arrested twelve-year-olds for murder.

"Had to try," said Joe.

"Always have to try," said Salvatore.

Joe had a brilliant and troubled brain. He had tested into the best school in the city, a tiny magnet located inside a big middle school on the East Side, where Austin Police Department had been called more than once to break up fights and drug dealing. As they neared the school, Salvatore slowed to park and walk Joe in, but Joe said, "I'm good. Just let me out here," in the low voice Salvatore was sure he practiced when he was alone in his room.

"Oh," said Salvatore. "OK." He stopped, and Joe jumped out, his Warriors jersey looking fine. "See you later, Steph Curry," he said.

"OK, Dad. Bye."

"Hey," said Salvatore. He felt sick when he tried to talk about emotional things with the kids. His father, a career Marine, had ruled his family with his fists. But the first time Salvatore spanked a toddler Joe (just a quick smack on his diapered bottom!), Jacquie had quietly informed him that if he ever touched *her* child in anger again, she'd be "gone without a trace." Her child!

Salvatore had been stunned. Not by her dramatic flair—he knew her tantrums well—but by the fact that he'd been so quickly eclipsed. Her fierce protection of Joe had shown Salvatore how strong she was. His own mother had been quiet and scared of his father.

When Salvatore, around age six, pointed to the bruise around his mother's neck and said, "Did Daddy do that?" she pulled her robe tight.

"Do what?" she said.

"The bad color," said Salvatore. He was dressed for school, a bowl of Cheerios in front of him. He had heard his mother being beaten the night before; he knew the thumps and cries.

"There is no bad color," said Salvatore's mother. "If you look away, it will go away."

He looked away.

JACQUIE HAD DEMANDED THAT Salvatore be a different kind of man than his father. She'd opened him up like a tangerine, like one of those clementines, a Cutie. She'd allowed him to be richer, to be tender. Knowing he was loved allowed Salvatore to be compassionate. He still thought the "time-outs" were a crock, but he'd never hit his children again.

He'd tried to become a strict but understanding father, but even so, Jacquie's warmth had enabled Salvatore to avoid getting involved with the "ushy gushy" stuff. "Hey, Son?" he said now.

"Yeah?" said Joe.

"Thanks for earlier. For your sister." He cleared his throat, then made himself speak again. "I appreciate—"

"That cat costume was pathetic," said Joe. "You gotta do better than late-night Primin'."

Salvatore closed his eyes, delight coursing through him. His nerdy son's transformation into a cool dude still seemed funny. "Late-night Primin'!" he said. "Is that a thing?"

"It honestly shouldn't be," said Joe. "Unless you're Primin' ice cream."

"Fist bump?" said Salvatore.

"Oh my God, Dad," said Joe, rolling his eyes but smiling. Salvatore was happy to play the innocent sap. He hoped that Joe knew nothing about the dark places where Salvatore spent his hours, the violence, the recent scourge of opiates in Austin.

It was a strange thing to be a parent. You spent so much time creating an alternate universe for your children's imaginations, convincing them everything was fine, whispering lies into their ears at bedtime: *Nobody could get into this house! I will protect you! If anyone tried to get into this house, my friends at the station would be here in seconds and arrest the bad person before you even woke up!*

Salvatore knew better than anyone how truly dangerous every moment was, but also how precious. It was saving him, minute by minute, to cultivate in his children a belief that they were safe, a belief he understood was false. These were kids who had lost their mother—they knew it was a sham, too.

"Dad?" said Joe. "Dad? You OK?"

"I'm here," said Salvatore.

"Later, Dad," said Joe.

"I love you, Son," said Salvatore.

"OMG," said Joe, slamming the car door.

Well, thought Salvatore, at least he hadn't said *FML*. He'd seen that on some teenager's Instagram and googled it. "Barton Springs closed on Mondays," the kid had written. "FML." It meant "Fuck My Life," Salvatore learned.

He watched Joe walk toward the school's entrance. Salvatore's eyes narrowed, monitoring a group of tall kids with their hoods up pushing each other and laughing. He saw a girl with sad eyes leaning against a tree. But what could he do? He couldn't save every sad girl.

As soon as his son was safely past the metal detectors and into his school, Salvatore put the car in gear and headed downtown to the station, to see what morning mayhem awaited him.

Call ME, Whitney Brownson, and Let Me Change Your Life!™

SOUTH AUSTIN NEIGHBORHOOD PROFILE:
BARTON HILLS

Welcome to BARTON HILLS, the best neighborhood in Austin, Texas! I'm Whitney Brownson, and I welcome the opportunity to show you around the place I have called home for twenty years! My children all went to the EXEMPLARY-RATED Barton Hills Elementary School, walking these tree-lined streets, and I love living near hiking trails into Austin's famous greenbelt, right next to Barton Springs Swimming Hole, where my fifteen-year-old son is a lifeguard this summer! Where else could you find a home in the middle of a city where you could walk to both Uchi Japanese sushi restaurant (my personal fave) and a swimming hole with a rope swing? It's the best of other worlds! Let ME help YOU find YOUR DREAM HOME!

Quick facts about BARTON HILLS:

 • Barton Hills is home to several attractions including the Barton Creek Greenbelt nature preserve and the Umlauf Sculpture Garden and Museum. Just north of the neighborhood are Barton Springs Pool, a natural spring fed by Barton Creek, and the 361-acre Zilker Park.

• Established in the 1940s and 1950s with construction continuing through the 1970s to the late 1990s, Barton Hills contains many different styles of single-family homes. In the 1940s, noted Austin-based architect A. D. Stenger designed and built a group of contemporary mid-century modern homes in a section of land bound by Arthur Street and Ariole Way.

• Average home cost: $790,000 and rising! Get your piece of paradise NOW!

• Urban but safe; in the middle of everything with room for your family!

Call ME, Whitney Brownson, and Let Me Change Your Life!™

-3-

Whitney

WHITNEY HEARD A CAR drive slowly around her cul-de-sac and woke with a start. It was 89 degrees already (according to her Apple Watch), her central air humming like a beehive gone mad. Whitney rose, her pajamas whispering as she went to the window and pulled back a velvet curtain. The car was gone.

Whitney peered out for a moment, watching the sun blazing through the trees, shooting darts of light through the worn-out leaves. No matter how much Rod watered the trees, summer was tough. Some of the newer homes on Whitney's list had Astroturf instead of grass, which struck Whitney as a frightening portent. When she'd been a lonely child, she'd spent entire days on her lawn with imaginary friends, the grass cool and ticklish on her bare feet. Whitney hated the thought of generations of kids growing up playing on Astroturf—or worse, only playing indoors, with their freaky VR headsets. She was glad her own twins had grown up with a yard. They were fifteen now, and Whitney scarcely saw her neighbors' younger children. Where were they? Where were the shrieks and whoops and trampolines?

Whitney knew she wouldn't be going back to sleep. She was a light sleeper on the best of occasions and hadn't napped in years. In their king-sized water bed (water beds were coming back, Whitney believed), Jules snored lightly. Above the bed was a giant photograph of Whitney performing Balanchine's *Allegro Brillante*, her dark hair pulled into a symmetrical bun, thin pink lips lifted only slightly at the corners. Her skin was pale, made even more so by the powder she wore to hide any damp evidence of exertion. Balanchine had famously said that *Allegro Brillante* "contains everything I knew about the classical ballet—in thirteen minutes." In the photograph, Whitney was at the height of her career—her hip problems would make her retire within the year, before her nineteenth birthday—but she didn't know it yet. Her face is triumphant; she is leaping with such power, her toe shoes five inches off the ground.

Whitney closed her eyes. She could still hear the Tchaikovsky. Reflexively, she held the heart-shaped locket she always wore around her wrist—it had been her sister's, and Whitney never took it off. She liked to place it between her thumb and forefinger and run the pads of her skin over its cool, smooth surface.

Jules still used Old Spice deodorant, like a teenager, though he was a decade older than she. Whitney put her face close to her husband's and breathed in.

Her lion. She'd once adored his authority, had allowed him uncontested rule over their company and family both. Obeying Jules made her feel protected. But even the wisest king needed to be watched and, if necessary, usurped.

Old Spice. Whitney and Jules's son, Xavier, used the same deodorant, which had rebranded itself as a kind of joke, targeting ironic millennials (Whitney supposed) with funny names on the containers, like Wolfthorn. Whitney,

Liza, and Annette had taken their boys to Target a few months before. (They'd always gone together on Saturdays; it was more fun as a team.) They passed the baseball and Pokémon cards. The women had spent so much time lingering while the kids perused over the years—Target should install a wine bar by the Pokémon cards, Annette had joked. Or at least a bench.

They entered the men's grooming area. "OK," Whitney told her son. "Pick a razor, some shaving cream, and deodorant."

Xavier, taller than Whitney and skinny, exhaled. "Mo-om," he said.

"And how about body wash? Any interest in body wash?" said Liza.

Whitney had taken Xavier's twin sister, Roma, to the adjoining women's aisle starting when she was seven. Roma's bathroom was filled with glosses, polishes, facial scrubs, and lotions. (As was Whitney's. She and Roma shared an interest in "product," as Roma called it.)

"Um," said Xavier, tucking his gorgeous hair behind his ears.

"Body wash? Or no body wash?" said Annette.

"Whatever, Mom," said Bobcat. "This is humiliating. Can we leave?"

So no body wash. They'd all stopped at the Village Soccer Shop on the way home for cleats (it was more expensive than Dick's Sporting Goods, but closer . . . and the women's time was valuable), then at Tequila's for nachos. At home, Whitney and Xavier sequestered themselves in what they called "the blue bathroom" (because of the tiny blue tiles). "OK," said Whitney. "You ready?"

"This is just . . ." said Xavier. He exhaled.

"So!" said Whitney gaily. She pulled the top off the Old

Spice and lifted her arm. "You just slide the stick right here," she said. "Got it? Now you try."

Xavier was red with embarrassment. Perhaps this was a job for Jules (or YouTube), but Whitney's grandmother had never talked to her about *anything*. "I've got it, Mom," said Xavier.

"Go on," said Whitney, raising her eyebrow in a school-marmish way.

He laughed, lifted his arm, applied the deodorant.

"Perfect!" said Whitney, in the same tone she'd used when he'd gone to the bathroom in his tiny potty. "You're amazing," she said.

"Can I go now?" said Xavier. (In the same tone *he'd* used when Whitney explained the birds and the bees as he'd stared at her, horrified.)

"Nope," said Whitney. "Let's talk about shaving."

NOW, SHE BREATHED IN her husband's Old Spice, and Jules said, "Mmmm." Whitney got back in bed, wrapped herself around him. She felt a momentary peace. But then it flitted away.

What had happened on the greenbelt?

She took a deep breath, pulled on her kimono, and wandered through the house, checking on her family. Her parents and twin sister had died in a plane crash when Whitney was eleven and at home with her grandmother. She'd grown up as an only child, yearning for a happy family.

Xavier kept his room locked, but Whitney had a key, which she wore on a chain around her neck. She turned the lock quietly and stood in the doorway for a moment. The boy smell was amazing—pungent, disgusting, beautiful. (With a top note of Wolfthorn.)

Since infancy, Xavier had slept the same way: on his back, arms thrown up—*I surrender*. Above his queen-sized bed, he had a framed papyrus from Egypt—actually from Amazon, ordered on his seventh birthday during his Egyptology obsession, which had replaced his truck obsession and was followed by obsessions with Rubik's Cubes (she could still hear the clicking and clacking as he spun the cubes), yo-yo tricks, and skateboarding.

Ribbons from Xavier's track meets were strung in a row over his bookcase. His lifeguard uniform lay in a heap on the floor. Whitney gathered it up, happy at the thought of handing him a freshly laundered T-shirt and red shorts. His fanny pack (blue—you couldn't wear a red one until you were sixteen) was tossed next to his whistle on his desk. Shoes were everywhere—sneakers that cost hundreds of dollars (Xavier had his own debit card that pulled from Whitney's trust), flip-flops, soccer slides—as well as countless socks.

Whitney moved close to her son. He was OK. He was in one piece. He was breathing. Anything else could be fixed, no matter what had happened on the greenbelt.

What had happened on the greenbelt?

Roma was asleep in her room. Ever since Whitney had read an article in *The New York Times* about nighttime screen use and decided that the twins had to charge their phones in the kitchen, Roma did seem to sleep more.

From the doorway, Whitney watched her daughter. Roma looked so sweet in slumber. They were all here, her family. Everyone was here. No one was hurt. Still, Whitney felt a scary loosening, as if a panicked rat were sprinting around the wheel of her brain. Spinning faster and faster, asking one question with escalating volume:

What had happened on the greenbelt?

-4-

Annette

ANNETTE STOOD OUTSIDE HER son's room. He'd hung a sign reading KEEP OUT on the door when he was eight, and she'd tried to be respectful, but she knew she needed to talk to Robert. A body, a woman's body on the greenbelt. It was the kind of thing you read about in Nuevo Laredo, the border town where Annette had grown up, but not here.

Read about! Not even. When Annette was eleven and had a sore throat, her grandmother brought her to work. (Her father and mother were needed at their custom boot shop.) Annette's grandmother cleaned gringo homes, and her second stop of the day was a giant ranch on land that spanned both sides of the U.S.-Mexico border. Wandering around the property singing to herself, Annette had seen a man lying on the ground. She ran to tell her grandmother. "Stay inside," her grandmother had hissed. "Must be someone who was trying to cross. Not our business."

Annette's expression must have shaken something in her grandmother, who put down her dust rag and sank to her knees. "Kneel down," she commanded Annette. "Now pray to God to send an angel to guide that man's soul to Heaven."

Annette had prayed for that man for over thirty years.

Now, she knocked timidly at her son's door, then turned the knob. "Honey?" she said. "Sweetheart?"

He was a giant mound in the bed. It was jarring to know that this *almost-man* was her son, the baby she'd nursed, the child she'd built endless pillow forts with, the youngster she'd walked to school two blocks away every day until he graduated sixth grade and started to ride the bus to middle school and then Austin High. He was *intense*, sure, but he did not have a dark side.

Annette touched him, wrapped her hand around the top of his shoulder. "Honey?" she said.

He stretched, made a sound like "Uuuugh." He sat up. "Mom?" he said.

"Honey," she said a third time.

Robert's room was navy blue and gray. Annette had bought a loft bed from Pottery Barn, a giant piece of furniture that had come with two white men to put it together. As they'd worked, she'd brought them lemonade. "Hi," she'd said, from the doorway.

They looked up, their faces flushed from carrying the mattress and hardwood frame.

"I brought you, um, lemonade," said Annette.

"Thanks," said one of the men.

Annette had placed the two glasses on the floor of Bobby's room. The man who had said *thanks* nodded, then returned to Bobby's furniture. (This had been called "white glove delivery"; Annette had checked the box easily, sort of assuming the furniture would be quickly installed in Bobby's third-floor room but not really understanding that two sweaty men would spend over an hour in her home.)

"ROBERT," SAID ANNETTE NOW. "We need to talk."

He looked at her fully. His brown eyes were clear. His black hair fell over his forehead. Annette was relieved, and not for the first time, that her son was white. She had wanted him to be biologically hers, of course—a baby who looked like her beloved family, as blond as she and her siblings—but when she couldn't conceive and the donor egg was white, the wistfulness was replaced with gratitude that she'd been able to carry him, to have him, her dark-haired, white-skinned son. He looked nothing like Annette and was hers absolutely.

It was not a fair system, and she knew this in ways her friends did not. They might have read about injustice in books, and Annette knew Liza had come from poverty, but, even in liberal Austin, even in Texas, where almost half the population was Hispanic, racial profiling was rampant. Annette understood the privilege that came with Robert's name and skin color. Her son would benefit from a corrupt and ruinous system, and she was ashamed to be thankful for this fact.

"I didn't do anything," said Robert in a flat tone. He did this sometimes, retreated into a shell of himself, almost robotic. Once, when he was asking endless questions about a graphics card at Fry's Electronics, the salesclerk said, "Brother, are you an Aspie, too?" Annette had heard of Asperger's, had even considered having Robert evaluated. But she knew how Louis would react—badly—and she had learned to avoid poking the hornets' nest. Familial serenity was her goal, even if it meant staying silent.

Responding to the clerk, who had been so friendly, Robert had just looked at his shoes and mumbled something incomprehensible.

"Sorry, man," the clerk had said. "But it's easier when you accept it. Just from personal experience."

"I DIDN'T DO *ANYTHING*," Robert repeated now.

"Did you know her?"

He sighed, broke his gaze from hers. "No," he said, looking at his navy sheets.

Annette felt her breathing quicken. She knew when her son was lying. She opened her mouth to ask more, but then closed it. She swallowed, tasting the familiar pain that came with choosing peace over truth.

Liza

CHARLIE AND I WALKED home from Whitney's house after Jules called 911 from his second cellphone, which he said was untraceable. (None of us asked questions like *why* a realtor would have a second phone or *why* we felt the need to remain untraced.) Jules had been insistent that the call be anonymous and we all agreed by not arguing with him: it was only ethical to report the woman's body, but there was no reason to have the boys' names caught up in the mess. Were we suspicious of our own sons already? It's possible this played a part in our decision. I *knew* Charlie couldn't have hurt anyone, but didn't every mother believe her son was only good, and completely known to her? Charlie was loyal to a fault, which worried me. But the way I had survived was by swallowing uncomfortable thoughts whole. Mysteries like *where is my sister now? Is my mother still alive? Is Patrick? What if he finds us?*

These questions made my stomach burn and my head spin, but I had antacids and sedatives.

Though my best friends and I were united in our plan of

action, each of us had different reasons: Annette was always sure Bobcat was at a disadvantage due to her lack of citizenship (and though I saw no evidence of this, I also knew it was impossible for me to fully understand her experience); Whitney and Jules were terrified of besmirching their real estate empire; and I . . . well, I didn't want to be found.

My son was quiet as we moved through the fragrant summer night, the air still heavy at midnight. Each home that we passed was utterly silent. I'd lived in Austin for almost sixteen years but the quiet was still revelatory—my life on Cape Cod had been noisy with arguments, sirens, traffic noise, and late-night television heard through open windows. The fence that protected us here in Barton Hills was invisible but absolutely airtight. I would never take for granted the safety of wealth and the luxury of soundless nights.

I could still remember leaving East Falmouth when I was a recent community college grad. I'd commuted to school and worked full-time; I'd scarcely ever slept away from the trailer we called home.

The night I left, my mom was snoozing on the couch, my little sister, Darla, curled beside her, Darla's bright red hair—so like Charlie's!—damp against her forehead. I'd smuggled a pregnancy test from the Stop & Shop, and in the cramped bathroom, I discovered it was positive. I saw my life in Massachusetts before me—making a bed somewhere in the trailer for a baby (Where? In *a drawer*?), continuing to work at the Falmouth Raw Bar, the scent of fried seafood clinging to my skin. I loved my mom and sister, but I wanted something else. Something more. I wanted to be named *Liza*, which seemed to me the name of a cool, wealthy, untouchable girl.

My old nickname, Weezie, was the name of a waitress, the name of a woman who'd work her ass off getting a college degree and then get knocked up and never leave the Cape. I abandoned that name the night I left Bluebird Acres, taking my mother's car keys from the seashell-shaped dish on the kitchen counter. I kissed Darla on the forehead. I stood at the front door and said a silent prayer for her. And then I disappeared.

I ditched my mom's Ford at the Peter Pan depot and stared out the bus window, tears in my throat as we crossed over the Bourne Bridge. I knew I'd never return. *Liza* and her son *Charlie* (a name that went with *Liza*, I thought . . . and somehow I knew I would have a son, though of course I had a high-class girl name, too: *Sarah*) would vacation in more glamorous places—Hawaii? California?

I can still remember the giant bag of Twizzlers I bought at South Station as I waited for my bus to New York. (I'd planned on getting off in Manhattan, but Penn Station in the middle of the night was scary. I gave in to my gut instinct and bought a ticket for as far as I could afford to go: Austin, Texas.) The Twizzlers had been sticky in my hand but sweet in my mouth.

EVERY WEEKEND, I WENT to open houses in the Barton Hills neighborhood, scanned the for-sale listings obsessively. I'd spent the last sixteen years scrimping to try to save a down payment, but something always came up to clean out my stash. It was possible that I could get a loan for a small place in another Austin neighborhood, but *this* was where I wanted Charlie to grow up, not in the cheaper places farther south or north of 183. No matter how many times Charlie found a new build off *Slaughter Lane* or in *Pflugerville*, texting me a listing or grabbing a flyer and sticking it to the refrigerator with one of our alphabet letter magnets, I knew where we belonged.

I had already run. Now I wanted only to stay.

"It just bothers me that you think you're not as good as Whitney and Annette," Charlie said once, after I'd asked him to toss our cardboard roach traps before I hosted Ladies' Night.

"I don't think that," I'd protested.

"Anyone who was your real friend wouldn't care if you had a roach problem," said Charlie. "Anyone who was a real friend *with money* would hire you an exterminator. She's our landlord now, isn't she? Call Whitney and tell her we need help!"

I laughed off his comments, but they stung. Because I *was* desperate to appear a certain way. I wanted my friends to think I had it all together. I asked Annette if she thought I should bid on neighborhood homes (though there was no way in hell I could), sending texts with "???" and listings featuring open kitchens and master bath suites.

I knew my friends loved that I was "eclectic," even that I was single, which seemed exciting despite the fact that I hadn't had a date in years. I didn't want them to see the grim underside of my life: staying up late whispering tarot card predictions to hapless callers; donning a red shirt, affixing a Target name tag, and bagging scented candles; rushing up to Round Rock to walk designer malta-poodle-doodles.

I wanted to be a rich person with a job that was my hobby. I wanted to own my own home. I wanted to pretend any college was possible for Charlie, to worry about highlighting my hair and making sure my gardener, Rod, had called my arborist, Brendan, to talk over options for treating my ailing live oak.

Whitney and Annette never would have even *seen* someone like Weezie. My friendship with them was my most valuable treasure. Next to Whitney and Annette, I was mistaken for one of the fortunate ones, and that felt wonderful.

Of course Whitney had had her share of tragedies—she

was orphaned as a child. Annette's family was loving and intact but she, too, had fought hard to forge her life. Our scars bound us, I knew—and our days in the syrupy terror of new motherhood. By the time we'd emerged out of those days, fragile and transformed, we were inseparable. I believed we were a family.

"Whitney's helped us plenty," I said that afternoon. "Now spritz that lemongrass spray around, will you? Nobody wants 'wine with a side of mildew' smell."

"Oh my God, Mom, if only you could see," Charlie said. "You're better than both of them."

"We *will* be better," I said. "We'll have our own house in Barton Hills, I promise. We're so close . . . I just need to work harder."

"Mom," said Charlie. "Are you listening to me? I *don't care* about staying in a fancy neighborhood. I don't even care if we own a house! I just want you to stop putting yourself down. It's depressing."

"Thank goodness I have you," I'd said, ignoring his words. He was a kid, and didn't get it (which was, I suppose, the point): my friendships protected us.

WE WALKED HOME IN the dark the night the boys found the body, and I could tell Charlie was shaken up. As I tucked him in past midnight, I sang him a lullaby like he was still a baby, my baby, because he was.

IN THE MORNING, CHARLIE'S big feet stuck out from underneath the covers, long and bony. I marveled at the sight of him: that beautiful profile, which I'd adored from the moment he was placed in my arms.

I lay down next to my boy. He smelled like soap and sweat socks. He was probably old enough to set his own alarm clock, but I woke him every morning anyway. "Good morning to you," I sang softly in his ear. "Good morning to you. Good morning, dear Charlie . . ."

"Noooo," he said.

"Good morning to you," I finished.

"No," he said. "Please, Mom."

I gave him one more squeeze and stood. "Coffee with milk and sugar?" I said.

"Coach Henrik said no sugar," he said, eyes still closed.

"So just a little," I said.

"Mmmmm," said Charlie, his assent.

Charlie had discovered track and cross-country during his freshman year. He was a natural runner, and most amazingly, he loved it. It had been hard for me to afford the expensive shoes his friends wore, but I told myself I would pay down the Visa debt (and my lingering student loans) someday. "I'll be sponsored soon," Charlie promised.

He never seemed embarrassed that he had no dad, that we were barely surviving on the money I pretended came only from freelance writing. My latest project was a collaboration with a local chef named Samantha, who combined Texan, slow-smoked meats with her mother's Thai recipes. Charlie seemed (how could this be true?) to be proud of me, stopping by Sam's restaurant, Thai Tex, with his friends, giving me a hug and saying once, "See? I told you she was writing a cookbook." Charlie and Whitney's daughter, Roma, did their homework some afternoons at a table right near the kitchen where Sam and I tested recipes, even though Roma had a giant "princess-themed" bedroom at home.

One of the hardest things about ghostwriting for chefs (especially famous ones) is getting the voice right. In the best scenarios, I can switch from my own stream-of-consciousness into the mind of whatever chef I'm working with. I sit down with a cup of coffee, close my eyes, and channel Vince Romaldi (*My Mama's Meatballs*, bestseller); Tracey Wills (*Even* More *One-Pot Pasta Recipes;* bestseller that led to the *One Pot with Tracey* cooking show on HGTV); or Kazra "The Sushi Queen" Tamiko, whose Roll Your Own book spent three weeks on the Nonfiction Bestseller list.

Kazra barely speaks English. After my trying to contact her for months, she'd emailed me the Wikipedia page for "sushi," flown me to her Tokyo home for lunch prepared by her mother (who spoke no English), given me access to her Apple photo stream, and told me to write whatever I wanted. The stories I'd conjured about her day-to-day life and her mother's hardscrabble upbringing had hit the right note: I was already under contract to ghostwrite her next two Roll Your Own books. (*Roll Your Own, Breakfast Rolls for Easy Mornings* and *Roll Your Own, Sweet & Savory.*)

But first I had to finish Sam's book, tentatively titled "Thai Cuisine for the Home Cook." (I knew we'd need to gussy up the name, though Sam was absolutely opposed to puns and rhymes using the word "Thai," like "Thai Me Up" or "Try My Thai.") I was thinking one word could be evocative, like "papaya" or "lemongrass." Sam was in her mid-fifties, and I could just see her elegant profile with one word in a bright, slanted font. When I wrote "as" Sam, I used calming, lyrical prose.

I MADE CHARLIE'S COFFEE as I heard him brush his teeth in the bathroom we shared. He lumbered into the kitchen in a Howler Brothers T-shirt (he saved up to buy four or five of the iconic Austin brand's shirts at their annual warehouse sale; today's featured a monkey wearing a bike helmet) and shorts. I put sliced melon on the table, as well as a bowl of mini-boxes of sugary cereals.

"Thanks, Mom," said Charlie, sipping. "Can I drive today?"

"OK," I said, though I hated Charlie driving. I was terrified from the moment I got in the passenger seat. He was a fine driver, even a good driver, but I couldn't help but feel as if we were about to get in an accident at every intersection.

"Have . . ." said Charlie, his voice fading out. He swallowed. "Have you heard from the police?"

"No," I said. "And, honey, we won't hear from them."

The boys had told us that they'd entered the greenbelt via an unmarked trail off Winifred Avenue, headed to jump off the Cliffs, and had seen a woman's body at the edge of the water. At first, they'd thought she was asleep. They tried to wake her, performed mouth-to-mouth and chest compressions. When they couldn't revive her, they biked home. They were still little kids, too scared to handle the situation on their own. We'd all vowed to erase the night from our memories and move on.

There was nothing else to tell, the boys had insisted. There was nothing else.

Still, a part of me felt nauseous, worried despite my assurances to Charlie.

He was quiet as he drove to work. Charlie had seemed down lately—I'd thought about trying to force some sort of heart-to-heart, but if I could avoid more awkward emotional conversations, I was all too ready to do so.

I wish I had made him tell me what he was thinking, what he was dealing with, who he loved. But I was weary. I had to walk three dogs in Northwest Hills before I could work on Sam's cookbook. I didn't want to contemplate the possibility that my son could be involved with a dead body. So I kept quiet, too.

Is it every mother's impulse to look away—look anywhere else—rather than delve into jagged details? Do the mothers of convicted murderers believe that their children are guilty? I don't think *my* mom even suspected I was planning a permanent escape.

There is a space, I think, between understanding that we are all alone—unknowable—and acknowledging this lonely truth. Some of us live forever in this space. I certainly tried.

CHARLIE HAD HAD HIS learner's permit for nine months, and was due to get his license on his birthday, though we had only one car so it wouldn't change his lifestyle much. He was saving for a car of his own, he'd told me: an electric car that wouldn't hurt the Earth. I didn't remind him that electricity came from somewhere, too.

"What are you doing after work?" I said. "Hanging out with Roma?" My son had been close to Xavier and his sister since infancy, though Roma seemed to be growing up faster than Charlie, with her heavy eyeliner, intimidating glare, and tiny skirts. For a while, I'd thought Charlie and Roma might be romantically involved, and though Roma was strange, I welcomed this possible union, even pushed it. But lately, Charlie had been resisting spending time with Whitney's daughter.

Charlie had brought home a boy named Amir a few months before, someone he'd met at school, but Amir was cagey when I asked him where he lived and mentioned that he was a senior (not a sophomore like Charlie and "the Three-Musketeers"). Later, I had a talk with Charlie about choosing friends who were right for him, and I hadn't seen Amir since.

"Roma emailed me that she lost her phone, so she's getting a new one and seeing a movie at the mall," said Charlie.

"But I got an extra shift at Deep Eddy, so I can't go." And then, as if he could sense the hurt I was *sure* I was hiding, he added, quickly, "I'm glad I have a job. It's so much better to be real."

"Oh, sweetie," I said. "What would I do without you?"

He climbed from the car, opening the back door and grabbing his backpack. I got out of the passenger seat and he gave me a hug. "You'd be a mess, Mom," he said. "You'd be lost."

He gave me a smooch on the cheek to let me know he was kidding, but he was absolutely right. As I drove toward my dog-walking job, I thought idly about how empty my life would be without Charlie. I would do anything to keep him safe.

Anything.

-6-

Salvatore

SALVATORE HAD BARELY ENTERED his office before he heard about the body on the greenbelt. An anonymous 911 call had led EMTs to a dead woman by the side of an unnamed swimming hole off an unofficial trail in the middle of the Barton Hills neighborhood, where Salvatore had grown up. Cause of death was suspicious, so they wanted Salvatore to weigh in.

Salvatore put in a call to confer with Katrina as soon as possible. He made himself a cappuccino—the department had chipped in to get him a De'Longhi after he and Jacquie had canceled their anniversary trip to Rome so she could stay home for more chemo—and sipped from his dainty cup as he booted up his Dell computer. His guys made fun of his beautiful cups—joking that he should hold up his pinkie while he sipped—but the Nuova Points had been his grandmother's. She'd been born in Naples, Italy, brought over kicking and screaming as a young bride, and had never stopped complaining about America in general and Austin in specific until the day she died. Every morning, Salvatore took a moment to hold a warm cappuccino and remember his loud and angry Nonna.

Nonna had lived to eighty-seven.

Using rage as fuel for living was a family tradition.

As he sipped, Salvatore read the daily reports from other agencies, federal and regional. He scrolled through wanted criminal reports, unidentified bodies, suspected car theft rings, and other assorted illegal operations. He caught up with paperwork, drank another cappuccino.

When Katrina paged him that she was ready, he got back in his car to head to the medical examiner's office on Springdale.

Austin had opened the new facility in 2017, giving Katrina and her colleagues nine autopsy stations and even a CT scan machine. Katrina met him in one of the waiting rooms, her white lab coat so crisp she must have ironed it or picked it up that morning from the cleaners. She was of Pakistani descent, tall with chocolate-hued hair she wore in a low ponytail.

Salvatore himself bought suits in bulk at Men's Wearhouse during their annual sale. Investigating homicides was a messy business: after one intense situation that had led to Salvatore's shoes, socks, suit, tie, and even *underwear* getting soaked by blood, Jacquie had told him to just "get naked in the garage and don't bring those nasty murder clothes into my house." Understandably, she didn't want the kids seeing him covered in gore, and she wasn't interested in any laundry that might include brain matter.

Jacquie had stashed a bin of clean outfits from Thrift Town in the guest bathroom. She'd instructed Salvatore to enter via the garage, shower, and then greet the family in fresh pants and T-shirts, depositing his "horror movie clothes" directly in the wash . . . or even the trash can.

Although he'd been brought up to wear clothes until they fell apart, Jacquie had introduced him to the thrill of throwing things away. Sometimes, it felt as if he could toss the trauma of his days into the bin with the stained linens.

But the memories usually came back.

"OFFICIAL CAUSE OF DEATH is drowning," said Katrina, bringing him back to himself. Salvatore could smell Katrina's lotion, something clean and sensible, like Lubriderm. "But opiate levels in her bloodstream were three hundred nanograms per milliliter . . ."

"So she overdosed."

"It's hard to tell what happened. That's why I called homicide."

"Three hundred nanograms? There's no way she was able to swim, right?"

"I'm not a detective," said Katrina, "but if she drowned, she would have sunk, not ended up at the edge of the water."

"So she wasn't alone." Salvatore inhaled. "And the 911 call was anonymous, untraceable phone. Did she have track marks?"

"None. And no evidence of any struggle."

"How old is she?"

"Nineteen or twenty. No ID on her, no phone."

"OK," said Salvatore. APD was still searching the greenbelt trails for any belongings she may have left behind, and he'd ordered a sweep of all the trailhead parking areas. She could have lived in the neighborhood or parked a car nearby. Salvatore needed to get his team to begin interviewing possible witnesses and going door to door.

He followed Katrina into the examining room, where the victim lay on a stainless-steel table. Salvatore tried to enter the tunnel. He scanned her body: no bruises, no burst blood vessels, the developed muscles of an athlete; if she were a junkie, she hadn't been one for long.

He stood close, trying to hear what she could tell him. *What happened to you?* he asked her silently, staring at her face. Often, their eyes were open, but this woman's were closed. She had a small tattoo of a teddy bear on her upper arm, the word "BEARY" underneath.

Who did this to you? Salvatore asked her.

Why the tattoo of a teddy bear?

Whose daughter are you?

Who loves you, and is wondering where you are?

He imagined her swimming, sinking, trying to claw her way up the side of the trail. Salvatore glanced at her fingernails: oval shaped. No polish. Clean. He saw her fighting to get air, but being held down by something.

Or by someone.

Barton Hills Mamas

CARLA G
Hey mamas, what is happening on the greenbelt? I took Waylon for a swim (I know, I know, the water's got all sorts of diseases. No need to tell me. It's 100 degrees and I needed a freaking break!) and down by Campbell's Hole, there are cops *everywhere*. Homeless person down? Drunk teens? What is happening?

MAMATOCHLOE
I heard they found a dead body.

VICKI B
Oh, no. That's so sad.

BOYMAMA
Jesus Christ, we left the UWS to move somewhere *safe*! What the hell?

NYCMOM
No joke, we paid almost two mil for a Brady Bunch house and

our neighbor has Trump signage. Where on the UWS?! We were in Morningside Heights! But when a dude flashed Finnian's nanny in Central Park (Finnian was asleep in the Peg Perego, *thank God*) I told my husband, "It's Westchester or Austin!" He picked Austin. I'm not so sure. I traded my job and my friends for this.

VICKI B

What is wrong with you people? Someone died! A moment of respect for a lost soul, please!

NYCMOM

You're right. I'm sorry.

BOYMAMA

Me, too. I get wrapped up in my own world sometimes. It is very sad that someone died. Homeless person? Please don't hate me for asking. I'm a Democrat!

MARYKAYMOM

Don't despair, ladies! We all need to stick together. LMK if you want an invite to my summer bash this Friday night. All are welcome! I just got the new City Gal Lip Plumper Kit in stock and I can't wait to show you the magic of lip plumping. Plus margaritas!

ADMIN

The board is moderated closely to make sure everyone feels safe and respected, and corrective actions will be taken if we feel someone is abusing that. Please no solicitation on the Barton Hills Mamas list.

Janine, if you spam again, you will be removed.

MARYKAYMOM

Sorry! Just trying to be friendly! Come one, come all to my summer bash! 2104 Side Dip Cove at 5PM Friday!

ADMIN

Janine, seriously.

MARYKAYMOM

I totally apologize. All invited!

-8-

Whitney

WHITNEY'S CLIENT, GEOFF, LIVED at the Four Seasons Residences on Lady Bird Lake. Jules and Whitney had been to parties there, sipped wine on a balcony that overlooked the whole glittering city. One night, Jules had gotten tipsy and stumbled into a grandfather clock, breaking off a piece of wood. A small sliver: Whitney told him to find the hostess and apologize. Instead, he wrapped it in a napkin, handed the evidence to Whitney, and went to refill his Scotch. She'd been on edge for the rest of the evening, watching him drink more (his British accent growing stronger with every sip), terrified someone would ask what had happened to the clock.

No one asked.

Wealth brought invisibility.

Whitney left the napkin in her empty champagne glass, placing it on the bar on her way out and trying to smile at the bartender who whisked the glass away.

———

AS GEOFF'S ASSISTANT HAD instructed, Whitney parked her car in the Four Seasons Residence Parking, then entered the Residence Lobby. Floor-to-ceiling white marble and a perfect temperature (she guessed 71 degrees) made Whitney feel as if she'd escaped hellish summer Texas, if only for a while.

In the center of the lobby, a Saarinen table held a stunning array of flowers in varying shades of lavender: dozens of glass vases holding delphinium and carnations surrounding a centerpiece of a hundred or more orchids. Whitney had read somewhere that Saarinen designed his iconic Tulip Table (a perfect circle of marble, quartz, or laminate somehow balanced on a single, cast-iron leg) to "clear up the slum of legs in the U.S. home." Whitney appreciated both Saarinen's creation and his sly, judgmental wit.

Circular orchid arrangements were hung overhead, in addition to at least a hundred exquisite, pale-purple, origami birds. Whitney moved toward the back wall of the enormous space, where a man with a white mustache stood between two towering birds made of paper. Whitney recognized them as the breathtaking work of the British sculptor Lisa Lloyd. Behind the man was a six-panel lacquer screen, golden cranes portrayed midflight. It was similar to one Whitney and Jules had seen at the Met during a New York trip. Painted in Japan in the late sixteenth century, the Met's screen was titled *Birds and Flowers of the Four Seasons*.

The Four Seasons. Clever, thought Whitney.

"Hello, how may I help you?" asked the mustachioed man.

"I'm here for Geoff MacKenzie." Whitney touched her silk caftan, her large gold earrings. Though Ballet Austin master classes kept Whitney a muscular size four, she'd stopped showing off her body recently. It felt freeing to wear flowing silks, though her Neiman Marcus shopper, Adele, had been surprised when Whitney sent a late-night, emailed request for caftans after watching a documentary about Elizabeth Taylor in her later years. "How about *very short* caftans . . . with heels?" she'd asked, and Whitney said sure.

"Can I get you a rainwater?" said the desk attendant—was that what he was called? "Butler" seemed apropos but outdated.

"No, but thank you," said Whitney. She rubbed her sister's locket between her fingers.

"Glass of something bubbly?"

"No, but thank you," she repeated.

WHITNEY WAS NO LONGER surprised when her client was a boy in sweatpants. His T-shirt was emblazoned with the word GUCCI, which had been Whitney's grandmother's favorite brand. Geoff ambled from the gilded elevator toward Whitney as if he owned the place. Which, who knew, maybe he did. "Whitney," he said. "I'm Geoff."

"Very nice to meet you," said Whitney. Geoff's clasp was moist.

"Can I get a rainwater?" he asked the desk attendant.

"Of course, Mr. MacKenzie."

"You da man," said Geoff. The butler was a pro—he didn't flinch.

As they climbed into Whitney's Model X, Geoff noted, "Your car is so clean."

"Red Bull?" asked Whitney. They always wanted Red Bull, these young internet-millionaires in sweatpants.

"You have green?" said Geoff, rolling down his window and tossing his rainwater into the street.

"Of course." Whitney gritted her teeth, did not mention his littering, and gestured to the Platinum Yeti cooler she'd had installed in the back.

"Epic," said Geoff. Whitney smiled. If he bought a dooms-day bunker out in Buda, her commission would top six fig-ures. He could have all the kiwi apple Red Bull he wanted.

In truth, Whitney felt compassion for Geoff. Climate change was obviously real, though everyone was trying their best to ignore it. Something about the impossible fact that life was changing, and fast, made it preferable to talk about Instagram, wine varietals, snacks. The strategy Geoff shared with many of his co-workers at Google—buy a luxury doomsday bunker and prepare for the hordes of starving cli-mate refugees by making sure your bunker was fortified and impossible to access—was both immoral and disgusting, but was it worse than ignoring the looming collective fate? This was something Whitney found it hard to discuss with her friends.

Five years ago—even two years ago—it seemed as if some-thing was going to change, someone was going to find a solu-tion. Scientists. World leaders. But as wildfires spread and glaciers melted, Whitney felt as if everyone just stopped pro-cessing. It was too horrible. Whitney admired the millennial millionaires for at least accepting the truth and making a plan, no matter how selfish.

Geoff was talking about "ecological burgers," made from an "epic meat substitute." Whitney made encouraging noises as they neared the turnoff for The Park, which was, in fact, a park on the surface but a sprawling world underground. Geoff fell silent, fingering his goatee as he surveyed the expanse of grass stretching before them.

"There's nothing here," said Geoff.

"The entire complex is underground," said Whitney. She cut her eyes to him, to see his reaction.

He raised his eyebrows and pursed his chapped lips, im-pressed.

"So no exterior walls," continued Whitney. "Instead, there is a series of tunnels and steel doors."

"Steel doors," he said, eyes narrowing.

"Concrete and steel blast doors," she elaborated. "They can withstand any catastrophic natural disaster or man-made event."

It was hard not to wonder, as Whitney put the Tesla in park, whether this could possibly be true. The nature of disaster preparedness was so weird, as no one actually knew which disaster to be scared of. Steel doors, for example, weren't going to help with anthrax. Fifty years of gourmet freeze-dried foodstuffs, which a nearby project promised, weren't going to fix a bad marriage.

Whitney made her voice bright. "Just *wait* until you see the pool, Geoffrey," she said. "They even have technology to turn the sky above it from day to night!"

"I'm not a super pool party person," said Geoffrey, looking unsure. He reminded Whitney of her son, Xavier, in that moment.

As if conjured from her heart, Whitney's phone chirped. "Pardon me," she said.

"My time is valuable," said Geoff. She'd heard this exact statement from other young men who worked in tech . . . was there a workshop?

"I'm well aware," said Whitney, stopping short of apologizing.

Geoff reached into the Yeti cooler, opened a second Red Bull. He looked pointedly at his wristwatch, sighing. Whitney, who had to study these things, knew it was a limited edition Carrera Calibre 1887 SpaceX chronograph watch, designed by Elon Musk. She smiled at Geoff, as if impressed. And then she answered her phone.

"Mom?" said Xavier. His voice was reedy, too high. "Mom?" he said again.

"Yes, honey?" she said. "What is it?"

"There's a big problem," said Xavier. "Mom! We're in trouble, Mom! It's Charlie!"

Whitney touched her fingertips to her forehead. Charlie was a bit naïve, not nearly as street-smart as her own children. He was . . . *ordinary*. Whitney doubted Charlie had anything to do with *what had happened on the greenbelt*, but if he'd done anything to harm Xavier—or Xavier's rocket ship of a future—Whitney would have to act fast. There was no question that she would protect her son.

"What is it?" she said, her mind turning, readying for battle. "What did Charlie do?"

Annette is an American!

LET'S PARTY!

You're invited to a pool party where we will celebrate
Annette Fontenot,
our favorite new American citizen!

WHEN?

June 4, from six P.M. to???

WHERE?

The Fontenot Home

DRESS?

Bathing Suit & Dancing Shoes

We'll have a buffet dinner, fireworks,
and dancing under the stars.
We're so proud and happy for our Annette!

Annette

"AMERICAN FLAG CAKE," SAID Louis. "Sparklers, Party in the USA playlist . . . what else?" Louis held a pen aloft, his MacBook Air balanced on his lap. When they had furnished the house, Louis had insisted on Ranch Luxe style, creating a living room reminiscent of the Driskill Hotel Bar, complete with cowhide furniture, a giant longhorn steer head mounted over the fireplace, and antique guns displayed as art.

Louis even hired Barvo Walker, famed sculptor of the Widow Maker statue in the Driskill (depicting life-sized cowboys getting tangled in their stirrups and falling to their deaths), to create an enormous bronze statue of Louis's beloved childhood pony, Red.

Annette had been unsure about the living room, but too busy with a new baby to protest. Now, she avoided the room whenever possible. Even Red had a maniacal gleam to his eye when the light hit him wrong.

"This party is too much," she said now.

"For my American citizen wife?" said Louis. "Who loves barbecue even more than a real Texan? Can't have too much,

Annette. I've got a call in to Aaron Franklin to see if he'll cater."

Annette swallowed a sour taste—she was just as much a "real" Texan as Louis. "I think Aaron is a bit busy," she said. "Didn't Obama go to Franklin's recently?"

"Can't hurt to put a call in, right?"

Gazing at her pudgy husband, Annette felt a wave of affection soothe her irritation. Louis was a quarter inch shorter than she was, but he loved her in high stiletto heels anyway. The way Louis allowed the world to delight him was a marvel to Annette, though sometimes his willful ignorance could grate.

Annette and Louis had met at the University of Texas. He was an oil heir from Midland, she an undocumented basketball superstar. It had been different in the nineties for border kids, especially gifted athletes. UT hadn't even mentioned Annette's status when they recruited her: She'd turned down full rides at small northeastern colleges because she wanted Div I, and she'd wanted to stay home. Or near home, anyway—Laredo was a three-and-a-half-hour drive from Austin.

The first time Louis introduced himself was after a game. Annette was on her way to the locker room and he'd stepped in front of her. "I'm going to marry you," he said.

Annette had sidestepped him—laughing, bewildered.

But Louis was sweet and serious. "I mean it," he'd said. "I'm Louis. Can I take you to dinner tonight?"

"Annette!" her assistant coach called.

Annette said, "I have to go."

"Mars Restaurant, eight o'clock?" he'd said. "It's on San Antonio Street."

"I . . ." she said

"I'll be there until you come," said Louis.

"Tonight's not good," she said.

"I can wait," said Louis.

Annette shook her head and jogged to catch up to her teammates. There was no time for anything but basketball. Annette had been the first person in her family to go to college and she wasn't going to screw it up for some guy, even a sweetheart who had somehow custom-ordered a jersey with her number on it.

Louis came to every game of the season, screamed every time she made a basket, began sending roses to her dorm room on Saturdays. Every bouquet had the same card: "Mars, 8 P.M., tonight?"

After the season ended, the roses kept coming, but Annette drove her beat-up Honda Pilot to Laredo every weekend to help in her father's boot shop. One weekend, she intercepted the floral delivery guy on her way to the parking lot, so she brought the roses with her, dumping them on her parents' kitchen counter when she got home late at night.

Her mother was waiting for her in the morning with a fresh cup of coffee and a hundred questions. Perhaps Annette had known when she brought the flowers home that she needed guidance. "He sends them every week!" she told her mother, as Maya arranged the bouquet in a ceramic vase.

Annette's childhood home was large—her father made beautiful boots and had done well financially. He'd bought the house on Bordeaux Drive with cash, adding on every time he had two cents to rub together. Her uncles and later her brothers helped out with the construction; Annette's mother was a gifted decorator who loved nothing more than a day spent shopping across the border or at her favorite store, Vega's Interiores Mejicanos. The house was filled with hand-carved tables and chairs (the dining room table was inlaid with horses) and Mexican hanging lamps and chandeliers that cast beautiful patterns on the orange and raspberry sherbet–colored walls.

Annette had not had to work. She'd just played basketball, and her family's financial success allowed her to train with the best coaches and attend all the pricey summer camps the white girls did.

Some of her friends had been born in Laredo and some had come over from Mexico as babies or young kids. Many students at her high school spoke Spanish at home and English at school. The border was porous in the nineties and early two thousands—Mexicans came over to work for the day or see family, and Americans swarmed from Laredo into Nuevo Laredo to go to bullfights, booze it up, and shop for pottery, vanilla, and diet pills. The bridge over the Rio Grande was a busy one in both directions.

Annette's parents, Maya and Roberto, wanted their family to perfect their English, so didn't allow Spanish at home. Annette's grandmother spoke little English.

When she'd visited a tiny, elite college in Massachusetts, Annette had definitely felt her skin color. On her student tour, she'd been the only nonwhite teenager. The blasé, appraising expressions on the other kids' faces gave her the creeps. The basketball coach had been kind, but the town had seemed like a cold and forbidding place; Annette had breathed a sigh of relief as she landed back home. Before she'd even seen her offer from UT, Annette had made her decision to stay. (A full ride, thank goodness, because without citizenship, she would have been charged out-of-state tuition.)

MAYA FINISHED ARRANGING THE roses. Her kitchen was stunning: the floor was created from square orange tiles and the counters were tiled in deep blue. A custom mural had been created as a backsplash behind her modern range. Thirty-six hand-painted tiles depicted a yellow-eyed coyote hidden behind a colorful spray of flowers. Maya had told Annette that in the Oaxacan village she was from, she could hear coyotes howling in the hills at night. "I should have been afraid, but the sounds helped me sleep," she said. "I felt like they were watching over me, keeping me safe."

Maya gestured to the roses and raised an eyebrow. "Mars, eight P.M., tonight?" she said. "Is this a code or something?"

Annette smiled shyly. "It's a boy from Midland," she said.

Maya whistled. Everyone knew that Midland was oil country, the epicenter of the Permian Basin, which had been gushing crude since the 1920s. An oil boom in the 1980s had created multimillionaires, and photos of private jets, a new Rolls-Royce dealership, and giant McMansions had fostered the image of Midland as the city of gaudy opulence.

(Annette would find this stereotype to be absolutely true, at least as far as her in-laws were concerned. Louis had grown up on a street called Charismatic Drive in a seven-thousand-square-foot home with a full basement bar and bowling alley; a pool modeled after a Dallas Marriott resort; a sunken living room with sprawling leather sectionals, a movie screen, and a popcorn machine; an art gallery with recessed lighting, a full-time guard in uniform, a small Monet; and a garage full of giant boats Louis's family had to drive at least a hundred miles to put into a body of water.)

"Yes, he's probably rich," said Annette to her mother, before she'd had any idea *how* wealthy Louis's family was. (And *what kind* of wealthy: they donated only to pro-life causes, choosing to use most of their money to show up their neighbors. For example, Louis's mother had a lighting specialist on retainer for holiday light shows and Halloween lawn theatrics.)

"What's he like?" said Maya. "Besides rich."

Annette laughed. "I have no idea," she said. "I've never gone. To Mars at eight. It's a restaurant."

"How long has he been asking you?"

"Since . . . months now. But I'm always here on Saturdays. Dad needs me at the register."

"You're fired," said Maya.

Annette smiled, looked down, and traced a tile with her fingertip.

"I mean it," said Maya. "We're not paying for that Jester dorm room so you can be here, taking up space every weekend. Dad can hire someone else."

Annette was quiet. She opened the cereal cabinet, closed it.

"It's time," said Maya.

"OK," said Annette. "OK."

The roses arrived on schedule the following Saturday. Annette's roommate went with her to Buffalo Exchange to find a vintage outfit for her date. "Mars is *so romantic,*" said Annette's roommate. Annette chose a black minidress.

At eight-fifteen, Annette approached the small, historic house where Mars was located. She climbed the stairs to the wide front porch and opened the door. Candles lit a red dining room, and Annette's eyes adjusted to the light, her shoulders falling as she heard soft jazz. At a corner table, Louis was reading a book, a plate of cheese and crackers and a Scotch in front of him. When Annette neared, he looked up.

"Hi," she said.

His eyes widened. "Is it really you?" he said, breaking into a grin. Annette nodded. When she saw Louis scramble to pull out her chair before she could sit, happiness coursed through her. Annette had never been the beautiful one. It felt so good to be admired—she didn't want the feeling to end.

When, months later, he first unbuttoned her shirt, the care

he took with the buttons and the way he trailed his fingertips so slowly over her skin, awestruck, thrilled her. She was used to hard work, grit, determination, and pain—the price of success. Wonder—inspiring wonder—was new, and Annette luxuriated in the feeling.

Later, she would question what life might have been like with someone who saw her as more than a gleaming trophy—a prize who began to lose her luster the moment she was won.

"WHAT IF I DON'T pass the citizenship test?" said Annette, eighteen years later. "Then what happens to the cake and the sparklers?"

"You'll pass," said Louis.

THE WHOLE PARTY MADE Annette a little queasy. While Louis insisted the event was to celebrate Annette's American citizenship, she knew (even if he did not) that it was truly to show off. It was tone-deaf, especially since the bizarre events of the night before.

When had Annette become the kind of woman who wouldn't say what she felt? Her transformation into the type of wife who sighed but stayed quiet had happened in tiny increments. But now and again, she felt her old self rise up. "Louis," she ventured, "do you think maybe we should postpone? It seems wrong, having a party when . . ."

Louis deflated. "Are you worried?" he said, taking her hand.

"Robert didn't do anything," said Annette, though her stomach ached. *Had* he done something? Or seen something—stood by when he should have intervened?

"That won't stop them!" said Louis. "They can accuse a boy of anything nowadays! It doesn't have to be true."

Annette was often disgusted by her husband's politics, but at the same time, she, too, was scared of Robert's life being ruined.

"You either control the story or you get screwed," said Louis grimly.

Annette exhaled. When Robert had thrown a whole watermelon at Xavier indoors during a neighborhood barbecue, the fruit smashing against a wall (Xavier ducked) and ruining the wallpaper and white couch, the neighbor called Annette to complain. Louis had called the woman back and told her it was her own fault for serving watermelon.

The year before, Robert had ridden his bike past a little girl on a narrow greenbelt trail. According to the little girl's mother, Robert had knocked the girl down and kept riding. (Robert insisted he hadn't seen the girl.) The child had ended up in the ER with a sprained elbow, but the version of the story from Louis was that the mother was litigious and needed to be taken down a peg. There was no reflection, no punishment for Robert (save a periodic threat to send him to Midland for a while if he didn't shape up). Louis's dad's lawyer had sent the woman a check and a cease-and-desist letter. The story had been controlled.

Sometimes, Annette was afraid she was raising a creep. She and her siblings had felt safe understanding the rules, knowing who was in charge. Still, she didn't want her son accused of something he hadn't done. He'd only found the body. He hadn't known the woman. That was what he'd said.

There were times when Annette's Catholic faith—her deep belief in what it meant to be good or evil—was at odds with her knowledge about how the world operated. She observed her white friends, surprised by their casual assumption that nothing bad could happen to them. Annette's life in the U.S. had always felt precarious. She could be deported in a day—that was not paranoia but reality; she'd seen it happen to relatives and Mexican friends.

Annette was protected by money and a white husband. She was *so close* to gaining citizenship. As much as she wanted to do the *moral* thing, examine more deeply how Robert may have been involved with whatever had happened on the greenbelt, Annette had too much at stake. For her, and for her family of origin, the choice to do the "right" thing could be a fatal mistake. And yet her Catholicism taught her the perils of dishonesty. It was anguishing, but despite believing in a vengeful God, Annette knew she would do whatever was best for her family.

"Everything is fine," said Louis, trying to convince himself. Annette squeezed his hand.

"Are you scared?" she asked.

"No," whispered Louis.

Everything was not fine.

Barton Hills Mamas

TESLALUVR

Good morning, Ladies! So my husband works downtown and he heard that it was kids from the 'hood who found the body on the greenbelt. ANYONE know more?! Has the body been identified? Please tell me it's not one of ours.

CHERI

That's really offensive.

TESLALUVR

What? That I hope it's not a child?

CHERI

No, that you hope it's not a *white* child.

TESLALUVR

I completely resent this comment. My sister adopted a child from Russia. Don't make this about race! I am just saying I hope whatever happened on the greenbelt last night didn't happen to one of the children from Barton Hills Elementary School. That's what I'm saying.

CHERI

All white kids at the BHE.

TESLALUVR

For one, that isn't true and for two, what does that have to do with anything?

KARENSMITH

BHE is pretty white! That's always bothered me. We tried to get into Zilker, which has a much more diverse student population, but they were not accepting transfers when Haven was in K. BHE is a great school, but I do wish it were more diverse.

CHERI

Plenty of "diverse" neighborhoods in the city, Sis! Try Rundberg & 183!

TESLALUVR

I feel like this discussion has gone *way* off course. Does anyone know anything about what happened last night on the greenbelt?

MARYKAYMOM

I suggest gathering information until Friday and then we can all present what we know at my house, 2104 Side Dip Cove, 5PM. We need to stick together! Free margaritas! (And did I mention Mary Kay's new City Gal Lip Plumper Kit?)

ADMIN

Janine, this is your third warning. Solicitation is not allowed on this forum.

MARYKAYMOM

Sorrrrrrrry!

-12-

Liza

AFTER CHARLIE GOT OUT of the car, I moved to the driver's seat and sat in the parking lot of the Deep Eddy Pool. A young family exited a Volvo station wagon, pulling swimmy diapers and floats from the back. The mother wore a tiny bikini and a big hat, her back covered with a large tattoo of an armadillo (the official small mammal of Texas). The father had a mustache and goatee. Each parent held a golden-haired toddler—were they twins? They had a Yeti cooler on wheels, Guatemalan blankets to lay on the grass.

I was pierced with jealousy. I missed my chubby little red-head boy, and I felt a familiar ache: wanting a family, a father for Charlie—even one as silly looking as the one before me, strapping a guitar on his back. (As if you'd have time to strum with two toddlers next to a pool!)

I rolled the window down to feel the early-morning sun on my face, and remembered my "young mother" years. Whitney, Annette, and I would meet with the kids at one public pool or another, in the days before both women had backyard pools of their own. We'd laugh, run after our toddlers, or perch a child on a hip and gossip, standing in the shallow end and bouncing. I'd dated for a while (before I gave up) and my friends wanted to know *every detail*. They were bored to tears of their husbands—did everyone hate their spouse in the baby days?

My friends had especially feasted on my story of a hot guy who'd claimed he was in the police academy and given me three orgasms after a concert at Stubb's. When I'd snuck out early to get little Charlie from Annette's house, she called Whitney and we drank coffee as I regaled my friends with the story of my fabulous new lover. But it had felt wrong to be away from Charlie—I'd never called the number the "officer in training" had written on my hand, and eventually it washed away.

In those early days, it had felt as if we were equal, all struggling with sleeplessness, all feeling (as Whitney once said) like we'd "woken up on a farm with no equipment or training."

As Whitney and Annette grew rich, though, the dynamic shifted a bit. Where once we'd all been up for "2-for-1 Margarita Night" at Güero's, now Whitney hated "crowds, millennials, and crowds of millennials" and preferred to make a reservation and pay whatever it took for her to get a nice table. She always offered to cover me, but it felt awkward. Annette and Whitney could drink wine and laugh, but I was mentally adding up the tab, feeling more nervous with each pricey sip.

I always paid my third, even when it meant rice and beans for a few nights. Even when it meant rice and beans for a week.

Sometimes, I dreamed of a rich husband emerging and taking care of me and Charlie. But I knew in my heart that I had only myself to rely on—myself and my friends. I wanted to touch base with Annette and Whitney now, to make sure everything was OK. I sent a text: DOG WALK TONIGHT?

Annette replied in seconds: YES!

Whitney sent a fat thumbs-up.

6 PM? I wrote. My two best friends liked the note, so it was set.

At happy hour, we often convened in the empty back-yards of Whitney's listings (or sometimes used her realtor code to drink margaritas in abandoned living rooms, perfectly staged fantasies of the good life). In a pinch, we met on the greenbelt, which we knew as well as our kids did.

Our neighborhood smelled of roses and fecund mud. It was the smell of the gardens planted by elderly women when they were young mothers, like my next-door neighbor, Beatrice. It was the fragrance of hidden waterfalls and creek beds, frogs hatching and college kids smoking pot and the taste of barbacoa and watermelon agua fresca and the feel of 68-degree water when you dove into the Barton Springs swimming hole or one of the secret ones only us locals knew about . . . Gus Fruh with its rope swing, Campbell's Hole, the rushing Sculpture Falls. You could hike from my house to every one of them, with a hammock over your shoulder and a taco detour along the way.

I loved my home, and who I'd been able to be there . . . though I still felt as if I were in disguise, a hot mess imperson-ating a well-bred, even *classy*, mother.

When I allowed my mind room to roam, I realized I was scared. Of course, I knew bad things happened on the greenbelt—murders, overdoses, idiots who jumped from cliffs and broke their necks. We heard sirens and saw Life Flight helicopters over Barton Hills regularly.

"Frog Island?" suggested Annette. This was a place along the greenbelt reached only via an unmarked trail near my home. The boys had named the place Frog Island after catch-ing tadpoles there. I had a photo of the three boys, naked toddlers, standing on a giant rock and beaming. Annette, Whitney, and I had sipped wine from our water bottles and gazed at them.

That was the same summer that Xavier had led the boys on an escape. I'd been in charge of taking the boys on a hike when all three boys started running, too fast for me to catch up. I'd yelled at them to slow down, but they disappeared and when I hit a fork in the trail, I'd freaked out, terrified. The boys were toddlers, and none of them knew how to swim. I'd heard the urban legend about a group of eight-year-olds who had gone looking for a place called Secret Cave and had never been seen again. I'm ashamed that I hesitated, wondering if calling the cops would make my friends mistrust me.

Finally, I *did* call the cops, and they found the children at a greenbelt exit, lost and scared. Xavier was apparently inconsolable, and fought the cop trying to bring him home.

IN RETROSPECT, MAYBE I should have asked Xavier what he was running from.

CHARLIE, HIS FACE TEAR-STREAKED, told me later that "Xavier said keep running," and the boys had listened to their headstrong leader. I wanted to tell Charlie to ignore Xavier, to stand up to him and do what he knew was right, but I'd swallowed the words. I didn't want Charlie to become alienated, and it had all turned out OK in the end. We'd laughed about it; started calling the boys "the Three Musketeers."

I wanted my son to be a musketeer.

I wanted to be the mom of a musketeer.

I had spent my childhood being anxious, and with good reason. My father was in prison (*good riddance*, said my mom) and my mother didn't always come home. The front lawns at our Cape Cod trailer park were filled with broken kids' toys, and the endless nights were punctuated by screaming arguments and women smoking and crying on front steps. We didn't have a phone. I remember being scared, holding my little brother close, knowing I couldn't protect him, though I would try.

One night, when I was twelve years old and Mack was eight, he got very sick. It came on suddenly while my mom was out. (Darla hadn't been born yet.) I made Mack a microwave pizza, carefully placing the frozen disk on the cardboard apparatus that was meant to "brown" the bottom in the microwave. I made us a pitcher of Crystal Light (my mom's favorite mixer with cheap vodka on a summer day—she drank it all afternoon from a Big Gulp cup). We had a small TV and I settled Mack on the couch with food and drink, angling the rabbit ears until I found cartoons.

"My head hurts," said Mack. "My neck hurts and my head hurts so much."

I found a bottle of Tylenol behind a bag of maxi pads under the bathroom sink. I crushed a pill with the back of my mom's hairbrush and mixed the powder in Mack's Crystal Light. He drank a few sips. "Does that help?" I asked. Mack shook his head, not crying, but pressing his lips so hard together they were white. He, like I, had been trained not to complain. I knew his pain was bad.

Mack didn't eat his dinner. He gazed dopily at the TV, his expression like a blasé summer girl's. His breathing was shallow and seemed to take a lot of work. When he exhaled, he made a groaning sound. Once in a while, he started crying and clutching his head or neck.

We didn't have a thermometer, but I could tell Mack was too hot. When he fell asleep, I ran through the trailer park in the dark to Mrs. Deacon's house. Mrs. Deacon was an elderly woman who seemed nice. She opened the door after I had knocked for a while. She wore a nightgown, smelled of beer, and seemed annoyed. I apologized and told her Mack was very sick. She let me in, and from her wall phone I dialed my mom's prepaid cellphone. She couldn't always afford minutes, but I closed my eyes and prayed it was on.

I guess I had believed in God, because I did pray that night. I remember putting my palm on the wall beside Mrs. Deacon's phone, the rough wallpaper. I asked God for help. I asked God to save my brother.

By morning, I knew God was a lie.

There was no answer on my mom's phone. The Clam Shack had been closed for hours but I called there anyway. The phone rang and rang. I tried my mom again. Hatred for her shot through me—what kind of a mother forgot about her children?

Finally, I asked Mrs. Deacon if she had a thermometer. "Honestly, honey," said Mrs. Deacon, "I have no idea where it is. Can we talk about this in the morning?"

I went home. Mack was breathing, but in a scary way. He was absolutely burning up, his eyes like hooks catching mine. "Help," he managed. "It hurts so much, Weezie. It hurts so much."

"It's going to be OK," I said. "I promise, Mackie. You're going to be OK. Sip the Crystal Light." I held the drink up, but when I tried to angle his head to the glass, he cried out in pain. "My neck!" he said.

After a while, I went back to Mrs. Deacon's. I don't remember all the details. I had been told *never, never* to call 911, as it was asking for trouble. Our next-door neighbor had called an ambulance once and the cost of the ride had ruined her. She'd eventually lost her trailer, because of calling 911.

My father had gone to jail after a bar fight during which a stranger called 911. "You hear me?" my mom had said, after one of these stories. There were so many of these stories, brought out on lazy nights for my mom and her friends to rehash, to reexamine, almost as if they could find another ending if they told the stories often enough. "Don't ever, ever, call the police. We handle things on our own in Bluebird Acres."

My mom was a bad mother—I allowed myself to acknowledge this. From Mrs. Deacon's, I called 911.

By the time the ambulance arrived, Mack was already dead of bacterial meningitis.

It was a tragedy, everyone said.

Mack would be thirty years old if he had lived. He loved microwave pizza, and dogs, and his bike. He would have been the best uncle, Uncle Mack, stopping by my Barton Hills house with a bike helmet on, and even those ridiculous biker shorts, saying, "Charles, my man, you up for a ride?"

When Mack had been dead a week, I stopped at a crosswalk on my way to work at the Woods Hole Beach Club. I watched a small white van pull into one of the mansions along Woods Hole Drive. On the side of the van was a red cross, but the vehicle was not an ambulance. Under the cross, I read the words CAPE COD CONCIERGE MEDICINE—KEEPING YOU SAFE. I watched the van park, and a young woman in a white doctor coat climbed out. She went to the front door of the mansion and rang the bell.

The door opened, and I heard a voice ring out. "Dr. Wilson! Thank goodness you're here."

Later that night, after work, I went to the Falmouth Library and typed "Cape Cod Concierge Medicine" into a web browser. I saw that rich people had their own doctors, who came right away when you called them.

It was clear: if you were wealthy, you were safe. I'd seen how the summer kids seemed braver than me, reckless, and now I knew why. They could dive off anything, because underneath them was an invisible net of parents, doctors, coaches, teachers, money. If they fell, they had Cape Cod Concierge. If we had been rich, Mack would be alive.

A TEXT FROM WHITNEY brought me back from the past: NOT FROG ISLAND. MEET AT PACKERS' POOL.

This was interesting. The Packers had put their enormous Cliffside mansion on the market over a year ago with Sotheby's. They must have moved it over to Whitney if she wanted to meet there. I'd never been to the Packers', just gazed at it towering above the greenbelt.

I was excited to see the inside of the Packers' compound at last. This would be our most glamorous "dog walk" yet.

None of us had a dog.

13

Salvatore

SALVATORE PARKED AT THE Gus Fruh entrance to the greenbelt. As soon as he opened his car door, a familiar smell washed over him and he was sixteen again, escaping from school, meeting his friends with a hammock and two pilfered beers—or three! The afternoon cracked open with possibility and sunshine . . . his high school girlfriend not exactly *promising* she'd show up, but a *maybe* just as thrilling . . . her nineties orange hair, bangs stiff with Aqua Net . . . smooth stomach and a high-cut Billabong bikini . . .

Salvatore's stomach cramped, making him crouch and almost vomit. How had he ended up middle-aged and alone? What could he have done differently? He bent forward, puked a watery stream of coffee-colored bile.

It hurt. It hurt so much.

Look away and it will go away. Salvatore made himself stand up, walk away from his puddle of anguish and toward the crime scene.

Barton Hills Drive was packed with cars on this 90-degree day: everybody wanted that feeling of flying through the air on the rope swing, letting go at the perfect moment and smashing into the water below.

And there was the usual chaos surrounding a murder: radio and print journalists, television news anchors (their heads shaking at a "senseless loss of life right here on our Barton Hills greenbelt"), concerned neighbors, rubberneckers, even local politicians wanting to attach their "tough on crime" sound bites to the latest grisly headlines.

SALVATORE, NONDESCRIPT IN PLAINCLOTHES and sunglasses, kept his head down. He made his way along the steep trail to the creek, ducking off the marked trail. The body had been found at a relatively unknown swimming spot surrounded by cliffs. There was no public parking near this place, so it was used almost exclusively by people who could walk from their homes along the greenbelt—in other words, neighborhood kids. Salvatore's team had blocked the scene of the crime with yellow tape, but had not released the location.

Salvatore tried to get into his mental tunnel. His job was not to discover the *why*. He was here for the *what*. If he had learned anything, it was that spinning a narrative before gathering all the facts was a mistake. He needed to focus on *what* had happened to his Jane Doe. (And, OK, *who* the hell she was.) All he knew was that she'd ingested opioids and ended up with her lungs full of water . . . but on land.

He'd always loved the canopy of trees, how it morphed as he descended to the creek bed. The light on the leaves changed by the hour—neon, noontime greens fading to otherworldly purples by nightfall.

This was no country club, though; it wasn't sanitized or safe. People had drowned down here; people had been murdered. Even as the houses around the greenbelt had changed hands from old hippies to Silicon Valley refugees, the trails remained open to everyone. Many Austinites wouldn't go near the greenbelt. It was intimidating—if you didn't know your way around, you could wander in circles. Phones didn't always work down here. The greenbelt might have been the one remaining place in Austin where you could get lost— where you could *stay* lost. Trails shifted with storms, and waterfalls appeared and disappeared. Sometimes, the turkey vultures winging overhead felt menacing.

When Salvatore reached the water, he crouched down. This secret swimming hole could be reached from two official greenbelt entrances: Spyglass Drive (you parked behind Tacodeli) and Gus Fruh (you parked on Barton Hills Drive). But you could also get into the greenbelt via hidden trails, or by bushwhacking a trail yourself. There was no saying how the victim had arrived here or why. She'd likely swallowed pills, gone swimming, and then . . . what?

Salvatore scanned the muddy bank, looking for footprints, for anything that didn't belong. He was in the tunnel. The sun played across the water. He saw minnows under the surface, a large turtle on a floating piece of driftwood. And then . . . at the far end of the swimming hole . . . something that wasn't right. He narrowed his eyes. A black object was half-submerged in mud; he could see why the previous team had missed it. It was probably nothing, trash. Still, he scanned the bank.

There was no way to hike to the spot.

Salvatore took his pager and phone out of his pockets and placed them on the ground. He dove in, propelling himself across. He saw a set of footprints, and in the shadows, so covered with mud it was almost invisible, a kneepad, like the one you'd make a kid wear skateboarding, or biking. Salvatore hauled himself out of the water and examined the pad. A small tag gave him his first clue:

IF FOUND PLEASE RETURN TO:
CHARLIE BAILEY
1308 OAK GLEN AVENUE
AUSTIN, TX 78704

14

Barton Hills Mamas

HIKRGURL

OMG, Mamas! I was trying out my new Burley D'Lite bike trailer and there was lots of action when I rode by the Gus Fruh entrance to the greenbelt. I slowed down and saw six uniformed cops gathered around something. I'm scared.

COFFEEISLIFE

Oh, no. Do you think it was a body? Also—unrelated—is the D'Lite worth the splurge?

HIKRGURL

No, it wasn't a body. Something small—a guy in normal clothes was showing the cops something in his hands. I should have snapped a pic. I don't know what it was. An animal? Jesus.

***And YES! My husband almost killed me when he saw the $850 charge but the D'Lite is awesome.

PACIFICHEIGHTS4EVER

I will head over to Gus Fruh with the triplets now to see what I can find out. I bet it was drug paraphernalia . . . needles, pipes . . . Always was in San Francisco~

COFFEEISLIFE

Ha, maybe you should change your name, @pacificheights4ever! Don't blame you, BTW.

PACIFICHEIGHTS4EVER

Sigh. #truth. Guess I am @pacificheightsuntillgetmuggedinbroad daylightandthenImovetoAustin

COFFEEISLIFE

Ugh, I'm sorry. Let us know what you find out by Gus Fruh.

-15-

Whitney

WHITNEY DROVE TOO FAST, taking the turn into the Four Seasons without waiting for oncoming traffic. "Whoa!" cried Geoff MacKenzie. Whitney slowed in front of the Residence entrance. "I apologize," she said.

"What's going on?" said Geoff petulantly. He played with the zipper of his hoodie, moving it up and down, trying to self-soothe. (Whitney, her sister's locket clasped in her palm, could relate.) He'd finished four Red Bulls and his hands were shaking.

"It's a personal matter," said Whitney. "I really am sorry. I'll be in touch to reschedule."

Whitney saw the kid pout and consider telling her (again) about the value of his time. On a normal day, she would placate, cajole, flatter, flirt. But not today. "You know . . ." Geoff began.

"I've got to go. I'll be in touch. I really am sorry," said Whitney.

"Wow, OK," said Geoff. He crossed his arms across his belly. (Why, though they lived on Soylent and Red Bull, were all the young millionaires chubby?) Whitney hit the button on her key fob, and the falcon door unfurled. Geoff climbed out, and when he was standing on the sidewalk, he glared at Whitney, inhaling in preparation for giving her a piece of his mind. Whitney clicked the button to close the passenger door (as silly as it was, she did adore the key, shaped like a mini-Tesla in her hand), and the sleek wing fit snugly into place before Geoff could convey his wrath. Whitney put the car in gear and depressed the pedal, zipping soundlessly forward, leaving Geoff openmouthed, still working his sweatshirt zipper.

Jules called as she merged onto Lamar heading south. She answered, and her husband's plummy voice rang through the premium sound system. "Darling?" said Jules. "I hear you have an emergency?" Jules didn't like thinking about "personal matters" at work, so she knew the "darling" took some effort.

"It's family," said Whitney.

"Noted," said Jules. He took her off speaker and went into the soundproof room, its door to the left of his desk in their shared office. (Only Whitney and Jules knew about the room; it required a retina scan to enter.)

"Carry on," he said, after a moment.

"Oh, Jules," said Whitney, "we have a problem."

"What is it?"

"Xavier just called me from work. He says Charlie thinks he left a kneepad on the greenbelt. With his *name and address* on it."

Jules exhaled. "Don't make a move," he said. "I'll speak with a lawyer immediately."

Whitney bit her lip. When she had first met Jules, his complete self-assurance had made her feel taken care of. How wonderful it had been, after a life of being self-sufficient, to have someone telling her exactly what to do! She'd agreed with everything he said, even getting her real estate license to join his agency. She'd reveled in the many (*many*) photo shoots they'd posed for—*Austin's Power Couple! Love & Real Estate! Riding the Wave of Austin's Population Boom, Meet the Brownsons!* (The last posed on their matching stand-up paddleboards in the middle of Lady Bird Lake.) But over the years, as he got American citizenship and they built a family and a business, his dictatorial way with her began to chafe.

Whitney didn't know what had happened on the greenbelt. But she knew what had come before, and she did not want a lawyer's sharp eyes on the case. She wanted some overworked cop who she could lead like a dog to his dinner.

Jules had made her into a sleek, powerful machine. Whitney flexed her muscles. "I don't think we need a lawyer," she said.

There was a silence, and then Jules said, icily, "Sorry, darling?"

Whitney looked at her face in her rearview mirror. She looked flushed, self-assured. She raised her chin. "I said, *darling*, that Xavier had nothing to do with whatever happened on the greenbelt. We don't need a lawyer. "

"I disagree," said Jules.

Whitney cut the call. When Jules called back, she did not answer. This was *her son*. Whitney knew Xavier. He was not a murderer, and she was not going to behave as if he were. She was certain that Xavier had no secrets.

Whitney, however, had many.

SHE TURNED ON BARTON Hills Drive and her front gate came into view. They had been the first in the neighborhood to install a security gate, but not the last. Whitney paused in front of the sensor and the metal door swung open slowly. She pulled the Tesla inside, waving to the men working on their new topiary garden, passing the pool guy's van. She waited for the garage door to lift, and slid her car into its spot, next to the Mercedes G Wagon, in front of the Jet Ski rack. (They didn't have a Lake LBJ home yet, but that was in the works. Waterfront lots on the constant-level lakes surrounding Austin were selling like gangbusters, and the Brownson Team planned to invest heavily in the area.)

Whitney had treated her two best friends to a weekend on the lake, even renting a pontoon boat so she, Annette, and Liza could watch the sunset from the water. They'd cued up a Yacht Rock playlist on the boat, drunk margaritas, and sung at the top of their lungs to "Come Sail Away" and "Brandy, You're a Fine Girl." Whitney loved her kids, but spending a weekend getting sunburned, reading *Us Weekly*, and letting Liza paint her toenails had made her feel as if she had a sister again. It had been so wonderful.

The garage door closed. Whitney's mind spun and she tried to stay still, to scan her body, taming the frightened parts. She climbed from her car and entered the house. A "Welcome" mat fully sanitized the bottoms of her shoes before she stepped inside. Blinding light filled her modern kitchen. Maybe white marble *everywhere* (except the obsidian countertops) had been a bit much. Whitney smiled weakly at her cleaner, Gilly, who was polishing the freezer drawer of the already gleaming stainless-steel refrigerator.

Jules had texted that he would be home in an hour, and Whitney knew she needed to be calm and collected by then. She went into the master bathroom, torn between playing a Breethe meditation through her bathroom speakers, taking a hot bath in her double-sized Jacuzzi (complete with lights that could be synced by Bluetooth to her favorite songs), or popping a Xanax. She stood before her bathroom mirror, letting the sensors measure her heart rate, BMI, posture, and blood flow. (Their toilet regularly tested their waste for signs of disease.) Whitney opened her medicine cabinet. She couldn't resist putting her hand on her Kate Spade makeup case. Liza had given her the case the year before "just because." Whitney had almost cried when she opened it, savoring a friend who thought of her "just because"! Was that love? It felt like love to Whitney.

Whitney started to unzip, just wanting to make sure everything was still in place . . .

The bathroom door swung open and Roma strode in *without knocking*. "Mom?" said Roma.

"Honey?" said Whitney, zipping up the case quickly and slamming shut the cabinet.

"What's going on?" said Roma, sitting on the edge of the Jacuzzi. Roma was deeply tanned, wearing a yellow bikini. Whitney felt a stab of jealousy at her daughter's youthfulness, followed by a wave of affection for her pinkish, sunburned nose. "Why doesn't anyone ever tell me anything?" said Roma, looking at herself in Whitney's bathroom mirror.

"Sorry, sweetheart," said Whitney.

"You probably think *I* had something to do with this," said Roma, standing up, opening Whitney's cabinet, helping herself to Whitney's hairbrush and running it through her glossy brown hair. "You always blame me for everything."

Whitney bit her tongue and sent a quick prayer: *Please don't let her open the Kate Spade case.*

Roma met her mother's eyes in the mirror with a strange expression. Whitney tried to convince herself that maybe . . . maybe? . . . her daughter was just looking at her with simple teen disdain. That was normal, right? Teenage girls were supposed to disdain their mothers!

From infancy, Roma had been worrisome. While Xavier latched right on, Roma would not nurse, turning her tiny head *disdainfully* and wailing. After three days, when Whitney was on the verge of a nervous breakdown, Jules came home with formula, a bottle, and twelve kinds of plastic nipples. "Leave her to me," he said. He took baby Roma (clad in her pink Vuitton pajamas, a gift from Jules's mother) and left the master bedroom, shutting the door.

"No!" Whitney had cried, a sense of failure descending. "Jules! No!" Whitney desperately missed Roma, but also (her stomach twisted when she admitted it to herself) felt enormous relief.

Jules had opened the door, peered in. "No?" he said.

Whitney felt guilty, but whispered, "Thank you."

Jules looked at her with tenderness (he had once been tender!) and shut the door.

Xavier nursed easily, gazing at Whitney. "My love," she said. His eyes fell shut and he nestled closer. Whitney breathed in the smell of milk and skin, leaned her head back against her silk headboard, and smiled.

NOW, WHITNEY TRIED TO hide her annoyance with her fifteen-year-old daughter. "Come on, Roma," she said. "I would never think—"

"Yeah, *right*," said Roma. Whitney gritted her teeth. She hated this expression. But this was normal! she told herself. A normal teen would be annoyed with her mother!

Whitney forced herself to move behind her daughter, put her arms around her. In the bathroom mirror, they looked peaceful, like a painting. Like the painting Jules had commissioned that now hung above one of their fireplaces. "You're going gray," said Roma.

"I love you, Roma," said Whitney evenly.

"Whatever," said Roma, walking out, taking Whitney's hairbrush with her.

WHITNEY TOOK A XANAX and a bath, hoping to halt her rising panic. Her shoulders loosened, and her mind slowed down, then fell silent.

She toweled off and put on a silk robe. In the kitchen, she found her husband and daughter. Roma was perched on a Lucite barstool, still barefoot and wearing her skimpy bikini. Jules was making himself a coffee. "If you take me to get a new phone like you *said you would*, Daddy, I could ask around and see what people know. I never connected my computer to my phone when I upgraded! I'm, like, living in the desert at this point. Like, a desert island. But in my house. In Texas. You know what I'm saying!"

"Coffee, darling?" asked Jules.

"Yes, Daddy," said Roma.

"He means me, Roma," said Whitney. "And no, but thank you."

"Can I have an espresso, Daddy?" said Roma.

Jules looked at Whitney: He wanted her to be the bad guy.

"No, Roma, no espresso," said Whitney, on cue.

Jules shrugged, as if he were as pained as his daughter. Roma sidled up to him. "Daddy," she cooed, "what about my phone?"

"I'll take you to the Apple store," said Jules. "Let me have a chat with your mother and then we'll go."

"*Finally*," said Roma, who had been without her phone for less than twenty-four hours.

"You can't just lose an iPhone and expect a new one for free," said Jules, sliding his reading glasses down his beaky nose. "I *told* you to turn on the Find My iPhone notification system. That application—Big Mother? They raised twenty million in their first round. You're going to get that app and the Find My iPhone thing, and you're paying me back every cent, you know," said Jules.

"OK, Daddy," said Roma, who had never earned a cent in her life. *What job could she possibly do?* wondered Whitney sadly. She'd always dreamed, if she had a daughter, that she'd raise her to be strong and brilliant. Come to think of it, Roma was both . . . just not in the way Whitney had ever envisioned.

"Very well," said Jules. "Go and put on some clothing, Roma."

"Yes, sir," said Roma, slinking out.

Slinking! Like a feral creature! Whitney couldn't believe she thought this about her own daughter! She shook her head.

Jules turned to Whitney, put his hands on the counter. "I have a call in. Ken Bauer is the best of the best, apparently."

"We don't need a lawyer," said Whitney.

"We do," said Jules. Whitney sighed, understanding this was done. She would have to reevaluate her plan, stay one step ahead. Or talk to the lawyer? How wonderful it would be to lay everything in the lap of the "best of the best" lawyer in town! Whitney knew it was impossible; she knew. It was too late, and yet she yearned to unburden herself.

"Whitney? Are you there?" said Jules, peering at her curiously.

"I'm having drinks at six," she said. "With all the moms."

"Ah, a secret dog walk," said Jules. He put his arms around her. "It's not one of ours," he said. "You know it's not."

"Right," said Whitney. She repeated, "It's not one of ours."

Jules touched her face. "It's just some awful event," he said. "It has nothing to do with us, not with our children."

"This *best of the best* lawyer will represent both the twins, right?" said Whitney.

"Why would Roma need a lawyer?" said Jules. He looked straight at Whitney, his jaw tensing, green eyes flashing with anger and pain. Roma had told them she'd been binge-watching television in her room all night.

Whitney had turned off the alarms and the video surveillance system as she always did when she drank wine with her friends, not wanting the piercing beeps as they went in and out of the slide door into the yard, grabbing drinks from the outdoor fridge, not wanting footage of moms sneaking cigarettes and sharing confidences.

No one had been watching Roma. She could have gone out, leaving her Netflix account playing. Both Whitney and Jules knew that if she'd climbed out her ground-floor window, she could have reached the side yard, Barton Hills Drive, and then the greenbelt.

Neither parent had asked how, if she'd been home all night, Roma had lost her phone. Whitney raised her palm and touched her husband's face. She didn't have to say a word.

Barton Hills Mamas

OAKLANDMAMA

Hi, Mamas! My hubby and I are moving from the Bay Area to Austin and I am wondering about your 'hood. Do you feel like it is safe? How is the elementary school? Parks & playgrounds? Is it as perfect as it seems??? I'm in LOVE with a house on Rae Dell Avenue!

CHARDONNAYISMYJAM

Welcome, Oakland Mama! Barton Hills is amazing but not so sure about safety . . . google "Barton Hills greenbelt dead body" for more. We are all pretty shaken up.

TESLALUVR

Anyone have any more info on this? I want to take the kids to Gus Fruh but not if there's a murderer around. Joking! Sort of.

OAKLANDMAMA

OMG I am so sorry about this news. I'm sure it is a one-time event. Still, I think we will look at other neighborhoods. Thank you for your candor.

MARYKAYMOM

Harsh! We need to stick together, Barton Hills gang. Hit my web site for details of a neighborhood watch and party!

CHARDONNAYISMYJAM

It is a city, ladies, like it or not. I'm scared, too. Please post anything you hear. Please don't let my property value go down!!!

QUEENYOGA

Now that we're on the topic, I have been alarmed by two men sitting in a Cadillac Escalade by the Zilker Elementary tennis courts smoking pot. I called 911 but no one came! Appalling!

ORIGINAL78704

Ha! That could have been my dad—he just retired from his corporate law practice. He and his friends say there's nothing better than getting high and watching tennis.

-17-

Annette

ANNETTE FELT SQUIRRELLY. SHE checked her watch—three hours until she would see her friends, and they could talk through what was happening. Thank goodness for Whitney and Liza: Inside their circle of three, she felt invincible. Ever since she had watched a nature documentary called *Wild Animals of Yellowstone* one night when she couldn't sleep, Annette had thought of her friends as a pack of coyotes, keeping each other safe.

In all honesty, though, none of them had ever really been tested the way the coyotes were tested. They had no visible predators, no deprivation or subzero temperatures. And who was the alpha dog in their crew? Who was the beta, the second in command? Was Annette the omega, the weakest coyote, the one who'd be left behind?

Robert was physically the strongest of the boys. But where was Annette in the pecking order of mothers? She was easygoing, and had a wonderful family back at home in Laredo. Whitney seemed like the pack leader, Annette supposed. An outsider might think Annette was the omega, but then again,

Liza's blind adoration of Whitney (and financial instability) might put her below Annette.

Had they always been competitive, jockeying for position? In Annette's memories, their coming together had been effortless. She could still remember the day she'd first joined Liza and Whitney for decaf lattes and cinnamon buns at Quack's after prenatal yoga class, the two friends inviting her to come with them. Whitney and Liza looked up and smiled brightly when she entered the café, welcoming her.

"I got you a pastry," said Whitney.

She could still taste the cinnamon, feel the warmth of being included.

The three women couldn't stop talking . . . about their worries, preparations, where they wanted to live and raise the babies who were due in a few weeks. They were scared, vulnerable in a way they hadn't been since childhood and might never be again. Pregnancy and new motherhood cracked Annette open—had she not met Whitney and Liza during this time, before her defenses grew back like armor, she might have remained stalwartly alone, driving home to Laredo every weekend for support.

The women had moved over to Matt's El Rancho for queso and chips and ended up sipping nonalcoholic beers and two-stepping, maneuvering their big bellies and laughing at the Broken Spoke dance hall. When she fell into bed at the end of the night, Annette knew that she had found the crew with whom she would travel the (metaphorical) seas of adulthood.

THE WEEK BEFORE, ANNETTE had been sitting on her upper deck when she'd glimpsed something moving by the edge of her yard—an animal. Their upper deck was enormous, with a gas fire pit and bird's-eye views over their lawn, which ran into the Barton Hills greenbelt. Louis had long argued for a big fence, but Annette liked feeling as if she were connected to nature, not walled off. For once, she had gotten her way, if only because Louis was lazy and erecting a fence would take effort.

Annette had stood up and squinted. The animal looked like a small dog. It was brown and gray, with large ears and a pointed snout. Its tail was large and bushy. Annette put her hand over her mouth, realizing it was a coyote.

An electric shock ran through her. A coyote! In her own yard! Annette stood at the edge of her deck, placing her elbows on the metal guardrail. She sipped her coffee, gazing at the wild animal. *Look at me, coyote*, she thought.

As if hearing her, the animal turned its head up, locked its yellow eyes with Annette's. She felt thrilled. The coyote turned and ran away, disappearing into the wilderness of the greenbelt.

The next morning, at dawn, Annette put turkey leftovers in the place where she had seen the coyote, then went to the deck with a coffee and binoculars. To her immense delight, the animal returned. She read about coyotes online, identifying hers as an adolescent by its size. It seemed to already be on its own in the world.

Annette became a bit obsessed with the animal, leaving it food every morning, then waiting for its arrival. The coyote was elegant and free. Why had God sent her a coyote? What was its message for her?

For three weeks, the coyote came like clockwork. It began to appear in her dreams as well. One day, when it met her gaze before leaving, its message was as clear to Annette as truth: *Look at me, running away from your house! Follow me! Escape!*

Oh, shit. Annette did not want this message, although she understood its power. How simple the solution was, in the end. Escape.

THE NEXT DAY WAS the first day of summer. Annette placed raw hamburger out for the coyote, then climbed to the deck. The sun rose above the greenbelt, igniting the treetops, and Annette waited. But the coyote did not arrive. She closed her eyes, summoned her spirit animal. But nothing happened. The coyote was gone.

That night, Annette met her friends for wine at Whitney's house. And her own son went down into the greenbelt, where the coyote had lived. By the same source of water that had kept the coyote alive, Robert found a dead body.

It had to mean something. But what?

USUALLY, AT NAP TIME, Annette curled up on a mat beside the kids at Hola, Amigos. Sometimes, she fell asleep, but more often her mind wandered lazily, pleasurably. Robert, Xavier, and Charlie had attended the daycare from their second birthdays until they went to kindergarten. Annette had fallen in love with the place when she toured it, the same day she found out the fertilized donor egg had implanted. She'd called Louis (who'd been in a meeting), called her parents, and then driven to Hola to put her future baby's name on the list.

When Bobcat went to Barton Hills Elementary School, Annette began working at the daycare. The founder of Hola, Amigos, Hank Lefferts, had bought four South Austin houses in the early 1980s and knocked down three of them, creating an enormous outdoor play space. The penned yard was filled with sprinklers, mud, paints, toys, and utter mayhem. Hank—handsome, tanned, and tattooed—presided over the magical place. Annette adored her days among children in diapers dancing, singing, smearing themselves with shaving cream and mud. It reminded her of her grandmother's house, where she and her cousins would run wild, only vaguely supervised.

Annette wanted to kiss Hank Lefferts, but she was not going to kiss Hank Lefferts. She'd once desired her husband, but now, when he reached for her, she had to swallow her repugnance (among other things). Annette was a good Catholic: She'd signed them up for marital counseling, but Louis had never filled out the presession forms, which were—fair enough—exhausting. Instead, Louis had come home with a bag of La Perla lingerie for his wife. He didn't seem to understand that trussing herself up for his ogling was the *last* thing Annette was seeking. She wanted Louis to love her when she wore sweatpants (like Hank seemed to). She wanted him to see her as who she was.

Who was she?

She dreamed of kissing Hank, leaving Louis, moving into Hank's bungalow behind Hola, Amigos. The sexy nights they'd share, the coffee made on Hank's stovetop percolator. But Bobcat might choose Louis and the wide-screen 5K TV, and Louis could block her American citizenship and wrest custody. Annette didn't really understand Robert and his computerlike brain; she wasn't sure of his allegiances, or if he had any. He was strangely . . . unemotional. So as hard as it was some days not to kiss Hank Lefferts, Annette knew that she was no lone coyote.

She needed her pack to survive.

EVIDENCE FILE 147

BIRTHDAY CARD RECOVERED BY APD
TECHNICAL FORENSIC DEPARTMENT

Dear Arlo,

Happy Birthday! I miss you SO MUCH. How is Beary?
Are you taking care of him? I know you are. I am working
very hard in the city and I hope you can come visit someday. Are you looking at the stars every night like I told
you to? It might seem like we are far apart but every night
I look up and think of you. I love you.

XXOOOOOOOOOO,
LUCY

*P.S. I have a new boyfriend! I think you will like him a lot.
He is as sweet as you.*
P.P.S. This squishy sloth can live next to Beary on your bed.
P.P.P.S. His name is Slothy.

Liza

I WAS GHOSTWRITING TWO cookbooks for local celebrities, both due in the fall. *Bring on the BREAD* was the brainchild of Lou Jenkins, a big guy with a wild beard who ran a brewpub and bakery in downtown Austin. I'd been stunned by the size of his book advance—who knew there were so many rabid fans of sourdough? But every time Lou had a local appearance, there were *hundreds* of attendees, many of them young men with beards similar to his. They lined up to ask him question after question about their yeast makeup, beerbrewing equipment, and sourdough starters. Lou was a king.

My second project was the cookbook I was working on with Sam, who had grown up in Thailand and attended graduate school at the University of Texas, where she met her husband, Brent. After obtaining advanced degrees in biology and history, respectively, they ditched academia and opened Thai Tex. It was a sleek and modern restaurant, its hanging lamps covered with large paper umbrellas to create a reddish glow.

Sam was much more hands-on than Lou, who was happy to have me write his book for him. She wanted to talk through each chapter of her upcoming book, and I loved spending afternoons in the sunlit kitchen of her popular restaurant, drinking lemongrass tea and listening to her stories, watching her craft recipes.

Sam was making fish sauce from scratch. "Really, there are only two ingredients," she explained. "Fish and salt. That's all! But it's a complicated process." My phone rang, interrupting the recording.

"Sorry," I said.

Sam stopped speaking and nodded as I took the call. She was short and lovely, her hair held back with a rubber band. She wore peach-colored pants and a fitted T-shirt, a blue apron wound twice around her waist. Brent and their daughter, Wren, sat in the corner of the kitchen working on Wren's seventh-grade algebra homework. Giving me privacy, Sam joined her family at the table.

I didn't recognize the number on my caller ID. "Hello?" I said.

"Is this Mrs. Elizabeth Bailey?" said a warm male voice.

"It's Ms., but yes," I said, immediately wary. Anyone who knew me would ask for *Liza*.

"This is Detective Salvatore Revello from the Austin Police Department," said the man. "I'm looking for the legal guardian of Charles Bailey?"

I cut the line on instinct, my heart racing. I stood. Sam turned to watch me. I sat. I pretended to speak into my dead phone. "Thank you, I'm so glad my library book finally came in!" I said loudly. "OK, OK, yes. I'll come after work to grab it. Thanks again."

I smiled at Sam, but adrenaline flooded my veins. Two words rang in my ears: *Protect Charlie. Protect Charlie.*

"Liza," said Sam, "what is it?" I hated her then, this kind woman with a husband at her side. She wouldn't ever be in the position I was in: completely alone with everything to lose.

-20-
Salvatore

THE GOLD TOYOTA TERCEL smelled of coconut sunscreen. It was rusty around the wheel wells, reported abandoned at a 7-Eleven at Lamar and Barton Hills Drive. Headquarters was running the license plates. It had almost been twenty-four hours since the woman's body had been found, and Ramirez wanted SOMETHING FOR 7 P.M. PRESS CONFERENCE, he'd texted. He'd followed up, saying:

NEED AN ID ON THE BODY AND AN ARREST NOW.

A PAIR OF SIZE six black pants and a white shirt were folded in the backseat; the victim had likely been a waitress or worked behind a hostess station or bar. After forensics gave him the go-ahead, Salvatore went through her belongings: a calculus textbook, makeup case with earrings, lip gloss, travel toothbrush, a cellphone with a password they would soon be able to bypass, a paperback copy of *Carrie* by Stephen King, and a pink towel.

He texted his boss: ALMOST THERE.

Jacquie had driven a Toyota. She'd worn black and white clothes to waitress at Vespaio on South Congress, paying her way through graduate school at the University of Texas. This car—though it was a different color than Jacquie's, smelled different, *didn't belong to her,* he *knew* that—made Salvatore woozy. He had the bizarre, déjà-vu-esque sense that he was trying to solve Jacquie's disappearance by going through the meager remains in this car. The painful hope that he could still find her, somewhere, somehow, made him feel both fabulous and sick. Was he going to throw up again?

He did not throw up.

Salvatore stepped out of the car into the hot Austin afternoon. The 7-Eleven where the victim had parked her car was a few blocks from the greenbelt entrance that led to the spot where she'd been found. What the hell was she doing here? Why had she gone down to the greenbelt at night?

He saw a car park across the lot, and his colleague, Tina Silver, climbed out. Salvatore preferred to work alone but was glad to see Tina, who was smart as hell and often considered angles that hadn't occurred to Salvatore. Tina was a blond woman in her late forties, a mother and grandmother who relied utterly on her husband, a librarian, who took care of all the cooking, cleaning, and childcare. The Silvers hosted a big Thanksgiving potluck every year, emailing an open invitation, Tina glowing as guests complimented her husband's famous sweet potato pie. Salvatore and Jacquie had spent every Thanksgiving with Tina and her family, and Salvatore planned to bring the kids in the fall.

Tina saw Salvatore and approached. "This the victim's car?" she said, when she reached him.

"Nothing concrete yet, but I'd bet on it."

"We have a name?" asked Tina.

"No wallet. Got a phone, but there's a password."

Tina took a deep breath, put her hands on her hips. "Katrina found semen in the body," she said. "No obvious signs of rape, but our Jane Doe definitely had intercourse the night she died."

"OK," said Salvatore.

"Water in her lungs, found on land, semen . . . you ready to call this a homicide?"

Salvatore nodded. "This is a murder investigation. Get the victim's phone unlocked, and get me her home address from the plates."

"I'm on it," said Tina.

"Salvatore?" It was one of the techs; Salvatore turned. "There's, uh . . . there's a photo in the glove box."

Tina and Salvatore rushed toward the passenger-side door. The tech held up a Polaroid print. The old-fashioned Polaroids were all the rage; Salvatore had given one to Allie "from Santa" the year before.

"It's just some kids," said Tina.

Salvatore stared at the photo. In the picture, three handsome teenage boys stood in the sunshine, their arms around each other's shoulders. One was blond, one with black hair, and one with hair the color of strawberries. They were tanned and smiling, wearing City of Austin lifeguard uniforms.

"Any idea who they are?" asked Tina.

"No," he said, squinting. They looked a lot like Salvatore and his friends, back when he was a carefree teenager. All three boys grinned, as if the world were a kind place, holding only joy in store for them. But Salvatore had met plenty of handsome teenagers who'd committed crimes.

He thought of the woman who had hung up on him earlier, then forced him to leave a message. He couldn't tear his eyes from the photo. He had a feeling that one of these happy kids would turn out to be Charlie Bailey, address 1308 Oak Glen.

Whitney

WHITNEY WAS A TERRIBLE cook, hated every step from making a grocery list to garnishing plates. And although she could afford someone to help, or at least order in once in a while, she made herself do everything. Cooking and serving was what a wife and mother was supposed to do, so goddamn it, she wasn't about to shirk her responsibilities.

Whitney understood that what drove her was internal, a voice that tore her apart and critiqued her every move. She imagined everyone was judging her constantly (and let's be honest, many *were*) but understood that the unkindest commentator resided in her brain.

Whitney refilled her wineglass, continued to chop. The menu included grilled chicken—she even grilled, for God's sake: was Jules the only neighborhood dad who didn't man his own barbecue? He was a husband who could assemble a charcuterie platter with ease, but propane and tongs confounded him. On the side: orzo with pistachios, roasted red peppers, and feta. She would eat only the protein; Roma would concoct some borderline anorexic plate (or just eat garbanzo beans from a bowl—had she seen this on some "pro-ana" TikTok video?); Xavier would eat heartily and compliment her, hugging her and thanking her a bit overzealously, as if he knew how much she relied on his appreciation; and Jules would chew and nod distractedly, expecting nothing less than the usual gourmet meal at 6:30 sharp.

Toast the pistachios. Whitney took one of her stainless pans from the hanging rack (she *hated* the pots hovering above her head, always felt a low anxiety, worried one would fall on her skull, but Jules wanted their gleaming pots and pans displayed) and placed it over a low flame, but stopped herself from adding olive oil.

She held the bowl of shelled pistachios. No one would know they weren't meant to be poured atop the orzo raw. Whitney felt a small thrill—she wasn't going to toast the damn nuts. She turned off the burner, exhaled. A small kindness to herself, but she already felt a bit less furious.

Roma and Jules burst in the front door, approached the kitchen. Whitney tossed her hair back and smiled. "Dinner in twenty!" she sang.

"We got P. Terry's burgers," said Roma, arching a perfect eyebrow.

"Oh," said Whitney, feeling hurt smash into her but recovering immediately, making her face impassive, moving to the sink to wash her hands.

"Sorry, darling," said Jules, slipping an arm around her waist.

"It's fine," said Whitney lightly.

Jules nodded, distracted already by his phone, making his way out of the kitchen. Whitney looked at the expensive ingredients laid out on the marble countertop: a perfect still life of wasted energy, money, and time.

"I wanted an iPhone Ten and Dad said OK," said Roma.

She placed three shopping bags on the kitchen counter, baiting Whitney to ask what else she'd suckered her father into buying, wanting her mother to be angry with them both. She leaned back and crossed her arms over her tiny chest. "Sorry we got burgers, Mom," she said, her voice saccharine.

"It's fine," said Whitney. "Sweetheart," she added, forcing the word from her mouth.

"I wish I knew where my old phone was," said Roma.

"Where did you go last night?" said Whitney. "Did you retrace your steps to look for it?" She swallowed. How could it have been less than twenty-four hours since the boys had found the body?

"I didn't go anywhere," said Roma. "I was in my room."

"Really?" said Whitney. "I saw your car leave, around nine."

"Oh, yeah," said Roma. "I went to the Barton Hills Food Mart to get Takis."

"What's a Taki?"

Roma laughed derisively. "It's a chip, Mom. Like Doritos. You're so white!" She waited, willing her mother to erupt.

Whitney did not respond.

"And I couldn't find my phone," Roma continued, "so I went without it. I was so annoyed. I missed *everything* last night."

Whitney's head throbbed. "Did anyone see you at the food mart?" she said.

"The food mart guy," said Roma, twirling a strand of hair around her finger.

"Did you use a credit card?" said Whitney. "For the chips?"

Roma stared at her. Her look was a bit menacing, and Whitney's stomach began to ache. "No," said Roma. "I used spare change. They're only, like, eighty-nine cents."

"There's probably a video," said Whitney, thinking aloud.

"What's going on, Mommy?" said Roma.

"Well, someone died last night, Roma," said Whitney.

"Yeah, I *heard*," said Roma, gathering her shopping bags. "Mom," she said. "Are you thinking I did something?"

"Of course not!" said Whitney.

"You always suspect me when things go wrong," said Roma, looking genuinely pained.

Whitney's mind spun. "Have you . . . heard anything else?" she said. Roma didn't answer, kicked off her sandals, and made her way toward the living room. Whitney touched her bronze shoulder and Roma flinched as if her mother had hit her. She whirled around.

"I had nothing to do with this!" she cried, her direct gaze chilling. *Don't think about New Zealand*, Whitney ordered herself. *No, don't think about the boy in New Zealand . . .*

"Maybe you should talk to your BFF *Annette*," said Roma, her glossy lips curling. "Maybe you should ask Annette where Bobcat goes at night."

"Bobcat?" said Whitney, bewildered.

"Yeah," said Roma. "Because one of us *has* been sneaking out late at night, and it isn't me."

"Bobcat's been sneaking out?" said Whitney.

"He's dating some older woman," said Roma, using her fingers to put quotation makes around the word "dating." "Bobcat's *dating* her in the middle of the night, if you know what I mean."

"What? I don't understand."

"Oh, you'll understand soon enough," said Roma, leaving the room, a burst of laughter echoing behind her.

-22-

Annette

ANNETTE STOPPED AT THE 7-Eleven on the way to her "dog walk," buying a pack of Camel Lights and stashing it in her jog bra. Whitney brought tequila in her Austin City Limits water bottle. Liza packed caramel corn and squeezed fresh limes.

They preferred fresh-squeezed lime juice and Cointreau to make "Mexican martinis." (Annette bit her tongue every time her friends used the stupid *and honestly racist* drink moniker.) But they *could* mix margaritas with lemonade, or nothing, in a pinch—they were Texan women, after all, and could drink tequila straight, especially if it were good tequila, which they called "sipping tequila."

Austin moms—at least Annette's friends—trafficked in *only* good tequila; not one of them had sipped bad booze since college. Whitney would get along with Annette's father— they could both discuss tequila for a long time, much longer than Annette thought was interesting or even healthy.

Every neighborhood mom had gone through a vodka phase, usually for a few weeks at the start of a bikinis-at-

Barton-Springs season. You'd notice a bit of winter pudge, vow to go carb-free, then realize the local vodkas *were* carb free. You'd buy one of the Yeti-brand stainless-steel travel mugs—bonus points for a neon monogram—fill it with ice at the start of an evening (the time might creep earlier as the hellish Texan summer went on), mix up your Tony's ATX vodka and Crystal Light.

Annette had met one mom who'd actually almost dated Tony himself; a friend had offered to introduce her to "a guy who makes vodka in his basement." Understandably, she'd been reluctant, but now the story was her claim to fame. Tony was a worldwide celebrity; Whitney told them she'd even seen a drink with Tony's ATX vodka featured at a chic bar in Hong Kong.

The end of every mom's vodka summer came with the realization that Tony's *flavored* vodkas allowed you to forgo the Crystal Light. The lemon and grapefruit varieties were so damn delicious you didn't need a mixer! So you filled your Yeti travel mug and attended the neighborhood pool parties, having a great few days (for some, a week or two) before you started blacking out, passing out, or being rushed to the hospital. Because straight vodka, motherhood, and high temperatures were a recipe for disaster. You'd survive—they'd all survived—but get a stern lecture about responsibility and a worried husband and eventually, you'd return to wine or LaCroix and chalk it up to a learning experience. All the moms went through it—it was almost a rite of passage.

Sometimes, when she woke with a piercing headache, Annette wondered if she (and her husband . . . and her friends) should seek out a better way of handling adulthood. Annette wasn't an idiot—she'd questioned the fact that the only way she knew to let loose was by ingesting booze.

But she'd also become someone who didn't want to chip away at cracks—if she started questioning her own tequila intake, she'd have to examine Louis's drinking, and then acknowledge the problems that existed in her cosseted life. She'd once been clear-eyed, but now there was so much at stake.

Annette missed the strong person she'd once been on the court. She'd been ruthless, willing to do anything to win. But once college ended, she lost direction. When Robert was born, she devoted herself to motherhood.

She was happy. She loved her life, her husband, her house, and her friends. Every day, she woke feeling as if this was where she belonged. She'd been working as hard as humanly possible for a long time—first at basketball, then at new motherhood. Now she had made it to the good part, the heart of her life. She was so lucky, and she didn't want to dive back into the shark-infested waters she'd swum through to get here. (Metaphorically, of course: there were no sharks in any Austin waters! Just trash and freaky snakes.)

When she arrived at the Packers' Cliffside address (although the Packers had returned to Silicon Valley, their "Austin experiment" apparently unsuccessful, everyone still referred to the mansion they had built by their name), Annette texted Whitney, who told her to come to the side gate. Past a topiary shaped carefully like Willie Nelson holding a guitar (complete with two braids of wisteria), Annette found a towering metal wall with a security camera on top. She peered into the camera's eye and waved uncertainly.

Whitney slid the gate open. "Hey," she said, embracing Annette.

"Hey," said Annette, relaxing into her friend's hug for a moment.

Whitney pulled back and wiped her eyes. Annette was moved to see that even Whitney was rattled by the body on the greenbelt. "I shut it off," said Whitney, gesturing to the camera.

"Annette!" called Liza, who was relaxing on a lounge chair in one of her long sundresses. Sometimes, Annette was jealous of Liza. For one thing, she was clearly Whitney's favorite: Whitney was always giving Liza clothes and spa appointments with her favorite aestheticians. It was a bit of an "Eliza Doolittle" situation, of course—Whitney obviously adored being admired by Liza, who wanted not only to be Whitney's favorite but to *be Whitney*.

Who was she kidding? Annette wanted to be Whitney, too. Whitney was effortlessly beautiful—imperial, even. The Jackie O of South Austin. Tonight, Whitney wore yoga pants and a top with multicolored straps that exposed her tanned collarbones. Her body was slim, bordering on bony, but in a pretty way.

Annette wasn't sculpted; she'd always been curvy, but she was strong. She generally hid her body in workout gear or drawstring pants and her favorite University of Texas tops. She dressed like an athlete, which she was, or anyway, *had been*. Louis loved her in tight, expensive outfits, but Annette felt most comfortable in the sports clothes she'd worn all her life. Her bright blond hair attracted enough unwanted male glances as it was.

The Packers' pool was stunning: huge, rectangular, surrounded by shade trees and furnished with modern loungers that looked like giant white balloons. At one end of the pool was a large gas fireplace. Annette felt her shoulders relaxing. "Do I hear a waterfall?" she asked. "Is there a waterfall?"

"Look, it's under the fireplace," said Liza. Annette squinted and could see a sheet of water falling underneath the flames into a hot tub, and then into the pool.

"Wow," she said.

"Mrs. Packer went to a Japanese spa that was heated by underground lava, and she wanted her yard to feel the same," said Whitney.

"Underground Japanese lava. It's fantastic!" chirped Liza.

Liza's obsequiousness irked Annette. But when Whitney looked at her pointedly, Annette said, "Wow."

Whitney smiled, placated. She stood by an outdoor kitchen with appliances almost as nice as the ones in Annette's own restaurant-grade kitchen. "Et voilà!" said Whitney, flipping a switch. Pool lights glowed, and three neon signs somehow affixed to the hedges ignited, reading AUSTIN, 78704, and LOVE. Annette sank into a balloon chair. It embraced her—it did! She must have looked unsettled, because Whitney noted, "It's memory foam. They all are."

"Wow," Annette repeated.

"And if I hit . . . *this* . . ." said Whitney, touching a keypad, "the entrance to the underworld opens . . ." The women swiveled as the pool fireplace moved aside to reveal a staircase.

"I feel like I'm in a Nancy Drew book," breathed Liza.

"Where does the staircase go?" said Annette.

"Sixties-style bunker," said Whitney. "To be honest, they didn't go 'top of the line' on the underground space. It'd be fine for a few weeks . . . nice living room, fake garden, windows showing Paris, plenty of canned goods, but they skimped on features . . . no library, no playscape, if you needed *anything* medical you'd have to resurface."

"Windows showing Paris?" said Annette.

"I know," said Whitney. She paused, then burst into laughter, breaking her realtor persona to be herself among her friends. "The Eiffel Tower from different angles—forever!" she said, giggling.

"Should I get a bunker?" said Liza, worriedly.

"We probably all should," said Whitney, clicking the buttons and restoring the Packers' regular, resort-style yard.

"I hate thinking about doomsday," said Liza.

"Me, too," said Annette. She bit her lip, trying to find a way to segue to the *other* topic she didn't want to think about.

"They want too much for this place," Whitney continued, clearly reveling in being able to relax and speak freely. "Three mil. It's just too much for the neighborhood. Tarrytown, maybe. Westlake? But not Barton Hills. Not yet, anyway!"

Liza queued up music—early Dixie Chicks—and began mixing drinks. Whitney went to the edge of the back lawn and lit a Camel Light, blowing the smoke toward the street. There was a long pause that felt uncomfortable to Annette: they were all waiting, she thought, for someone to talk about the boys and the body.

Annette felt weary. It had been a long day at Hola, Amigos. She wanted to hear what her friends knew and go home. "Can we . . ." she said. "Can we talk about it?"

"Yeah," said Whitney, finishing her cigarette and walking toward them, accepting a drink from Liza.

"The police," said Liza, her voice low, as if they were being recorded. They probably were being recorded. "The police called me."

"Goddamn it," said Whitney. "Why didn't you tell us earlier?"

Liza looked as if she were about to burst into tears. "I didn't . . . I don't know. I'm sorry. I . . ." She shook her head.

"How would they even find your number?" said Annette.

"Please don't be mad at me," said Liza, blinking back tears.

"My cell rang. I answered. A man said he was looking for Charlie and I . . . I hung up."

"Do they think Charlie had something to do with this?" said Annette. She was ashamed to feel relieved: Robert wasn't a suspect. Nobody had called *her*. Immediately, she berated herself. They were a team. If Charlie had done something wrong, she would protect him, too.

Wouldn't she?

"Look," said Whitney, lighting another cigarette. "There's something you both need to know."

They turned to her. Annette's stomach clenched. "What?" she said. "What is it, Whitney?"

"Charlie left a kneepad at the . . . scene of the crime, I guess they call it," said Whitney, gravely. "Xavier told me. The boys went back to get it and it was gone."

"That's not true," said Liza, alarmed.

"It is," said Whitney. "I'm so sorry."

"But why wouldn't Charlie tell me?" said Liza. "Why wouldn't he ask me for help?"

Good question, thought Annette.

"You need to lawyer up," said Whitney, putting her hand on Liza's knee. "We all do."

"You mean hire a lawyer?" said Liza.

Annette drew a breath. While she envied Liza many things—a bed to herself, time to do whatever she wanted, take-out pizza for dinner—at a time like this, she was glad to have a bulldog of a husband. Annette knew that as soon as she texted Louis, he would have the Fontenot family lawyer fly down from Midland. It was nice to be safe. It was nice to have a "family lawyer."

"But Charlie didn't *do* anything," said Liza, getting hysterical.

"Jules will get you a lawyer," said Whitney, her brow furrowed with concern. Annette knew Whitney felt responsible for Liza. They shared secrets, too, like who Charlie's father really was. Annette wished Liza would confide in her. It made her feel lonely, always being the third wheel.

"Really?" said Liza.

"Of course, Liza. Of course."

Annette's heart ached for Liza, who seemed so fragile. When she thought of kissing Hank Lefferts, Annette needed to remember Liza's face in this moment, the anguish Annette saw there. Annette hoped she would never feel the sense that she had no one and was completely alone. "This is all going to blow over. I know it," she said soothingly, trying to convince herself as she spoke.

"Maybe," said Whitney. "Who knows?" She turned to Annette, and her expression made Annette's stomach flip. Whitney looked at her with pity, as if she were worried about her. As if Whitney knew something, and whatever it was would put Annette in danger.

"Why are you looking at me that way?" said Annette.

"What way?" said Whitney.

"Like you feel sorry for me!"

"Oh my God, what?" said Whitney. "I just—" She stopped, inhaled. "Annette," she said, looking her directly in the eyes, "I have to ask you something. OK? Can I ask you a question?"

"Go ahead," said Annette.

"Was Bobcat dating anyone?"

"Dating?" said Annette, her heartbeat quickening. The week before, Bobcat had left his phone to charge in the kitchen, and Annette had picked it up. She'd put in his passcode—78704—and scrolled to make sure he wasn't dealing drugs or watching pornography. She'd known all the numbers . . . his friends, his dad, his coach. And she'd actually smiled when she saw a few notes from a girl—she'd *thought* it was a teenage girl—named Lucy. "Why do you ask?" said Annette.

"Roma mentioned he'd met someone," said Whitney. "That's all."

Annette made herself stay calm. She closed her eyes, listened to the sound of the cicadas in the Packers' fantastic yard. "I don't know anything about a girl," she said.

It was the first time she had lied to her closest friends.

The Lifeguards

THE DAY LUCY DIES

MORNING

Xavier

NOW THAT HE LOCKS his door—even secures it with a bolt
he bought at Home Depot and installed himself before anyone could stop him—Xavier can sleep, his descent into black
nothingness steep and quick. It's like falling into a vat of
black soup. He lies down, he falls deep, and it is morning, too
early, impossible to rise. He is making up for fifteen years of
lying awake and waiting, worried about what his twin sister
might do.

The day they find the body on the greenbelt begins with a
tapping at his window. The tapping is forceful and insistent: it
can only be Roma. Xavier tries to ignore it, to roll over and
press his pillow around his ears. But she keeps rapping, tapping, as if she is a woodpecker, and this image, at least, makes
him smile as he abandons sleep and moves into the day. Roma
as a sharp-beaked bird, all spindly legs and claws, her head
jutting back and forth endlessly.

He pulls open his blackout curtains. She is there, one hand
on her hip, one raised to continue the endless knuckles-

against-the-window barrage. Xavier stares at his sister, who begins talking, though he cannot hear her through the thick security glass. Xavier glances to the camera in the corner of his room. He unlatches the window and waits for the piercing alarm, but there is only Roma's voice.

". . . long enough," she says. "Now the screen, little brother. Let's go."

Roma calls Xavier "little brother," though she beat him into the world by only three minutes and twenty seconds. She also calls him "boy," or "boi," as if she is a rapper, when she's just a fifteen-year-old girl, cruel and spoiled, deranged. Xavier hesitates.

"What?" says Roma.

"What are you *doing*?" says Xavier. "You turned off the alarm?"

She grins and shrugs, thinking he is calling her smart. She raises an eyebrow. "Open the screen or I'll cut it," she says.

He laughs. "Oh, you have a knife now?" he says. "You're a full-on gangbanger now?"

"I don't have a knife," says Roma. She rummages in her miniature pink backpack and pulls out child scissors, holds them up triumphantly.

"I don't care if you cut it," says Xavier. He wants to shut the window, to go back to sleep, but he knows from experience that Roma will have her way. He opens the screen.

"Many thanks and happy returns," says Roma, climbing nimbly inside. She stretches, exposing a belly ring. She's wearing tight jeans and a midriff-baring top. Her makeup is a mess.

"Where were you?" says Xavier.

She crosses his room without answering.

"Roma," says Xavier, "where have you been all night?"

She unlocks his door and steps through it. "Wouldn't you like to know?" she says. She slips the child scissors into her back pocket and is gone. Xavier shuts and locks the door. But there is no going back to sleep. The first day of summer has begun.

Bobcat

BOBCAT BIKES PAST HER apartment on his way to the pool, and then—compelled by a magnetic force—he veers into a parking space, locks his bike, and runs up the stairs. Outside apartment 5B, he pauses, honestly kind of scared.

(There could be someone in there with her.)

(He should leave.)

(Something is wrong with him.)

He knocks.

From the landing outside her door, he can see the condo complex pool where he works on weekends, not because he needs money but because he wants to be away from his house. His dad's "Mr. Good Time" act and his mother's face, her smile a frozen mask of effortful joy. The air around them is toxic. He only wants to breathe.

Lucy opens her apartment door. She wears pink pajamas and looks so beautiful he almost tells her so. "Robert?" she says, sleepily. Her eyes are unfocused, as if she is stoned. It scares him. "Are you high?" he asks.

Instead of answering, she takes his hand and pulls him inside.

Lucy's apartment is an adult's apartment: framed posters, a bowl of fruit, a neatly made bed with accent pillows, no socks on the floor. Bobcat looks around. Where is her laundry? Lucy is even neater than his mother and their housekeeper combined. Bobcat thinks of asking if she cleans her own apartment, or complimenting her on her countertops, which gleam and smell of lavender. But that would be weird.

There is no pot smell. Only the lavender counter spray, the smell of her sleep, and some kind of fruity lotion.

As soon as her door is locked behind them, she falls to her knees and takes him in her mouth.

(He stops talking.)

When, later, she says, "I'm sorry, did you ask me something?" He shakes his head.

(He wants to say, "I love you.")

(But that would be weird.)

-3-

Charlie

CHARLIE'S PHONE HAS TWELVE Snapchat messages before he even wakes up. Only one has words, and it's from Amir. Charlie smiles, just thinking of Amir. They've been together about a month, only Charlie's third relationship since coming out. Amir is more experienced but just as nervous, just as smitten, Charlie thinks. They've gone shopping three times at Flamingos Vintage, held hands under the table at Kerbey Lane once, and on the last day of school, Amir had come up behind Charlie at his locker and kissed his neck.

"Get a room!" said Van, who was on the basketball team with Amir.

"Only if you pay for it, brother!" cried Amir.

"Hot couple," said Sophie, the girl with the locker next to Charlie's.

Charlie had blushed, turning to smile at Sophie, and Amir had leaned down to kiss Charlie on the lips.

Heaven!

Amir's message reads: HIIIII. WHAT SHOULD WE DO TONIGHT? MEET AT THE 7-ELEVEN FOR SNACKS AND THEN???

Charlie answers with an emoji of a cat in a party hat. He immediately wishes he hadn't sent such a stupid emoji, but it's already done. He gets up to shower and pee. In the shower, he thinks about how he should change his Snapchat avatar's outfit. His avatar wears basketball shorts and Jordan 1s, but he's more preppy now, less into sports gear. He loves the band Vampire Weekend and wants to copy the lead singer's boarding school style—Birkenstocks and slim-fitting khaki pants. His mom is obsessed with seeming rich, so she was thrilled when he asked to buy some J.Crew and Abercrombie off eBay.

He hasn't come out as bi to his mother officially, but he assumes she knows. Charlie's mom doesn't like to talk about uncomfortable topics, and Charlie figures that if *she* wants to keep his father a secret, *he* can keep his sex life a secret. It angers him; it's bullshit. Charlie wishes he and his mom could just have a big cryfest and be real about things. It's exhausting to live the way they do, his mom pretending she can afford things she can't, Charlie pretending he is seeing his lifeguard friends when he is seeing Amir.

Xavier and Roma and Bobcat are fine, they are his everything, his best friends. But they're kind of strange about Amir. They *like* him—he's on the basketball team, after all, and leaving for Tech (Div I, full ride) at the end of the summer—but Charlie knows his being *in love* makes them feel uncomfortable. Maybe jealous? Nobody cares that he's bi; it's more that he has a lover and the rest of them don't. Not yet. Not really. Unless you count Bobcat's Lucy, which to be honest, Charlie doesn't.

He even tried to bring Amir to the house, warned him to wear the collared shirt they'd bought together, giggling and kissing in the Flamingos Vintage dressing room. But his mom immediately acted like an idiot, with the high voice and constant "are you sure you boys don't want some nachos" bullshit. By which she means Costco cheese microwaved on tortilla chips.

Charlie's mom has nothing but him, he gets it. But after Amir left, her inquisition about him—what did his parents do, was he a good student—was too much. He watched her mouth move, and he thought, *I don't even know you.*

Worse, he thought, *I don't want to know you.*

His mom! They'd been so close. Pizza and movies on Saturday night, "us against the world," et cetera. But the story she'd been telling him unraveled when he started to examine it around sixth grade. *Why* was his father a lie about a heart attack on a ski slope? Who was he really? Why didn't his mom trust him to understand any situation that had gotten her pregnant?

Had she been raped?

Who were her family?

Where were her family?

Who was *he*?

What was his DNA?

Where did he belong?

Eventually, his anger about the questions she refused to answer turned to contempt for her. He hid it well, he knew. She thought he was easygoing, without cares. Worse, she thought she'd given him a perfect childhood. Honestly, he was done with her. Especially after that speech about Amir. Fuck her.

So he'd gotten a DNA test. He'd found his family, even his father, who was not dead after all. Charlie had ignored all messages from ancestry.com except the one giving him his father's contact info and name: Patrick Hamilton. (So regal!)

His dad definitely seemed sketchy, what with no Facebook, a hotmail.com email, and needing three hundred dollars sent via PayPal, but Patrick Hamilton was flying into Austin that afternoon. Fine, he would pay his dad to see him, whatever.

Charlie would work his lifeguard shift, then meet his dad, then end up next to Amir, who would make it all OK.

There's also a party tonight in the neighborhood, a big one. A kid he doesn't know, a younger kid, posted on his Snapchat story that his parents were away. A hyped-up video of him yelling about a rager on Barton Skyway. Any idiot who would post his address on Snapchat was asking to have his house burned down. It was like buying drugs on Snap. Just dumb.

Everyone knows: if you want drugs, you text.

The
Third Day
of Summer

2019

Austin American-Statesman

AUSTIN POLICE CHIEF JOSÉ RAMIREZ VOWS TO PROSECUTE "CRAIGSLIST DRUG DEALERS"

In the first arrest of its kind, Austin Police Chief José Ramirez has charged seventeen-year-old Cameron Levy, a so-called Craigslist drug dealer, with murder. Levy allegedly sold fentanyl-laced pills to Jessica Finlay, a classmate at Live Oak High School, who died of an opioid overdose. Investigators say that Levy knew about the deadly overdose risks of fentanyl consumption—he had used his smartphone to search "fentanyl overdose death" the same night he met up with Finlay in the parking lot of a Braker Lane Taco Bell restaurant.

"These illegal opioids have ravaged many parts of the United States," said Ramirez. "We will not allow this to happen in Austin. Not on my watch. If anyone sells these extremely dangerous, illegal drugs, they will be prosecuted to the full extent of the law, regardless of their age."

The Austin Police Department determined that the victim bought pills from Levy on March 30, meeting him at Taco Bell. She overdosed later that night at her family's home in the exclusive Central Austin neighborhood of Tarrytown. Jessica was found by her younger sister when she did not come downstairs for breakfast, according to EMS reports.

When police tracked down Levy, also a Tarrytown resident, they seized Xanax, more of the fentanyl-laced pills, and an array of other drugs including LSD, ecstasy, cocaine, and codeine, and a digital scale. He had also advertised these items on Craigslist. A search of Levy's phone also showed a Google search for "what does aspiration mean," which investigators believe refers to pulmonary aspiration, a common cause of death from a drug overdose due to the inhalation of saliva or vomit.

A murder charge for an underage teen is the first of its kind, and will require proving that Levy knew his conduct was so dangerous that it could lead to someone dying. Jurors could believe risk is accepted by both parties in an illicit drug deal. "You can't prosecute every drug dealer as a murderer," says criminal defense attorney Raj James. "That's ridiculous."

Ridiculous or not, Austin Mayor Remshart Janicki supports the murder charge. "We're going to do what we have to do to stop opioid abuse, especially by teenagers in our community," says Janicki. "I am making opioid prevention the cornerstone of my reelection campaign. If you're a drug dealer—whether you're on TikTok, Twitter, Snapchat, Tumblr, Craigslist, Instagram, Instacart, or a street corner—listen up: we will catch you, and we will put you in jail for a very long time."

-2-

Liza

I GAVE UP TRYING to sleep at 5:00 A.M. and made a pot of coffee, sprinkling cinnamon over the grounds for a bit of spice. I loved sitting on my front step, waving to the early-morning joggers, watching the birds. I kept a bird book and a pair of binoculars by the door, and sometimes Charlie and I sat side by side, crying out, "Blue jay! Look!" and "Ugh, another grackle." Our lawn was small and neat, watered by a lone sprinkler and kept trimmed by Charlie borrowing our neighbor's mower twice a month. We even had a live oak tree, which cast intricate shadows.

It started to heat up by six, so I went inside to begin work. Sam wanted a chapter on breakfast, so she'd submitted a list of recipe ideas. I started with *kao tom goong* soup, a traditional Thai dish that Sam made her own by adding grilled vegetables and shrimp. When Charlie woke, he padded into the kitchen in running shorts and an Austin City Limits T-shirt.

The shirt was from the year when his elementary school choir opened for Charlie Sexton. *That* had been a weird experience—I'd once owned a poster of Sexton, and had gazed at his full-lipped pout, his extravagant hairstyle, full of teen lust. He'd seemed the epitome of the bad boy who could get me out of Massachusetts, show me wild worlds of dimly lit bars and poolside parties and making out during rainstorms. And so to be standing in an audience of moms (all of us dressed up as teenagers—jean shorts, trucker hats, spaghetti-strap tops) watching my own flesh-and-blood sing "Blowing Up Detroit" and "Cruel and Gentle Things" earnestly, sweetly, his chubby twelve-year-old face and Sexton's wizened visage and a few morning mimosas . . . I had felt swoony, enjoying the rare sense that all the pieces had come together in my jagged jigsaw puzzle of a life.

"WHOA," SAID CHARLIE NOW, using a worn-out pot holder to lift the top off my concoction, inhaling the fragrant steam.

"It's Thai," I said. "*Kao tom goong.*"

"Hmmm," said Charlie.

"In other countries, shrimp for breakfast is a thing," I said. "Sit down and let me ladle you a bowl."

"Sounds good." Charlie leaned against the avocado-colored laminate counter. It was trimmed in gold, with a patterned wallpaper backsplash. Our floor was green-and-white linoleum. Our wooden kitchen table had come from an estate sale years before.

Charlie and I loved attending estate sales and snapping up furniture, clothing, and kitchen stuff. We were both moved by peeking into what remained of a home when the owners had passed. I'd once bought four tubes of unopened, frosted lipstick, and Charlie, a skeleton that must have been used in a doctor's office to point out spine deformities. How strange, I'd said to Charlie, to put price tags on everything you'd accumulated.

Nothing in our Oak Glen home was worth much at all . . . though I had pilfered my mother's measuring spoons, feeling sentimental as I was jamming stuff in my backpack on my way out of town. The metal spoons were a bit rusty, but I treasured them. By the time I'd left, my mother no longer cooked anyway. I wondered if she'd even noticed they were missing.

Sometimes, I thought about emailing my mom, or calling her. Sending a postcard? I didn't even know if she was alive. And then there was my sister, Darla. She would be nineteen now, likely lost the way most of us kids on the Cape got lost, our frustration assuaged by getting pregnant, taking drugs, or both. I had taken care of Darla like a mother before I left. Who had cared for her when I was gone? When I thought about her—acknowledged how much Charlie looked like her, especially his red hair—I felt a searing pain.

Why not go back to visit Falmouth? Charlie was fifteen, grown and intelligent. Maybe knowing my mom and Darla would be good for him. About once a year, after a wine-filled evening, I googled my mom's name, Darla, and Patrick. I never found anything, not even on Facebook.

Besides, I didn't want Charlie feeling (like I did, every day) as if he didn't belong in our bright life. Bringing him to that trailer park, poisoning him with the knowledge that his dad was an addict, that his biological family was poor and struggling . . . no. I had worked so hard to get us here. I didn't want to look back. I didn't want him to know I was white trash. I didn't want anyone to know. I wanted to be Liza Bailey.

If I really examine it, there's also a part of me that was afraid Charlie *would* love his dad. Maybe Patrick was better, maybe he was better than me. Maybe he lived in a fancy apartment in Beacon Hill, and Charlie would choose to join him and leave me. What would I have then?

I couldn't afford plane tickets anyway, and Charlie was not the type of kid who traveled on smelly, long-haul Greyhounds.

At our kitchen table, Charlie seemed distracted. "Mom?" he asked.

"Try the soup," I answered.

Charlie swallowed, seemingly weighing a decision. I knew—I *knew*—he had something to tell me. I think now, *Jesus, Christ! Ask him what he wants to say!* I can't explain why I didn't. Why I couldn't. It was a wall of blue fear, making my mouth dry, keeping me silent. I just wanted things to go on as they had been. I just didn't want him to speak any words that would end our dream of a life.

Charlie looked at me pleadingly. I turned away, toward the stove. Eventually, as I had hoped, he returned to himself. He picked up a spoon and took a bite. "It's awesome, Mom," he said, his voice a bit flat, false.

I exhaled. "Really? You like the soup?" I said, my voice reedy, a bit hysterical.

"I was dubious," said Charlie. "But yum."

I laughed, then startled when a voice from the front hall said, "How come my kids don't know words like *dubious*?" I looked up to see Whitney stepping into my kitchen.

"Smells amazing in here." Whitney grinned. She wore exercise clothes, a visor in her black hair. "Can I have some? I just finished a paddle on Lady Bird Lake," she said, opening a cabinet and taking a bowl, ladling soup. She joined us at the table. I loved how at home she was in my kitchen, like a sister.

"Um, I better get going. I have an eight-mile today, and then I'll be at Barton Springs," said Charlie. He lifted his bowl and finished every drop of his *kao tom goong*. "Mom, can we drive tonight?" he asked.

"Reverse parking on Congress and then Home Slice?" I

said. Home Slice was our favorite pizza joint; we always split a pear gorgonzola salad, pepperoni and mushroom pie, and garlic knots.

"Awesome," said Charlie, leaning in to give me a hug from behind. His smell, his smell. I closed my eyes to savor it.

"Maybe Roma could join you guys at the springs?" said Whitney.

"Um, yeah, maybe," said Charlie. "OK, bye, Mom. Thanks for the shrimp soup." He touched his toes, then slammed out the door and down Oak Glen. His eight-mile would wind him through the neighborhood, then up Lamar to the University of Texas and back again.

Whitney smiled. "What a sweetie," she said.

"He is," I said, grinning despite myself. I added quickly, "So are yours!"

"Do you have any of that amazing cinnamon coffee? I'm dying," said Whitney.

My Mr. Coffee was empty. I felt a tension in my jaw and almost wanted to say, "Sorry, I don't." But I swallowed my annoyance and stood. "Let me just make a fresh pot," I said.

"I love you," said Whitney, lifting her phone to check her messages while I ground the beans from my Costco-sized bag, breathing evenly to dispel my irritation. I was barefoot, still in red-and-green-plaid Christmas pajamas.

I tidied up the kitchen while I waited for the coffee to brew, making notes on Sam's "breakfast soup" recipe, which maybe needed something to make it sweeter for American palates.

When the pot was full, I retrieved one of the two nice mugs I'd found in the sale room in the back of the Anthropologie store, filled it, and brought it to Whitney with one Splenda and a dollop of milk.

Whitney sipped, still not looking up from her phone.

"Mmm, perfect," she said. Whitney loved being cared for, and she did look after me as well. If sometimes it felt as if she treated me like staff, I could live with that. Wasn't I using her, too, in my own way? Would I still love her if she were poor, or less influential, less glamorous? I liked to think I would, but I couldn't know for sure.

As Whitney scrolled on her phone, I tried to think of a way to say, *Are you hiring me a lawyer? If I coddle you and make you coffee, will you take care of me and Charlie?*

Whitney began tapping an email. I was silent, all the words I wanted to speak forming a ball in my gut. Or maybe it was the spicy soup.

Finally, Whitney put her phone down. "I'm scared," she said.

"What?" I said. I hadn't ever heard her say these words before.

"Can you promise to keep a secret?" said Whitney.

"Of course," I said. "You know you can trust me."

"I do know," she said. "And by the way, we need to talk about a lawyer for Charlie. I haven't forgotten. But this . . . I don't know where to . . . who to tell. But I can't . . . I don't know what to do. Jules won't . . . he refuses . . ." Whitney's face transformed before my eyes. Her polished veneer cracked, and she looked almost feral. It was such a dramatic transformation that I wondered if it was fake. I had a strange feeling, as if Whitney was acting.

"I'm only telling *you*," she said, putting her hand on mine.

"What is it?" I said. "You're scaring me."

"This is only between you and me, OK? You're my best friend."

"Yes, of course. I promise," I said. As always, the term "best friend" made me feel warm—chosen.

"It's Roma," said Whitney, her tone grave.

"Roma?" I was surprised, though I knew Roma was a perennial problem. She could be cruel, but despite a few truly alarming incidents, I tried to believe that Roma was, at heart, a good person. Charlie had once asked, "Mom? What do I do if every time I see someone, I feel bad about myself?"

"Sweetheart," I'd said, "you can try to make friendships work, but it's OK to just let some people go."

Charlie had nodded grimly. I felt that I'd taught him a good lesson . . . until Whitney called, crying, saying Charlie had told Roma they couldn't hang out anymore. I confronted Charlie, and he'd said, "Mom! You told me it was OK to let people go!"

"But not Roma," I'd said, pleadingly.

Charlie had looked at me with disgust. I pretended I hadn't seen it, inviting both the twins over that evening for "Make Your Own Pizza" night, ignoring Charlie's withdrawn demeanor.

"ROMA?" I REPEATED NOW, taking a gulp of hot coffee. "What happened?"

Whitney took off her visor, and her hair fell into her face. She rubbed her eyes. Was she crying? I didn't see any tears, berated myself for checking for moisture. "You can trust me," I said. I moved to her side of the table and hugged my friend. Usually, I felt comforted when I was near Whitney, but today, I just felt raw.

Whitney lifted her head. Her eyes were reddish but dry. "I don't know where she went night before last," said Whitney. "She left the house while we were drinking wine . . . she says she lost her phone. And I don't know where she was. I'm afraid . . . I'm just afraid. Do you think Roma could have had something to do with that woman's death?"

Whitney certainly looked afraid. I tried to speak sooth-ingly. "Come on, Whitney," I said. "You know she didn't."

Whitney nodded, but this news really was worrisome. It was another item on the list of disturbing events involving Roma. There had been the fractured elbow. The neighbor's cat. Xavier's mysterious poisoning. And worst: the incident in New Zealand. Whitney had confided in me in the early years about Roma's troubling behavior, but a wall had come down sometime in the last few years. Was it possible Roma had been on the greenbelt and somehow hurt the woman, left her for the boys to discover?

If so, why?

"Promise you'll never say anything?" said Whitney, putting her hands around my wrists. "I had to tell someone. I had to."

"I promise," I said, biting my lip. Whitney's grip was pain-ful, but I repeated, "I promise, Whitney."

But I knew, deep down, that if betraying Whitney meant saving my son, I would do it.

-3-

Salvatore

WHILE HE RODE THE exercise bike he kept in the garage, Ozzy Osbourne blaring in his headphones, Salvatore tried to solve the problem of having a job he loved too much and kids who needed him. Jacquie had accused him of being selfish, attending to his work and not his family. She'd complained, but she'd made it all OK. Better than OK: when he was jacked up from one horror or another (the worst were the kids, the kids), she would let him talk in the hushed, sacred space of their bedroom, unloading the worst of it, listening, staying next to him. Now, all the stories were crammed in his brain with no off-ramp. And at 2:45 every day, his own two babies needed him. It was impossible.

Salvatore didn't have time for the plaintive texts he got from Joe, the guilt trips from Allie when he finally made it home completely wiped out. He needed to find a solution and fast. He couldn't afford a nanny, but he was going to have to afford a nanny. That would fix it: a nanny! He had a vision of a competent young woman, maybe in a blazer, who would handle his kids so he could stop worrying about messy domestic intricacies.

Solving murders was what he was meant to do, what he *could* do. Work was a balm. Adrenaline distracted him from sorrow.

When he finished his ride to nowhere, pedaling furiously yet traveling no farther than his perch in front of the plastic bins of Christmas decorations, he googled "How to Find a Nanny Austin," and ended up on "Nanny Poppinz." He filled out the forms quickly, entered his credit card with a sigh, and "matched" with three people. He copied and pasted the same message to all three and logged out in time to take a quick shower before Joe and Allie woke up. He was out of soap. He would ask the nanny to buy soap! Naked, he rummaged under the sink, then washed himself with years-old baby shampoo.

Salvatore didn't really listen to Allie and Joe as he drove them to school. Something about a bully, something about a jerk, Joe kept poking his sister. Salvatore was so tired.

RAMIREZ WAS LIT UP and waiting for him in the office. "So," he said, "you saw the conference?"

"I get the gist," said Salvatore. "Arrest someone, anyone. Rich kids are ODing and that's not acceptable."

"Fair summation," admitted Ramirez.

"So if Teen One gives Oxy to Teen Two, and Teen Two OD's, that's a murder charge now?"

"For Teen One, yes." Ramirez leaned against Salvatore's desk. He crossed his arms over his chest. Ramirez was younger than Salvatore, single, a go-getter. Salvatore had never seen him appear troubled. "Best solution we've got, apparently," said Ramirez.

Salvatore respected his honesty and told him so.

"You take a child, she breaks an ankle, needs surgery," said Ramirez. "You give her some Percocet, open those receptors, you can never go back. Once you crave these drugs . . ."

"Yeah, I know. We all know," said Salvatore.

"You got an ID on the greenbelt body?" said Ramirez.

"We got a car registered to Lucy Masterson. Twenty-one, Austin Community College student, part-time waitress, from Sugarland. She lived in a condo complex near the greenbelt. We've notified the family. They're on the way." Salvatore winced, remembering the wail of Lucy's mother over the phone line, the sobbing of a young boy in the background.

"Anything else?"

Salvatore listed the facts. "I thought it was an OD . . . it *was* an OD. But she had water in her lungs. Someone dragged her to shore. And Katrina found semen from recent sexual activity."

"OK . . ."

"At the crime scene, I found a kneepad with a name tag and address. It belongs to a kid who lives near the greenbelt named Charlie Bailey. Could have been down there awhile, not sure. There was a photo of three boys in the victim's glove box. They were wearing City of Austin lifeguard uniforms. One of them could be Charlie Bailey. I can't reach his mother or the kid, went to the home three times. Could be no connection, but I'll stay on it. That's where I am."

"OK. Get the kid in here before he lawyers up. Head to the City of Austin pools, find out who the boys in the photo are. We'll need their DNA, so get warrants ready."

"On it," said Salvatore.

"Arrest them if you have to. We need some progress on this."

"Got it, boss."

Ramirez paused. Salvatore willed him not to say it, but Ramirez cleared his throat. "Look, Revello," he said.

"I know," said Salvatore.

"It's been awhile now, and . . ."

"Yes, sir. I get it."

"I cut you slack, but . . ."

Salvatore met his gaze. Ramirez didn't mention the late reports, the botched cases, the time he was caught at Jacquie's hospital bedside during his shift. Ramirez didn't have to say it: *This is your last chance.* "I know you're a good detective," said Ramirez. "And if you need a break . . . ?"

"Thanks," said Salvatore. "I don't need a break."

Ramirez nodded. "OK," he said.

"Thank you," said Salvatore.

When the chief was gone, Salvatore checked his email. One of the nannies had written back. Her name was Mae Mae, she was an English major at St. Ed's, she listed references. Salvatore called the first three, and each confirmed Mae Mae was reliable and fine. Salvatore did not call the fourth reference. He knew he should, and he would, just later.

He wrote the nanny back, sending the times the kids needed to be picked up, telling her his home address, where he hid the key. His children were a messy situation, and he needed clarity. When Mae Mae said she'd take care of it, of them, he ignored the hot feeling in his gut and wrote, "Thanks."

Look away and it will go away.

-4-

Whitney

AS SHE DROVE HER morning client back to his steel-and-glass rental home above Lady Bird Lake, Whitney's mind wandered. Despite the punishing heat, her client, who made millions of dollars by streaming himself playing videogames on Twitch, wore a black sweatsuit and dirty socks with Gucci slides. (The hideous shoes were worth $400; Whitney had to keep up with all the trends. These young men didn't always shower, but they kept their shoes immaculate.) Luckily, her client was the "ignore humans and listen to AirPods" type. Whitney guessed he was just a year or two older than Xavier.

Whitney tried to pay attention to her driving. She was furious about Charlie and his forgotten kneepad. She needed to know *what had happened on the greenbelt.* Questions scrolled in her mind:

Why had the boys been on the greenbelt late at night?

Was it possible that the boys had had something to do with the woman's death?

Had they known her?

Who was she?

Had Bobcat really been seeing an older woman, as Roma accused?

Was the dead woman Bobcat's girlfriend?

Had Bobcat killed her?

Bobcat was, despite his size and strength, a sweet boy. Xavier was a bundle of nerves, and Charlie could be broody, but Bobcat had always been open and enthusiastic, easygoing if a bit wild. He had a wide and generous smile.

Bobcat's father was crass and a loudmouth, but as far as Whitney knew, Louis had never raised a hand to his son. The boys saw physical altercations only in movies and videogames. Whitney cut her gaze to the gamer dozing in her passenger seat. Could the creepy videogames the boys played have resulted in real-life bloodshed? Xavier got so worked up when he played, wearing his silly headset (it reminded Whitney of her aerobics instructor in 1998), screaming and shooting and having an absolute meltdown when Whitney called him to dinner.

She'd certainly read about the problems of boys these days, the way they didn't know how to regulate the emotions these games elicited, how to process rage. And everyone knew social media apps eroded attention spans. She and Jules had a glossy shared Instagram page that was so far from their day-to-day reality it was laughable. Sometimes, Whitney scrolled through images of her twins posing in sunlight, her husband gazing at her, and the one time they went to BookPeople (pretending to browse in Austin's iconic bookstore but not even buying anything! Well, Roma had bought a muffin), marveling at how happy her family seemed, lasciviously reading all the over-the-top comments: *You guys are so cute! #goals.*

Whitney remembered the summer the kids were twelve. How had that been only three years before? The kids went from chubby to rail-thin during those few, hot months, it had

seemed. One afternoon, Whitney sat by her pool with Annette and Liza. The boys tackled each other on the lawn, then
ran and cannonballed into the pool. "I'm jealous of my own
son," said Liza. She tried to laugh, but the sound was stran-
gled. "Imagine this being your childhood," Liza continued,
gesturing to the house, the pool, the outdoor refrigerator full
of cold drinks.

Whitney's childhood had been bitterly lonely. She'd
missed her sister and parents every single day, and she'd spent
her summers in punishing ballet classes, pushing her body
beyond what it could bear, as it turned out. But then she had
created this life; she'd used iron will and cunning to get herself here. The money didn't matter to Whitney the way it did
to her friends—what she craved was *love*.

Whitney, too, was envious of her own kids.

Annette had been thoughtful that day, playing with her
blond ponytail and not looking at Whitney and Liza when she
said, "I was lucky. My childhood was the best."

"In Laredo?" said Whitney. She sounded more shocked
than she should have. She had never met Annette's family:
the Fontenots went to their parents' houses, alternating holidays.

"Yeah," said Annette. "My brothers took care of me, and
my mom is an amazing cook, and my dad's the best man I
know." She looked up, almost embarrassed. "He's famous in
Laredo," she said. "Everyone wants his boots." She laughed
and shook her hand in front of her face, as if to dispel her
pride. "Sorry to be a show-off," she said. "I should bring you all
there. My parents would love you."

"Wow," said Whitney, suddenly jealous of Annette, whom
she'd always kind of looked down on: the sloppy athletic
clothes, Annette's muscular thighs, her penchant for messy
ponytails. Whitney hated the yearning that rose in her chest.

Just then, Bobcat had emerged from behind a live oak tree with a water gun. "Moms, get in the pool!" he'd cried. Whitney and her friends protested happily, running to the pool, joining in the fun. Whitney tried a cannonball and failed, cherishing a brief respite from being perfect, thanks to Bobcat.

WHITNEY'S CLIENT WAS TALKING. Whitney—part of her still trapped in her lonely childhood room, those endless days in the ballet studio, the smell of resin and sweat; part of her feeling the cool water on her skin as Bobcat shot at her with a water gun—tried to morph back into an adult, a realtor, a cool cucumber. She tried to hide her desperate need.

". . . move to New Zealand," concluded the gamer, whose name Whitney kept forgetting. Was it Mongrel or Meathead? In any case, his real name (Gene Willoughby) was not one he used anymore.

"Tell me more," said Whitney. These rich young men, many of whom had bought their real mothers houses and cars, clearly missed having a maternal figure in Austin. They had money and power, and some of them had worldwide fame, but they all seemed to want someone to sit with quietly, to listen as they spoke. "I'm listening," said Whitney.

"I mean, it's safer in New Zealand. In terms of the class war. You'd need your own plane, if they shut down commercial travel."

"I've surveyed properties in New Zealand, and I'd be happy to send you an information box," said Whitney. These kids loved "boxes" of all kinds. They spent thousands of dollars for "Mystery Hype Boxes" containing old sneakers and T-shirts. Maybe it was because they lived their lives online that a real box was such a thrill. (They even filmed them-

selves opening boxes, and watched videos of strangers opening boxes . . .) Whitney's packages contained house listings,
foodstuffs, and rare clothing and shoes. Xavier helped her find
good stuff. If a thousand-dollar shoe in a box made a child
billionaire buy a ten-million-dollar home, it was a great in-
vestment.

"I'd love an information box!" said Mongrel/Meathead.
When they pulled into his driveway (where three cars were
parked: a Tesla, an electric Porsche, and a Ferrari), Whitney
had him click a few items on her phone (square footage
needed, waterfront?, pool?, shoe size), and promised him
she'd be in touch. The kid unfurled himself from the Tesla
and said goodbye. Whitney shook his hand firmly, and told
him it was a pleasure to get to know him.

"Me, too," he said. As she turned the car around to exit,
Whitney glanced back and saw her client taking a breath and
looking around. He looked so young, this kid named Gene, a
lost boy in the city. Whitney hadn't even asked where he was
from, and if he'd told her, she'd forgotten. She'd seen him
only as a commission, and she suddenly felt a twinge of shame.

Tears welled behind Whitney's eyes. It was the thought of
Gene wandering through his rental mansion with no one to
greet him, or make him a snack. It was the vision of Bobcat in
a concrete prison yard instead of running down the basketball
court on a perfect fall evening.

Was Xavier involved with this dead body?

Was Roma?

Was the young woman who died the one who bought the
pills?

What had happened on the greenbelt?

Craigslist > Austin > Community > Childcare

Warning BEWARE!!!
DO NOT USE Nanny Poppinz Caregivers!!!

Warning! Fraudulent childcare in South Austin. Nanny Poppinz sent me a nanny with a fake name. They said they had completed a background check but THIS WAS A LIE!!! She stole checks and a phone from my bedside table when she was SUPPOSED TO BE WATCHING MY BABY!!! Her fake name was LISA STEPHENS but her real name is TIFFANI BUSTELLO!!! She is in trouble with the law for lying about her identity to police and a hospital. She will be looking for more children soon or skip town. DO NOT USE NANNY POPPINZ and if you do, use at your own risk!!!!

-6-

Annette

ANNETTE SAT ON HER upper deck, hoping to see the coyote, sipping a cup of coffee. Louis came through the sliding glass door in his work suit. "I wonder what happened to the coyote," said Annette.

"I told you, those things are dangerous."

"Not this one," said Annette.

Louis sat next to her, took her hand, began planting kisses on her palm. "Come here," he said. Annette smiled tightly, tried not to move away. She wasn't in the mood for sex *at all*. "I just . . . I liked taking care of it," she said.

"Forget the feral animal," said Louis. "I'll be your coyote." He leaned toward her, and she did not allow herself to rear back.

Don't lose Robert, she thought. *Don't lose everything you have built.*

It took all her strength just to remain where she was.

A Remembrance of Lucy Masterson

SPECIAL TO THE *SUGAR LAND HERALD*

By Junie Levine

Graveside services for Lucille Rose Masterson are
scheduled for Saturday, June 8, 2019, 3PM,
at the Wheeler Cemetery in Sugar Land, Texas.
Viewing will be held at Robertson Funeral
Directors Saturday, June 8, 2019, 10AM–2PM.

She flew through the air like an eagle, landing somehow
on her feet each and every time, her grace provoking
gasps and standing ovations. Lucy was a hometown hero,
shining brightly for a short time before shooting like a
comet to Austin, where she died last week, a fallen star.
Her cause of death has not yet been released.

Lucy was also my best friend, and while I stayed here in
Sugar Land, jettisoning my dreams of becoming a big city
reporter to become the manager of Panera Bread at the
Sugar Land Mall, Lucy went for her aspirations, leaving
the day after graduation with one pink duffel bag and the

money she had saved when she worked with me at Panera Bread, before I became manager.

I will never forget the days we spent behind the counter, joking around and talking about Lucy's many boyfriends. (I only dated Todd Levine, who is now my husband of three happy months!) Lucy adored her baby brother, Arlo. She also had three older brothers—Grant, Christopher, and Walter—who made sure that no one messed with her. One time, Lucy was having a romantic interlude with her high school beau when Grant and Andrew burst into her room with baseball bats! That was the end of that romantic interlude.

Lucy and I became friends when my family moved to Sugar Land. I was eight years old, new in third grade at Sugar Land Elementary. We had moved from the Pan-handle, and I'd never really thought about my bowl haircut or wearing my older brother's hand-me-down pants and T-shirts. I mean I guess I had *thought about* it, but I hadn't wanted to make my parents feel bad or I don't know but the point is I showed up for my first day wearing a T-shirt with a picture of a train and below that the word TRAIN.

I will never forget seeing Lucy that day. She wore pink, pleated corduroy pants, an aqua T-shirt, and a headband with pom-poms that matched her outfit. She had a rain-bow backpack and silver sneakers that lit up when she jumped around, which was always. At this point, she was already kind of famous for gymnastics. She left class at one P.M. every day to go to the gym and everyone said she was going to be in the Olympics someday.

Her father of course is Jim Masterson of Masterson Honda, and they always had a new car. Also, all of Lucy's spiral notebooks had animals on them and her pens and pencils had pom-poms like her headband but in different colors from the ones on her headband.

When I say she was my best friend I do not mean to imply that I was *her* best friend. I was maybe her fourth best friend, depending on if Skye Gutierrez and she were in a fight.

After her shoulder injury, Lucy valiantly found a new dream: to move to Austin and go to college. Understandably, all her brothers decided to work for Masterson Honda (except for Arlo, of course, who is only eight!).

I visited Lucy one time in Austin. She was super busy and had to work at her waitress job all three nights I was there (and forgot to call me when she went out one night after work) but I was able to get a glimpse of her sunny days. One morning, we went to get pancakes at Kerbey Lane Cafe and they were the best pancakes I've ever had. I told my husband Todd we have to go to Austin just for those pancakes sometime. Maybe like a romantic surprise getaway or something, since our honeymoon was one night at the Sugar Land Ramada.

Lucy was like this:

Her hair was spun gold.

Even after she had to quit gymnastics, her body was strong.

She always loved silver and pink, even when she was older.

Three days before she died, she answered when I called and told me she thought she might have fallen in love for the first time.

She was a strong swimmer. She had a pool and even when her brothers said they were joking and tried to hold her under, she could fight them off.

She loved red roses.

Her favorite shoes were a pair of black Steve Madden high heels with feathers.

She loved true crime shows like *20/20*.

I can still see her in that pom-pom headband.

8

Liza

I WAS IN THE middle of chopping scallions to prepare Sam's Noodle Salad with Smoked Brisket and Lime when my cellphone rang. I rinsed my hands, dried them, and picked up the vibrating phone, which informed me I had a "Private Caller."

It had to be the police officer. I let the phone go to voicemail, but then it started ringing again immediately. I knew I had to answer, if only to buy time. "Yes?" I said.

"Elizabeth Bailey?"

"Yes?" I said, using the back of my damp hand to push my hair from my forehead.

"This is Detective Salvatore Revello with the Austin Police Department."

"Yes?" I managed a third time. I forced myself to take a deep breath. If I had known this call was a fuse, and my response like a match—countdown to explosion—would I have cut the line?

"Am I speaking with Elizabeth Bailey?"

"You are," I said quietly.

"Mrs. Bailey, I'm on my way to interview your son, Charlie

Bailey, at his place of employment, the Rosewood Park and Pool. This is just a routine interview but I wanted to give you a courtesy call, since he's only fifteen."

This was happening. This was real. A cop was going to interview my son. How could I make this stop? How could I make this go away?

"Mrs. Bailey?" said the detective.

I began moving quickly, putting the brisket back in the fridge, turning off my stove top burners, and tossing my Target purse over my shoulder. "No. I don't give permission," I said. This was happening too fast, and after Whitney had left, promising to text me my new lawyer's name immediately, I had been biting my fingernails to the quick.

Whitney had not texted a lawyer's name immediately. She had not texted at all. I'd considering googling lawyers, but didn't want to make a mistake. Why should I hire some janky, affordable guy if Whitney was going to come through with a winner? *Was* Whitney going to come through? Jesus, I hated asking favors of people, of *her.* I knew it was time to find a way to get free of my dependence on Whitney. But how?

There was a pause, and then the detective said, "Is there a problem, Mrs. Bailey?"

"No," I said quietly. Of *course* there was a problem. Fear reared up inside me: if Charlie was arrested and his photo—or God forbid, *my photo*—was in the paper, Patrick might see it. My *mother* might see it, or Darla. Everything I'd run from could find us here. Even the *thought* of Charlie seeing Patrick in whatever state he was in now . . . Charlie taking in the fact that his roots led back to tattooed, chain-smoking Cape Cod people . . . it made me want to run.

But I'd made us a home here. Where could we go?

I should have been thinking of the woman. Of what had befallen her, and if my son had been a part of it. I should have been thinking of Charlie, what he had experienced and how to help him through it. But I was not.

I was thinking, *Run.*

Searching frantically for shoes, I found one pink flip-flop by the front door and a silver-colored one under the couch. I slipped them on and went outside into the 94-degree morning. "No reason . . . I just . . ." I stammered, jamming my key in the Mazda 5 ignition. "I'll bring him in. I'll bring him to you," I said. "Would that be OK?"

He sighed. "That's fine. When can we expect you?"

"Right away," I said.

"OK," said Detective Revello. "Do you need the address? I'll text you my information."

"Thank you." I hung up, feeling crazed. I called Whitney again, and she didn't answer.

I parked and slogged through the heat to reach Rosewood Pool. There he was, my adorable son, leaning against a guard stand holding a red flotation device. He was smiling up at the willowy brunette in the chair.

Oh, how I loved this boy in the red shorts I'd bought for him when he'd forgotten to buy his own pair at the end of the six-week Lifeguard Training sessions! His knees. His hair. The hair on his knees. Charlie's brilliant blue eyes—they were Patrick's eyes, I'd give his father that.

"Mom?" said Charlie, spotting me. "What are you doing here?"

"Hi, hon," I said. "Can I talk to you a sec?"

"Um, OK," said Charlie, sending a look to the girl that made her laugh. I knew I was being made fun of for some reason, which made me self-conscious.

"See you later, *Charles*," said the girl.

"See *you* later, Kelsey," said my son. (Of course her name was Kelsey.) She ran a hand underneath a curtain of hair and

swung it over one shoulder like a horse's mane. Ray-Ban sunglasses covered half her face, but I could still see her smirk.
Why a smirk?

"What's up, Mama Bear?" said Charlie as we walked
toward the shaded entrance. (I loved this nickname, and the
confident way he strode across the pool deck. His lifeguard
swagger! It was different from the way he acted at home, def-
erential and quiet. I swelled with pride seeing my son so confident and self-assured.)

"A detective from the Austin Police Department called," I
said.

"Oh," said Charlie. His demeanor changed immediately,
and he looked terrified. My heart sank, his reaction confirm-
ing my fears.

"He says it's a routine interview," I said, the hope in my
voice sounding a lot like desperation.

"I need to check my phone," said Charlie. "They make us
lock it up while we're on duty."

"I think you better tell your boss you're going home."

"*Now?*" said Charlie.

I bit my tongue. Sometimes, Charlie seemed a bit naïve, or
maybe self-centered was a better way to put it. I was glad I'd
raised him to feel invincible, but had I made him think the
rules didn't apply to him? That his lifeguard shift should take
precedence over a police investigation?

My anxiety spun out. Was I one of the mothers I saw on
TV who excused their sons' heinous acts? Who said, "One
event shouldn't ruin *my son* and his *precious future*"?

"Yes, now," I said.

"I'm supposed to work till three," he whined.

"A woman is *dead*," I said.

"But how do they know I—" he said, stopped himself.

There was a long pause. His words hung in the air. I found it hard to breathe.

"Let's go, Charlie," I said, almost choking on the words.

He nodded.

In the Aquatics Office, we found John, a middle-aged guy who was probably younger than me with gray hair and a pot belly that hadn't kept him from taking his shirt off. He was halfway through a breakfast taco, which he held suspended in midair when we appeared in his office. "Charlie!" he cried. "My man! What up?" He lifted the hand not holding a chorizo-and-cheese and gave my son a high-five.

"Um, this is my mom," said Charlie.

"Hi, Charlie's mom," said John, smiling.

"Hi," I said. "We have a family . . . situation . . . and I'm going to need to bring Charlie home for an hour, or maybe a few hours."

He nodded, chewing. "A *situation*, eh?" he said.

Neither Charlie nor I responded. On his desk, I saw the *Austin American-Statesman*. Had the body on the greenbelt shown up in the paper yet?

"Hokay, then!" said John, seeming a bit nervous at our silence. "You going to be back today?"

"I don't know," said Charlie. His swagger had vanished. "Mom?" he asked.

"I don't know," I said.

John looked from me to my son. "Hokay, then," he said, eyes narrowing as he sensed our worry and began to understand this was not a jovial *situation*.

"Thanks, John," I said. "Goodbye."

Charlie grabbed his bag from his locker and was texting before we reached the car. "They're calling all of us," he said.

"What?" I said.

"They know," said Charlie, under his breath.

I broke my silence with effort. "They know what?" I asked.

He was reading his phone and scowling. "Oh my God," he said. I did not repeat my question. I should have. *I should have.* I started the car and after a moment, the hot air pumping from the AC began to cool. "Mom," said Charlie. "There's something I have to tell you."

This is where I could have become the mother I wanted to be, the one who listened without judgment, who allowed any confession and made room, allowed sadness and shame, all of it.

Spoiler alert: I did not become this person. Charlie was looking at me, almost willing me not to break contact with him. But my phone chirped and I glanced down. Whitney had texted: GOT YOU A LAWYER. DON'T TALK TO POLICE.

"Mom?" said Charlie. "Mom, there's something I need to—"

"Charlie!" I said, awash in relief, cutting him off. "We've got a lawyer! He's going to handle this."

"A lawyer?" said Charlie.

"Don't worry," I told him.

"Mom, listen—" said Charlie, his voice rising.

"You're fine," I said. "We're *fine,* honey. I'll handle this." I put my hand on his knee. "You can go back to work," I said.

"Fuck you!" yelled Charlie.

I gasped, "Charlie!"

"You never listen to me!" he cried. His face was filled with rage. "You never want to hear anything! You don't even want to know what's actually going on. It's *bullshit*!" Charlie opened the car door and got out, slamming it behind him. He sprinted toward the pool.

I got out of the car and ran after him. "Charlie!" I called. "Charlie!"

He turned the corner past the front desk and was out of

sight. A teenage girl in a red guard suit with a head full of blond braids stared at me. "Can I *help* you?" she said. I stared at her nose ring, at her pale eyes.

"Charlie's my son," I said.

"Do you want me to . . . go get him?" asked the girl, seemingly taking pity on me.

"No," I said, shaking my head. "No," I repeated.

"OK . . ." said the girl. I turned to walk back to my car. I felt humiliated, heartbroken. The girl called after me, "Have a nice day!"

9

Salvatore

THE DNA WARRANTS WERE ready. If Salvatore's job had taught him anything, it was that every person was capable of darkness, even a group of seemingly innocent fifteen-year-old boys. Salvatore had been frustrated when every one of the lifeguards was walled off by their parents (and pricey defense lawyers), but he understood—if one of his kids was involved with a dead body, he'd call the best attorney he could afford, too. Salvatore emailed the kids' lawyers, all the paperwork attached.

He stood. Lucy Masterson's body had been identified by her landlord, a man named Jay Cutler. Lucy had lived in a condominium complex not far from the greenbelt called The Gables. Salvatore's team was interviewing the homeowners near where Lucy's body was found, and he decided to visit her condo to see if there were any clues that might explain why she'd been found dead by the side of a muddy swimming hole.

Salvatore pulled into The Gables, a sprawling complex with not one single tree to shade its blindingly bright parking lot. Cutler led him to unit 33. "She never caused any trouble," said the landlord, a forty-something man who wore jean shorts with a sleeveless T-shirt. "I think she worked at the Chuy's over on Barton Springs Road." Salvatore nodded. He was a big fan of the Tex-Mex institution, which was decorated with bright-colored booths and pictures of Elvis made from velvet.

Jay Cutler had the leathery skin of a man who spent a lot of time outdoors, and appeared to be wearing eyeliner. Salvatore quickly shuffled through his options of how to handle the guy. He tried for vulnerable confidant. "Thank you for your help identifying Lucy's body," said Salvatore. "That must have been very hard."

Jay shrugged, closed off. Salvatore switched tack. "Did she have any close friends that you know of? Any regular visitors . . . maybe a boyfriend?" He wanted to establish how well this guy knew Lucy from the get-go. The eyeliner signaled gay to Salvatore, or maybe straight-but-artistic.

They reached Lucy's apartment and the guy inserted his key. "Last weekend, she was grilling by the pool," said Jay. "She must have had a friend over, right? Nobody grills by the pool alone, right?"

This question did not seem to require an answer. Salvatore handed Jay his card. "Will you call me if you think of anything else?"

"Sure, of course," said Jay. He paused on the stairwell, not opening the condo, so Salvatore waited. (A classic "hand on the doorknob" revelation . . . it was a common phenomenon that Salvatore or a colleague would conduct a long interrogation and get nothing from a witness or suspect until the person got up to leave, and then—hand on the doorknob—started to spill.)

"She was really gorgeous," said Jay, looking not at Salvatore but at Lucy's rubber doormat. "I wondered if maybe she danced or something. You know, at the Yellow Rose."

The Yellow Rose was a strip club on the outskirts of the city. It wasn't as seedy as some of the clubs and "spas" Salvatore's colleagues in trafficking had to frequent, but it was a bit run-down. Salvatore and Jacquie had gone there once, before they'd had kids, when they were a bit drunk and feeling frisky. They'd thought it would be transgressive and fun, but Salvatore just found it depressing. In order to enjoy yourself at the Yellow Rose you had to be able to silence the part of your brain that wondered about the dancers' inner lives, what they had to do to turn on their smiles each night. Salvatore couldn't silence that part of his brain.

"The Yellow Rose?" he said. "You mean you think she was a stripper?"

"I don't *know* anything," said Jay in an insinuating tone.

"What makes you think she may have worked in the clubs?"

"Nothing," said Jay. "Nothing. A lot of these girls, though . . ." His voice trailed off. He looked at Salvatore pointedly, though what the point *was*, exactly, Salvatore wasn't sure. Was he claiming that most waitresses were strippers? Or that many strippers lived in this particular condo complex?

Salvatore waited, but Jay shrugged and said no more. Salvatore made a mental note to speak with him again, maybe at the station. "Thanks for your time," he said.

"Well, just let me know when you're done," said Jay. "Her family's coming to get her stuff this afternoon. They're from Sugar Land."

"Have you ever met them?"

"Me? No. I think she'd come to Austin to grow up, be an adult," said the man. "You know? Austin . . . it's everybody's dream to get here."

Salvatore nodded, considering. He got the sense that Jay Cutler knew Lucy better than he was letting on, but direct questioning hadn't seemed to work. "I guess so," he said.

"Yeah," said the landlord. "Doesn't always turn out like you think it will, though."

"How long have you been here?" said Salvatore, trying the "buddy" approach.

"Twenty years," said Jay. "Came from upstate New York to go to UT and never left."

"Seems like a common story," said Salvatore.

"Not Lucy, though. She went to Austin Community College."

"Hm," said Salvatore. "Any idea what she was studying?"

"I'd guess physical therapy, from all the books," said the landlord. "You'll see."

Salvatore swallowed. So Jay had been in the apartment, had checked out Lucy's bookshelf. "She was an exercise fanatic," Jay went on. "Asked me to run with her once, but I knew I couldn't keep up."

Salvatore decided to go for broke. "Did you ever suspect Lucy was using drugs?" he asked.

"Is that what happened?" said Jay. "She OD'd?"

"We're not certain yet," said Salvatore.

"I don't know anything for sure . . ." said Jay, leaning toward Salvatore.

"Any info you could give me would really help," said Salvatore.

"She wasn't a junkie," said Jay. "I don't want to give her a bad name, you know? She was a nice girl, studying at ACC, like I said. I went to Chuy's, sometimes, to have the Chuy's Special, keep her company."

Jay was clearly a lot more informed than he'd originally let on. Salvatore switched into his "I'm an idiot" mode. He used it with defensive or angry suspects. In the interrogation room, he'd blather on about anything *but* the crime—the Longhorns game, the weather, his own bad back. Many suspects would warm up, and eventually sing like birds. Most people *want* to connect. Many murderers *want* to confess. The "I'm an idiot" mode continued to surprise Salvatore with its effectiveness.

"I love Tex-Mex," said Salvatore. "What's the Chuy's Special?"

"Oh, man, it's blue-corn tortillas, chicken, cheese, and tomatillo sauce," said Jay.

"Sounds incredible," said Salvatore. He stretched and grimaced. "Jesus, I need to get in shape," he said. "Maybe jog."

Jay said, "I go to Gold's Gym."

"I should, too," said Salvatore. "You said Lucy worked out?"

"Not at Gold's," said Jay. "She was a famous gymnast, but in high school. Did her own workouts."

Salvatore nodded. "Maybe she had an injury," he said, fishing. "A lot of gymnasts, they end up hurt."

"She did!" said Jay. "She told me she had a shoulder problem. Asked me once if I had any pain pills. For her shoulder. I had some old Percocet from when I got my wisdom teeth out. She just . . . didn't have insurance."

Salvatore nodded. "Yeah," he said.

"I maybe shouldn't have given them to her," said Jay.

"When was this?" asked Salvatore.

"She had just moved in," said Jay. "Last August. I thought . . . It sounds ridiculous now. I thought maybe she liked me."

So he'd been wrong about Jay being gay. Maybe he was bi. "What happened?" said Salvatore.

"She said she'd cook me dinner. Spaghetti. With homemade sauce; it was delicious. And garlic bread." Jay looked utterly forlorn, and Salvatore had to prod to keep him talking.

"Sounds great," said Salvatore.

"It was. It was so great. And then she told me about her shoulder, and I got the Percocet. And . . . well, I tried to kiss her, which was obviously stupid. I misread the situation. But I mean, homemade spaghetti sauce! It seemed like more than friends."

"I've been there," Salvatore lied. He'd had a few dates since Jacquie's death, but he'd always been the one who stopped calling. He wasn't ready to love anyone new. He might not ever be ready.

"So I tried to kiss her—this is so embarrassing—and she turned away. She was nice about it. She *claimed* she was in a serious relationship. She *claimed* she just wanted to be friends."

Salvatore nodded. If Jay were involved in Lucy's death, it would not be the first time a scorned person's rage got the best of him. (Or her.) "Did you see her again after that?" said Salvatore.

"I told you, I saw her at the pool sometimes."

"But not socially?"

"No," said Jay. "She *didn't* really want to be friends, as it turned out," he added bitterly.

"Damn," said Salvatore.

"Well, thank you for—" But Jay cut him off.

"I can't believe she's gone!" he cried.

"If you could send me a list of employees," said Salvatore. "Custodians, workmen. I'd like to interview . . ."

"Sure, sure," said Jay. He sighed, seemingly close to tears.

"Thank you very much."

Jay nodded and walked toward the metal staircase. Salvatore pushed open Lucy's door and stepped inside.

Seeing Lucy's painstakingly decorated condominium made Salvatore ache. Over an eggplant-colored couch with pale pink throw pillows, Lucy had framed a print titled *1964 Amsterdam Women Gymnastics*, depicting a woman's abstract figure wearing a red leotard. A coffee table held a neat stack of books and class notes, three sharpened pencils beside them. Lucy's bed (located in the corner of the studio) was neatly made. Elegant gray floral sheets and pillows (Salvatore could imagine Lucy purchasing the set to begin her "adult" life) contrasted with a threadbare pink bunny, its legs carefully tucked under the comforter. On a plywood bookcase, Lucy kept rows of well-read paperbacks and scented candles. There was only one framed photo: Lucy in a cap and gown, hugging what must have been her mother. Lucy's eyes were closed and her smile was wide and her mom embraced her. The pride in the older woman's face was piercing and radiant.

Lucy's bathroom was spotless, cheery yellow towels hung next to the shower, bottles of Sunshine and Citrus shampoo and conditioner, a fresh bar of soap, and a razor on a shelf. In the medicine cabinet was the usual array of over-the-counter medicines, and a prescription bottle with the label torn off: a bad sign that she'd bought the pills on the black market. Salvatore would know more when his tech guys filed their report detailing her phone and banking information.

Salvatore moved to the refrigerator. If Lucy was OK, Salvatore knew he would find dinner ingredients—either fresh fruit and vegetables or Diet Coke and Lean Cuisines. It was only the late-stage addicts who barely ate, saving every cent for their drugs. These poor souls could live for a long time on ramen noodles.

Salvatore opened the fridge and sighed. There was nothing—no milk, no butter, no Diet Coke, champagne, or juice. No Tex-Mex leftovers brought home from work.

And in the cabinet: no coffee or tea.

Just three ramen packets in a lonely pile.

-10-

Whitney

ON THE DAY THEY got Roma's diagnosis, four years before, Whitney and Jules had left the doctor's office without speaking; they were silent during the whole ride home. As Jules turned onto their street, Whitney's shoulders eased a bit, relieved that at least there was an answer. She and Jules could be on the same page now; it was no longer her opinion versus his. They just needed to sit down together, as they'd done so many times—talking about college 529 funds for the twins, planning vacations, working through mortgage documents—and discuss their next steps. Some sort of fancy mental hospital? An intensive, inpatient treatment center? The doctor had been grave, but Whitney believed that everything could be solved. It was just a matter of work, period. Nothing was truly uncontrollable if you worked hard enough (and had money).

That afternoon, the doctor's words still ringing in her ears, Whitney held her tongue as Jules paused by their safety gate, letting the scanner register his identity, then maneuvered the car into the dim garage. He turned off his Mercedes and it made the ticking noise as its complex engine cooled.

"Jules," said Whitney.

"Darling, I have a surprise," he said.

"Jules," Whitney repeated.

He turned to her. "New Zealand," said Jules. He put his hand on her knee. He was exactly the prize she wanted . . . or the prize she had been *trained to* want. Her grandmother had been so pleased. But now Gram was dead and Whitney could wonder: did she want her husband anymore? Had she ever *loved* him—or just mistaken security for love?

Ballet trained you to obey orders. Your job was to become your teacher's vision. Nobody wanted a dancer with opinions.

"We should go to New Zealand," said Jules. "A vacation. All of us—together."

New Zealand? It was useless. Ridiculous. A big expensive itinerary that led them right back to this horrible place.

The doctor had said: *We call it conduct disorder with callous and unemotional traits. I'm sorry.*

"That's your surprise," said Jules. He alighted from the car and walked into their house, already calling someone about something with his Bluetooth headset.

In this moment, Whitney wondered if Jules's remote aloofness, his inability to be won, was not a positive characteristic but rather a symptom of a disease. The same disease, maybe, that their daughter had just been diagnosed with—it ran in families, the doctor had said.

Roma, Whitney saw clearly, was *her* problem. Jules would never take action to help.

This burden was Whitney's alone. But what could she possibly do?

THE TRIP WAS A write-off. Many of Whitney's clients were interested in New Zealand—it was where they wanted to be when the upcoming apocalypse hit. The idea (and they all had the same idea) was to be as far as possible from the U.S., but also in a place that was just like the U.S. They wanted ski mountains and beaches, but none of the starving hordes. These people were . . . Whitney didn't want to say *cold and calculating*, but honestly, they were cold and calculating. They could compartmentalize. Perhaps they were like Roma, truly.

Jules bought first-class tickets. They sat in a row: Jules, Whitney, Roma, and Xavier. They hadn't been on the plane for ten minutes when Xavier cried out, "What the *heck*, Roma!"

Roma didn't move. Her pearl-colored headphones covered her ears and her eyes were closed. Whitney had always admired her daughter's eyelashes—they were long and lush, unlike Whitney's. When Roma's eyes were closed, Whitney could pretend things were different. It was like a drug, this lovely forgetting. She'd imagined so many futures for her girl, so many adventures for the two of them together.

As a little girl, Roma had slept next to Whitney every night, Jules banished to the guest room. Roma would fall asleep before Whitney, her two "stuffies" gathered close to her heart, her face flushed pink. Whitney would read for a while longer, then turn out the light and put her nose to Roma's hair, inhaling. Roma smelled like ice cream melted in the sun: faintly buttery, sweet, a bit tangy. Whitney would cradle her head, touch her nose to Roma's. Roma had once been hers.

THE AIR NEW ZEALAND flight attendant smiled at the Brownson family and continued down the aisle. The twins were twelve and looked angelic. As soon as she was out of earshot, Xavier, said, "Roma pinched me."

"Honey," said Whitney.

"Look!" he insisted, showing Whitney his thigh, where a purple welt bloomed. Whitney's stomach went sour.

"Jules," said Whitney. He was also pretending to be asleep.

"Hm?" said Jules, opening one eye.

"Roma pinched him."

"Dad, look!" said Xavier. It was there—it was a fact. A painful-looking bruise on his fair skin.

Jules stared at his son's leg. "Well," he said, finally. "Roma's asleep."

"Dad . . ." said Xavier.

"I don't know," said Jules.

"Come on, Dad! You think I did this to myself?"

"Settle down, all of you." Jules closed his eyes again. Xavier looked at Whitney.

"Sweetheart," she said, her voice pleading.

"It hurts, Mom," said Xavier. He swallowed. "She did this," he said. The defiance in Xavier's eyes faded slowly when Whitney didn't answer, but it did fade.

"Would anyone like a drink?" said the stewardess, on her way back down the aisle. Xavier shook his head and turned away.

"I'll take some champagne," said Jules. His hand on Whitney's knee was warm.

-11-

Annette

ANNETTE AND LOUIS'S LAWYER was on speakerphone, the volume high. "OK," said Louis, standing next to his statue of his childhood pony, Red, tugging at his too-tight jeans. "OK, listen. We're just speaking to you as a precaution, Toby."

"Robert didn't *do* anything," said Annette.

"Right! Right!" said Louis. "Toby, I just want you to know. This is a good boy we're talking about."

"I absolutely agree," said their lawyer, who was Louis's parents' lawyer, currently en route from Midland to Austin. "But . . . Are you sitting down, Louis?"

"Yes, Toby," said Louis, annoyed. He looked at Annette, daring her to disagree.

"OK, so here's what's happening," said Toby. "I just got an email from the Austin Police Department. Louis, Annette, they're asking for Robert's DNA."

"What?" cried Louis. "His DNA? Why?"

Toby sighed. "I honestly don't know," he said. "I'll be there soon. All of you need to sit tight, OK? Especially Robert."

"Of course," said Louis. He turned to his wife. "Where is Robert, anyway?"

"He's in his room," said Annette.

"Oh, he won't say a word to anyone," said Louis. "How soon will you be here, Toby?"

"Two hours tops."

"I'm having a drink. You want a drink?" said Louis, walking to their full bar, a replica of the historic mahogany bar at the Menger Hotel in San Antonio (complete with a framed photo of Theodore Roosevelt at the famous watering hole). Louis lifted a bottle of Herradura tequila.

"No." Annette went to the sliding glass door that led to their outdoor patio. Louis did not follow, pacing back and forth across their tricolor patchwork cowhide rug. She walked toward the place where she had last seen the coyote. Where had it gone? Was it alive? Annette sat down at the edge of the yard, the grass damp on her bare legs. She closed her eyes.

Maybe, in devoting herself to protecting her son, she had been mistaken.

Maybe keeping *him* safe hadn't been the problem.

-12-

Liza

CHARLIE'S LAWYER'S OFFICE WAS located downtown, at Fifth and Congress. I parked my Mazda, got out, and gazed at the capitol building, glowing under the merciless sun. I could have gone home to change into matching shoes, but I was too eager to meet Hilary Bensen, who Whitney had told me was "the best of the best."

Clearly, Hilary was *not* the best of the best, because she wasn't representing Xavier. I'd asked, and Whitney had said, "Well, it just seemed like a good idea to get them each their own lawyer, you know what I mean?"

I *did* know what she meant. She meant that she was going to save Xavier, and if that meant throwing my son under the bus, so be it. "Clearly my lawyer's the *second* best of the best," I commented.

"You're hilarious!" said Whitney.

Still, it had been kind of the Brownsons to get me a lawyer at all, to tell me we could worry about her fees later. When I searched her name, a posting came up saying, "If you're guilty, Hilary's the one you want to call."

Why would Whitney hire me a lawyer known for defending criminals? It seemed strange. If I didn't trust her, I'd wonder if she were trying to frame me.

I walked into the lobby of the art deco building, rode an elevator that smelled of brass polish to the tenth floor. A secretary behind a giant desk told me Hilary would be out soon. I sat uncomfortably in the lobby pulling at my Artz Rib House T-shirt. It was so cold in the building; I felt goosebumps on my arms and wished for a cozy cardigan like the one the secretary wore.

My lawyer strode into the lobby in a red pantsuit and heels. She wore her blond hair in a motionless bob. (In fact I could still smell a bit of hairspray; she must have applied a coat before coming to greet me.) Her makeup was sparing but elegant: a bit of mascara, lipstick matching her suit. Her face was absolutely smooth, free of any lines at all, so it was hard to tell if she was thirty or fifty years old. She was beautiful in an unapproachable way, as if she'd perfected every piece of her visage, but it added up to more of a blurry photo of someone "pretty" than anything concrete or interesting. Hilary's handshake was firm, and I liked the fact that she seemed oblivious to my disheveled appearance. "Let's talk in my office," she said.

Hilary had a framed JD from Harvard above a large, sleek desk. She had no photos, no tchotchkes, soda cans, coffee mugs, or snacks. "Have a seat," she said.

"Thanks," I said. "Look. I don't even know that I need a lawyer. All the boys did was find a woman on—"

"Stop," said Hilary, holding up a hand. "There's a warrant for DNA now. This is serious. Where's your son? Why isn't he with you?"

"Oh, I wanted things for him to . . . stay as normal as . . ." My voice trailed off.

"Mrs. Bailey—"

"Call me Liza, please."

"Liza, this is a murder investigation. There's a warrant for your son's DNA, which means they have something—semen, blood, don't know yet, but something—and they think your son's DNA might be a match."

I felt my mouth open slightly, made it close. "Oh my God," I managed.

"Sorry to be abrupt, but this is very serious."

"OK," I said, biting my lip, a useless anger toward Hilary Bensen rising in my throat.

"Listen to me," said Hilary. "I need you to go get your son and bring him to my office. We'll administer the DNA test, and the three of us can have a long talk, decide where to go from here."

"DNA test?" I said.

"Charlie is going to be OK," said Hilary. "You hear me? It's going to be OK. But you need to get him and bring him here. Now. There are going to be photographers looking for him; it's just hitting the news cycle. Park in the garage—here, use this pass."

"Reporters?" I said weakly, taking the laminated parking pass.

"Liza," said Hilary. "Snap out of it. It's *go time*, you hear me?"

I met her gaze. "I hear you," I said.

As she walked me out of her office, she came close, and said, "Don't talk to any of the others, OK?" I must have looked puzzled, because she said, "The other lifeguards. Don't let Charlie speak with them. He's on his own now."

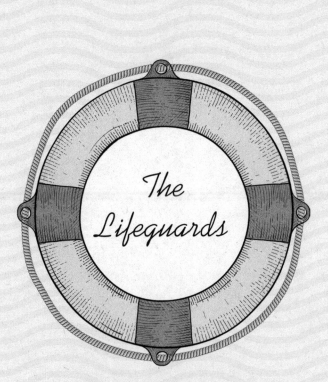

The Lifeguards

THE DAY LUCY DIES

LUNCH BREAK

-1-

Xavier

XAVIER'S STOMACH BEGINS HURTING after breakfast. He knows he should not have taken the smoothie from Roma. She'd been so nice about it, saying she was going to JuicyJuicy and would be happy to grab him a Peach Melba.

"I added protein powder," she'd said, handing him the orange cup as he walked out the door to work. Would he ever stop being a fucking idiot? But they all wanted to believe she wasn't what they all knew she was. The amazing part was that even though he knew her better than anyone—she'd taken his favorite blanket and hidden it when they were babies; she'd almost suffocated him but always stopped in time; she'd held him underwater in the pool but let him free before it was too late; she'd sent texts to friends and strangers from his phone; and on and on—he, more than anyone, wished she was the sister he wanted. His twin.

"Don't you trust me?" she'd said, holding out the orange cup.

So he'd taken the smoothie. He'd sipped it in front of her: *Yes. I trust you.*

By the time he gets to work, he can barely drive. He rests his head on the steering wheel, but then opens his car door to vomit on the pavement.

He is going to have to drive himself to the hospital. Wrenching pain seizes his stomach, and he feels boiling hot.

Xavier blacks out.

-2-
Bobcat

ROBERT'S BOSS AT THE Rosewood Pool stops him on his way to lunch. John is a funny guy. He obviously misses being a teenager (like every other grown-up, as far as Robert can tell) but he seems to have made peace with adulthood, getting a job where he can be in the sun, enjoying his conversations with the guards and the old ladies who swim laps every morning.

Honestly, Robert would rather be John when he grows up than any other adult he knows. Even his mom makes herself smaller all the time, trying to wedge herself into some role that was never made for her.

("Fancy Oil Wife.")

It kills him. Can't she just be herself?

(Guess not.)

Robert wants a different life than his parents'. He wants to *do* something, to *adventure*, maybe be an astronaut or a smoke jumper. His great-grandfather struck oil! But what's left for him? Robert doesn't want to end up like his father, living off his inheritance, talking about mortgage rates or whether a particular Scotch is "peaty." Even his parents' parties lack fun. They get drunk, sure—his dad more than his mom—but then talk more about mortgage rates.

"Bobcat?" says John.

"Yeah?" says Robert, pausing.

"Xavier never showed today," says John. "No call, nothing. Can you stay late and cover his shift?"

"Really?"

"Yeah. It's not like him, is it?"

"No," says Robert. Of all of them, Xavier is the most organized. Charlie is the nicest, Robert is the strongest, and Xavier is the genius. They'll be fine, as long as they have each other. In an apocalypse or whatever.

"Can you cover?"

"Sure, I guess so," says Robert reluctantly. He wants to see Lucy before her shift at Chuy's, and then hit a raver some Snapchat idiot posted about. He and his friends will either stay at the party or jump the Cliffs. The moms have already planned one of their epic booze fests, this one supposedly to celebrate the first day of summer.

(Which means no one will notice if they're gone.)

Robert stops at his locker to retrieve his shirt and phone. He groans when he sees his father's text: FATHER SON LUNCH! MEET YOU OUTSIDE POOL AT NOON.

(Fuck.)

Robert's dad is obsessed with making his son "a man." He roughhouses with him, takes him to the Austin Gun Club every weekend. Any excuse to act "manly."

There's nothing from Xavier. Robert messages Roma, asking her where her brother is, and she doesn't answer. He messages Charlie, who sends back a "shrug" emoji, followed by a "sick face" emoji, followed by a question mark. Robert pulls on a T-shirt, calculating how to evade his dad, grab his bike from the rack, and zoom across the bridge to Lucy's.

Robert walks toward the pool exit and sees his father's gleaming truck. "Crap," he whispers.

"Hey! Son! Over here!" yells his dad. Everyone in the parking lot turns to look. Robert's dad is playing loud eighties rap.

("Fight for Our Right to Party.")

(Oh my God.)

"Nice ride," says Carrie, who's working the front desk. She wears her hair in cornrows even though she's white.

"Jesus," mutters Robert.

"Is that your dad?" says Carrie.

"Yup."

"Wowzers," says Carrie.

Robert goes to the truck—there's no avoiding this—and gets in. "Dad," he says, "I have plans for lunch. Sorry, Dad."

"Open the glove box," says Louis. His voice is low and serious, as if he's starring in some Wild West movie and he's the sheriff.

Robert doesn't want to open the glove compartment. He knows what's inside. "Dad . . ." he says.

"Open the glove compartment, Son," growls Louis.

Robert grits his teeth. He wants to find Lucy, to make love to her, and then have a P. Terry's double cheeseburger and a strawberry milkshake before returning to work. He is so sick of his dumbass father. Robert opens the glove compartment and sees the gun.

"Take it out," says Louis.

"Dad, come on," says Robert. "Mom said—"

"I don't see your mother here," says Louis. "Do you, Robert? Do you see your mother here?"

Robert is filled with a white-hot fury. It takes him over almost instantly. His rage scares him sometimes.

"Take it out!" yells Louis.

(His dad is a fucking clown.)

Robert takes out the gun. He aims it right at his father's face.

Louis smiles. "Let's do this, Son," he says.

-3-

Charlie

THE FIRST DAY OF summer and Charlie should be in the water. Instead, he's nervous at Austin-Bergstrom Airport. Of course he's nervous! He's about to finally, finally, meet his father. Jesus, he'd wanted to bring Amir or someone along for this event, but it seemed like a strange request. Charlie is scared. Seriously, he's scared. He wants this random man to love him—there, it's true.

He considers making a TikTok of the reunion: turn the camera on himself, hold out his arm to capture the moment they embrace, edit it later with captions. This seems crazy but also a way to diffuse the situation, to make it content rather than pain. Rather than terror. Life hurts less when made into funny videos.

At baggage claim, Charlie looks at the screen to see that his father's plane from Boston has landed. Charlie scans the waiting area for the restroom: he might actually puke; he feels bile in his mouth.

He turns on his TikTok, flips the camera, hits record. The

timer counts down and he's on. All he has to do is smile. He ruffles his hair, tries to look pensive. Acting like a scared child makes him less actually scared—he imagines some sorrowful song, like "Jocelyn Flores" by XXXTentacion or "If the World Was Ending" by JP Saxe.

He'll put captions above his forlorn face, one by one:

I HAVE NEVER MET MY FATHER.

MY MOM WOULDN'T TELL ME WHO HE WAS.

I FOUND HIM AND PAID FOR HIS PLANE TICKET TO AUSTIN.

I'M ABOUT TO MEET MY FATHER FOR THE FIRST TIME.

(FOLLOW ME FOR PT. 2)

He feels immediately better, endorphins or serotonin or whatever they are flooding him even at the *thought* of posting his video. This is what cutting feels like, Roma told him once—you press a razor blade into your skin and feel immediately better. She used the word "released."

Jesus, Roma. Charlie can't help but think about her sometimes, even though they slept together only that one time, ruining everything. He misses her. She's scary but also exciting, showing up in the middle of the night when you don't expect her, being kind when you thought she was angry. She has problems for sure. Charlie wishes he knew how to solve them, how to help her, but she uses that feeling against him. Amir says she's a psycho. He might be right.

Charlie watches the escalator. He sees men of all shapes and sizes and colors, imagines each being his dad. But as soon as he sees Patrick Hamilton, he knows. His father is wearing slim jeans with loafers, a white button-down shirt. He looks wealthy, confident, a bit skinny. Charlie tells himself his father's hair is *fashionably* long and *fashionably* disheveled.

Charlie hears his own inhalation of breath. His father looks just like him.

He cannot help himself: he runs. He runs to his father and his father, looking dumbstruck, breaks into a huge smile and opens his arms.

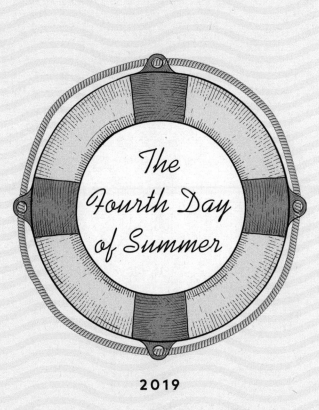

The
Fourth Day
of Summer

2019

-1-

Salvatore

THE NEW NANNY, MAE MAE, showed up promptly at 6:00
A.M., parking a black Crown Victoria in Salvatore's driveway.
Salvatore opened his front door and raised an eyebrow. Mae
Mae, a fifty-something woman in camouflage pants and a
tight black T-shirt, smiled sweetly. "Detective Revello?" she
said. "I'm Mae Mae."

"Is that your Crown Vic?" said Salvatore.

She smiled. "Sure is. I got it at CarMax, but I like pretending I'm a cop's daughter, you know? Or a cop's wife. Or a
cop!"

"Huh," said Salvatore.

"I never get pulled over, and I like to think you guys are
looking out for me." Mae Mae wore lavender eye shadow and
maroon lipstick, her silver hair brushing her shoulders. Salvatore's take was that she was a low-key lady who had made an
effort this morning, but might not wear makeup again. All of
the visuals added up, but something needled at Salvatore. He
made a mental note to call her fourth reference when he had

a moment. The first three had checked out and he'd been tired.

"Nice to meet you," said Salvatore.

The kids approached, smiling shyly. Salvatore felt a wave of sweet relief. He could do his job now, knowing they were safe.

Weren't they?

Mae Mae followed them all into the kitchen. Salvatore filled his travel coffee mug and listened to Mae Mae listening to his kids. God, they had so much to say. His stomach ached at the thought of how long they'd kept silent around him. "OK, guys, I'm off," he said.

"Bye, Dad!" said Allie.

"See ya," said Joe, not looking at Salvatore.

"You OK, buddy?" said Salvatore.

"They're fine," said Mae Mae. "Have a great day! If you're not home by six, I'll drop them with the woman next door."

"Peach," said Salvatore.

"Peach," Mae Mae repeated.

"But I'll be home by six," said Salvatore.

"Whatever," muttered Joe.

Salvatore paused, but he wasn't paying Mae Mae half his salary so he could stand around and worry. He headed out the front door, climbed into his car, and left, feeling lighter the farther he got from his house and his children.

Salvatore sipped his coffee as he made his way to Barton Hills Drive. No alternative suspects had turned up yet, so he was going to troll his childhood neighborhood, drive by the teen lifeguards' houses, wander the green and swampy trails.

The first kid, Charlie Bailey, lived with a single mom on Oak Glen Avenue.

As he turned in to the neighborhood, a boyhood emotion

rushed over him—*look! I'm a cop now! Driving a cop car!* He felt lit up, proud.

The history of the area had always fascinated him. A pioneer named Barton had set up his homestead on the southern banks of the Colorado River in 1837; almost two centuries later, the springs still bore his name. Sections of the twisty hiking trails held secrets—Salvatore and his friends had discovered a cave they'd christened Smoker's Hollow, storing pilfered cigarettes there. But now the neighborhood he'd roamed with his friends was in transition. Some of the old ranchers remained, including the one his mom had sold for peanuts in the eighties. But parts were unrecognizable, giant mansions sprawled over the large lots, fancy cars parked in gated driveways.

THE BAILEY HOUSE WAS one of the original ranchers. It was in OK repair, needed a new roof, the front lawn a bit overgrown but not unkempt, a gorgeous live oak well watered and healthy in the corner of the lot. There was no car in the driveway. This was the kind of house Salvatore dreamed of, actually. If only he'd bought one like this in 2000, or before the boom, anyway.

There wasn't anything wrong with Slaughter Lane (besides the name—my God! Were his kids really going to grow up between Slaughter Lane and Convict Hill Road?). Honestly, his "way South" neighborhood was made up of guys like him, guys who'd grown up in Zilker or Hyde Park and couldn't get near Central Austin with a normal salary. But he missed these streets, living in a place where you could bike to Barton Springs and jump in anytime you wanted. The Barton Creek Greenbelt was the heart of the city.

Salvatore slowed and parked across the street. Framed by what might be the living-room window, he saw a woman at a desk, pecking at the keyboard of a laptop. She was in her mid- to late thirties, closer to his age than he'd realized. Her short hair was tucked behind her ears as she focused intently on her computer, the screen's glow lighting her face.

Salvatore's eyes widened. He knew this woman. From his memory, he heard her speak her name, playing with the label on her Shiner beer, tucking that short hair behind her ear: *I'm Liza. Hey.*

Liza.

Elizabeth Bailey.

It was so long ago, before he'd even *met* Jacquie. He and Liza—Elizabeth Bailey—had danced together, both pretty buzzed, the fabric of her dress silky in his hands. Her lips had tasted salty, pressed to his. Her hips, underneath his fingers. He'd lived in a cramped apartment then, and in the morning she was gone. They hadn't exchanged numbers. He had no way to find her. He'd actually thought about her—the woman he'd met at a Damnations concert—for a long time.

Liza Bailey.

An almost—but not quite—forgotten lover, now before him, the mother of a murder suspect.

Liza stopped typing, placed her chin in her hand and gazed out the window, lost in thought. She wore a gauzy white blouse that skimmed her cream-colored skin. He had kissed a freckle on that collarbone.

Salvatore watched her for a moment, overcome with yearning. For her? For who he'd been, a young man who could get drunk at a Damnations show? For a life where anything was still possible?

Salvatore swallowed. He had to do his job, which was in- terview Liza Bailey. He gathered himself.

He approached the front door and knocked. She did not answer. He knocked again, but there was no reply. Stepping back, Salvatore saw that Liza had shut the shades to the room where she was working. Knowing she was inside made him feel a weird, hot thrill. He peered into the side yard, spying a Big Green Egg smoker next to an outdoor dining set. The smoker was filmy with pollen and one of the patio chairs had fallen over on its side. It had been over 90 for *a month*, so it made sense that nobody had been grilling recently.

"Hello?"

Salvatore turned. An older man was walking toward him from the house next door. He was heavyset, his hair in a long braid. "Can I help you?" he asked, crossing his arms. Why he was wearing wool socks and Birkenstock sandals in the insane heat was a mystery that was not Salvatore's to solve.

"I'm Detective Revello," said Salvatore, pulling out his badge.

The man peered at it; his brow furrowed. He nodded, seemingly satisfied, but his arms remained crossed. "Yes?" he said.

"I'm trying to find Elizabeth Bailey," said Salvatore. "But she's not answering her door."

"As far as I can tell, you're trespassing," said the man.

Salvatore rubbed his eyes, dismayed by the neighbor's antagonism. "Can I ask you a few questions?" said Salvatore.

"No, you may not," said the man.

Salvatore handed the man his card. "Well, give me a call if you change your mind," he said. "I'd appreciate it very much."

"Goodbye," the neighbor said. He stood sentinel on Liza Bailey's lawn, watching Salvatore like a hawk until he drove away.

I'm Liza. Hey.

Salvatore saw her in his mind's eye, thought of her naked

on the futon he'd discarded long ago, the pale green sheets, her eyes looking up at him, giving him a sly grin as she moved down his body . . .

Salvatore pulled over. He looked at himself in his rearview mirror: grizzled, perspiring, old. He was an adult. With adult responsibilities. He tried to dispel the thought of the mother of a murder suspect with her lips opening to his. Her tongue.

Barton Hills Mamas

CHARDONNAYISMYJAM

Does anyone know how early a child can be tested for dyslexia? Lulu Rosemary is three and when I do her letter work in the mornings, she consistently thinks the "B" is a "P"! I'm so freaked out but I don't want to scar her by seeming alarmed. I try to be low-key and gently correct her. I know BHE has a great dyslexia specialist (part of the reason we moved here from Boston in the first place!). Can I contact her now? I do feel it's important to intervene early so Lulu Rosemary doesn't fall behind. Help!

LIBRARIANMUM

I think what's important now is for you to read to Lulu Rosemary and instill a love of books. The rest will fall into place! Join us at "Story Time" at the Twin Oaks Branch of the Austin Public Library every morning at ten!

TESLALUVR

I just want to say that for those of you who imply that Barton Hills is all rich white people, you can see above that a librarian can afford to live here! It's a mixed community!

LIBRARIANMUM

Ha, true, but my husband was #3 at Uber and is now retired. You might see him around the neighborhood on his recumbent bike! He has a new, unfortunate man bun.

KRISTA-G

Ladies! Newsflash! I live next door to one of the older moms in the 'hood, Liza Bailey. (OG rancher and I think she rents, single mom—not saying that's bad!) Her 15-year-old son, Charlie, is a lifeguard at Rosewood. Super-nice kid, he plays soccer with the twins out front sometimes and not even paid. Anyway, there was a cop car on our street and a hot cop was just lurking around her lawn!

CHARDONNAYISMYJAM

Hot cop alert! Much more interesting than Lulu Rosemary's probable dyslexia!

KRISTA-G

#waitingwithbatedbreath

-3-

Whitney

JULES WAS FURIOUS AGAIN. He drove with a cool precision, switching lanes soundlessly, too fast. "Please slow down," said Whitney.

"I'm in a bit of a hurry to get to our lawyer's office so he can handle this *disaster*," said Jules.

"It's not a disaster!" cried Xavier from the backseat of the Mercedes. He was still in his running clothes; his father had told him to get the hell in the car and had then screamed for Whitney to join them. They'd left Roma asleep in her room.

"Calm down," said Whitney. "What happened?"

"I'm having a coffee, scanning the security system," started Jules, his voice growing louder and louder, "and there's my own son talking to a *police officer* in front of the main gate!"

"Honey," said Whitney, turning around to face Xavier, "why did you talk to the policeman?"

"I was finishing my run," said Xavier. "And he was parked in front of the house. I didn't know he was a policeman! I thought maybe he was lost or something. I just . . . I didn't *do anything*. Why are you acting like I'm guilty? Do you think I killed her? Dad? Mom? Do you think that about me?"

"Of course we don't!" said Whitney.

"We're just trying to keep you safe," said Jules. "And they don't make you give a *DNA sample* if you're not a suspect."

"Honey," said Whitney, trying to placate her husband. "Xavier didn't do anything and he wanted to tell the detective exactly that. We don't need to make this a bigger deal than it is. He hasn't been accused of anything and he hasn't been arrested."

"Do you understand the optics here?" said Jules, his tone black.

"Oh my God," said Whitney. "The *optics*. Can you hear yourself?"

"I hate you sometimes, Whitney," he said.

"Dad!" said Xavier, from the backseat.

"I'm sorry. I'm sorry. I just . . . I'm under a lot of pressure. What I don't need is my *son* being led off in *handcuffs*."

"I wasn't in handcuffs, Dad!" said Xavier. "Why doesn't anyone ask me what happened?"

Whitney turned around to face him. "I'm sorry, sweetheart," she said. "What happened?"

"OK," said Xavier, his voice becoming grave. He took a breath. "So we were going to jump the Cliffs—"

"You didn't even know her," interrupted Jules.

"Of course he didn't," agreed Whitney.

"It's like I'm not even here!" said Xavier. "I'm try to tell you—"

"You *didn't have any idea who she was*," said Jules, cutting him off. "We talked about this, Xavier."

"Fine," said Xavier. His voice was low, ice-cold. "Fine," he repeated. Whitney was silent, watching her son dim. He could turn himself off, turn inward. Whitney wanted to tell him the truth and explain that it would all be over soon.

But if she spoke, Jules would stop it.

Jules thought he was the absolute authority, which Whitney had once found comforting. But once you stopped believing your partner knew what he was doing, life was scary indeed.

Annette

TOBY TOLD ANNETTE TO go ahead and take her citizenship test, attend her naturalization ceremony, pose in the outfit her Neiman Marcus shopper had bought her: a blue-and-white, long-sleeved—but very short—Valentino dress with six-inch, fire-engine-red, tasseled Louboutin heels. No news from the Austin Police Department was good news, said Toby. DNA analysis took awhile, and besides, Robert was innocent. Toby would be in his suite at the Driskill keeping an eye on the situation.

After the citizenship test, which was complicated but rote (Annette had studied the flash cards endlessly, her friends reading the questions aloud and quizzing her, laughing that they could scarcely answer a single one), Annette made her way down the hall to the Texas State auditorium. Some of her fellow new Americans carried tiny flags. Some cried. Many were stone-faced, conflicted, even at this final moment.

Louis and Robert and Annette's parents waited for her in the auditorium. Annette sat in between her mother and father, who held her hands. She felt teary.

"What are you *wearing?*" asked Maya. Annette smoothed the skirt of the Valentino, which barely covered her underwear.

"It cost eight thousand," she whispered to her mother and the two women began tittering.

"When you were a baby," said Maya, trying to control her laughter, "I wrapped you in your great-aunt's dish towel."

"It had flowers on it," said her father, leaning in with a smile.

"Tulips!" cried her mother, laughing hard now.

"We should have named you *Tulip*," said her father.

The three of them collapsed into giggles as a man took the podium, ready to address a room of new American citizens. "What's so funny?" said Louis, leaning in, wanting to be inside the joke.

Annette didn't answer. Louis would pity her if he knew that she'd once been a scrawny baby in a dish towel. But it wasn't a sad story to Annette and her parents—it was about bravery and hard work and God. Robert looked at Annette, his eyebrow raised, shooting her a grin. Her son, who had never known hardship, never been wrapped in anything but the softest fabrics. Which side of the joke was he on?

When she'd been announced an official American citizen, Annette posed in front of the flags at the front of the room. She hugged her family, and everyone from Laredo headed back. They had declined to attend her "Annette is an American" party, to Louis's dismay.

"We'll have our own party, next time you come home," said Annette's father, embracing his daughter. He held her for a while, whispered, "You deserve all of this. You can have whatever you want, my love."

"Thank you, Dad," said Annette. "For everything."

Annette stood before her parents for a moment, imagining

how scared they must have been, swimming against a current with a baby held aloft. "You're so brave," she said.

"So are you, Annette," said Maya. "Come home soon."

Annette had once been annoyed that her parents still called Laredo her home, but now the words rang true. When her family exited and Annette was left with her husband and son, she felt lonely.

"Come on, gorgeous!" said Louis. "The caterers are already at the house making American flag fruit cups and your signature cocktail!"

"Signature cocktail?" said Annette, suddenly exhausted. She could barely walk in her heels.

"Something with crème de cassis; I don't know," said Louis.

ANNETTE'S PHONE RANG AS she was changing for the party—a blocked number. She let the call go to voicemail. She bound her hair in a pink scrunchie and began applying mineral makeup. Her complexion wasn't as perfect as she'd like, so she'd worn "base" since high school, dusted with Revlon powder. Her mascara and eyeliner were Maybelline. Although Annette could afford expensive makeup now, she stuck to what worked, including platinum highlights from a hairstylist she'd visited in the Barton Creek Square for decades.

Outside her bathroom window, Annette could see three large tents. Her kitchen was filled with caterers making every possible iteration of red-white-and-blue foods: skewers of raspberries, blueberries, and light melon shaped like stars; blue crab cakes with multicolored dipping sauces; blue corn mini-empanadas.

The signature drink, the American Annette, was revealed to be a fruity concoction with a flag affixed to the glass. Louis had spared no expense: Dale Watson and his band, fireworks, the pool filled with inflatable Texas-shaped floats, spangled outfits for the catering staff. Even Hank Lefferts was coming to the party on his bike (he'd never gotten a driver's license).

Annette told herself she could huddle with Hank and her friends, sneaking cigarettes, later downing a few "American Annette" cocktails and dancing barefoot to Dale Watson . . . all in her very own yard. God knows they all needed a break.

With the house abuzz, Annette tried to feel happy.

Instead, she stared at her phone, a premonition creeping slowly up her neck like a scorpion. Images flashed before her: she and her son, walking across the bridge between Laredo and Nuevo Laredo, a small apartment with a handheld shower, her mother visiting for fresh coffee.

Annette put her hand on the vanity to hold herself up. Her heart beat powerfully in her ears.

Louis appeared in the doorway. Annette looked at her husband. He grinned, then dropped his pants to show that he was wearing a Speedo bathing suit printed with American stars and stripes. He opened his arms.

"Louis . . ." said Annette.

"My love," said Louis. "Are you ready to party?"

-5-

Liza

MY WORLD WAS CLOSING in. I had waited for Charlie to return from work the previous day, readying myself to bring him to Hilary Bensen, but he texted that he was staying at Bobcat's house and that his phone was dying. He had track in the morning, he texted, and then would meet me at Bobcat's party. I responded that he should come home immediately. He did not answer. When I called his phone, it went to voicemail.

This was not uncommon. Charlie dropped his phone and fell into sleep (or videogames) and emerged as if from underwater hours (or even a day) later, texting me back. I knew he would text me back. I prayed he would text me back.

I almost went to find him, but that would be shredding the fabric of our normal life. I wanted everything to be the same. I didn't want to show up, frazzled, yanking Charlie from his friends and taking him to a lawyer's office.

I did not want what was true to be true.

———

AS THE SUN SET, a police car parked in front of my house and I heard the doorbell ring. I was frozen, holding my breath until the car drove away. I stayed up much of the night. When I woke—too early—I waited with difficulty until 7 A.M., and called Charlie again: no answer. I tried Annette and Whitney, but no one took my call.

Finally, I went on foot to Annette and Louis's house, in case someone was following me. I knew my brain was misfiring, but I couldn't rest. It was midmorning, and the person who answered the Fontenots' door was a party planner who said none of the family was home. Still, I searched the house.

No Bobcat.

No Charlie.

The boys often spent their days off together or with other friends from the track team, roaming their city, sneaking into hotel pools, thrift shopping or gorging on Panda Express. As I walked home, Charlie texted at last. WENT SAILING ON LAKE TRAVIS W/ GUYS FROM XC. THEY GOT A BOAT CALLED BLUE ROOSTER. IT'S SO COOL! LOVE YOU SEE YOU LATER! He sent a photograph of himself with two friends in the background, grinning—blond boys I didn't recognize. I exhaled, gritted my teeth, decided to let him have the day, the lake, the sunshine. We would meet with Hilary Bensen as soon as he returned.

I sent a thumbs-up emoji.

Finally, around 5 P.M., another text: PLUGGING IN PHONE AT BOBCAT'S AND CRASHING FOR 1 HR. SEE YOU AT PARTY? CAN YOU BRING ME NICE CLOTHES?

I texted back: I NEED YOU TO COME HOME NOW.

He did not respond.

Finally, I showered quickly and went to Annette's. I held a pair of khakis, clean socks, and a button-down shirt for Charlie.

———

A PART OF ME still hoped there was some path that could lead me back. Wasn't the bond I had with my two best friends stronger than this mess? We had always discussed how to keep the kids safe—we'd made plans and hired driving instructors and tutors and enrolled the boys in swim lessons before Annette's pool was even finished. Couldn't we handle this situation in the same way—together?

Austin was my home—I wanted to stay. (An embarrassing truth: I'd imagined myself as an old woman, maybe wearing a sun hat and orthopedic sneakers, walking with Annette and Whitney through the neighborhood . . . even donning old-lady bathing suits and meeting at the Springs.)

I was sad for the young woman named Lucy Masterson. From the few mentions of her in the paper and an article in her hometown news, I saw she had been a waitress and a student, just starting her adulthood, the first in her family to go to college. I ached for *her* parents.

Everything had moved so fast—with the lawyers and defense strategies and DNA warrants. We'd all jumped right over trying to discover the *facts* and become obsessed with the exit strategy: protecting the boys from prosecution and harm. The last time we had all spoken, the night Whitney had shown us the Packers' underground doomsday bunker entrance, we had believed everything was a mistake that would blow over. We'd talked about the right lawyers to ensure there wasn't any lasting damage. Now, just three days later, it was seeming as if the event hadn't been blameless. The DNA warrants meant that the police had reason to suspect one (or more) of our boys.

Was it possible that in a dim corner of Annette's expansive yard, my friends and I could air our fears and lessen their power? As I approached her house—blazing with light, fabulous music spilling from her backyard into the street already—I nursed a tender shoot of hope.

But not for long.

6

Salvatore

SALVATORE PARKED HIS CAR at 1009 Slaughter Lane. It was 5:00 P.M. on the dot and he was absolutely bone-tired, done. He didn't want to get out of his car. His children, his loud, energetic, beautiful children, and the knowledge that one of the summer lifeguards could be a rapist and murderer . . . it all felt overwhelming. Was this depression? Could a pill fix him, make him want to stay in his life?

Salvatore's team had combed the neighborhood surrounding the greenbelt, interviewed Lucy Masterson's neighbors, co-workers, family, friends. They had not uncovered any other possible suspects.

One neighbor had seen "a teenage boy" entering Lucy's condo the week before but had seen him only from the back and didn't remember any identifying details other than that he was tall. Lucy's professors at Austin Community College either couldn't place her or had nothing to add. Her hometown doctor had stopped refilling an OxyContin prescription he'd written two years before for a rotator cuff tear. (Dr. Garcia talked to Tina for close to an hour about the painkiller problem in Sugar Land.)

Lucy Masterson had had sex the night she died, and the lab had promised to "ultra-rush" the process of analyzing the teenage suspects' DNA to see if it matched the semen found inside the victim. (Salvatore had called the lab himself, and assumed Paul Jackson had been joking when he said, "Oh, we're not just rushing, Detective. We are *ultra-rushing.*" Salvatore could never tell when Paul was being sarcastic or earnest or what; Paul was a weird guy.)

They hadn't yet received a DNA sample from Charlie Bailey. After dinner, Salvatore was going to have to follow up again with the kid's lawyer, the fearsome Hilary Bensen. She'd kept some gruesome criminals out of jail. The fact that she was representing Charlie Bailey looked very bad for the kid—everyone knew you didn't pay for Hilary unless you were scared. Salvatore wasn't sure what the DNA delay meant in terms of her strategy. She was smart as hell—he respected her legal acumen, if not her ethics.

Salvatore plodded up his walkway. (Someone needed to replant the window boxes and that someone was going to have to be *him.*) He made small talk with Mae Mae and bade her good night, assembled something like dinner. He felt half-asleep as his kids chattered and ate the meal, the very sad meal—deli meat, a stack of bread, sliced cheese, a jar of mayo on the table with a knife stuck in it.

Salvatore tried not to think of Jacquie, up in Heaven, wearing her favorite shortie pajamas with a matching silky robe, saying, "Sal, honey! The mayo jar *on the table?*"

He had to do better.

Allie was talking—maybe to herself?—something about lima beans, and Joe was dancing in his seat. As soon as they'd wolfed down the "dinner," Joe cried, "Time for football!"

Football meant that Salvatore was supposed to change into his running shorts (still on his bedroom floor, filthy) and sneakers and teach his son about the game. Throw the ball. Listen intently. Somehow also entertain Allie, responding in a somewhat human way to her entreaties, and meanwhile, dessert would appear after *football*. There would be homemade cherry pie . . . or maybe pumpkin? Yeah, pumpkin, with freshly whipped cream.

"Dad!" said Joe. "Come on, Dad!"

He couldn't do it. He. Could. Not.

"And then there are *pinto beans*," said Allie. "And black beans, and the round ones that aren't really beans. What are they, Daddy?"

"Come on, Dad!" said Joe.

"Daddy? The round ones? They taste like lima but they are *not* lima beans. Daddy?"

Salvatore's head hurt so much. *This must be depression*, he thought. He wasn't just tired, though he'd never been so tired. There was simply no joy. Even looking at his precious children, all he felt was an almost unbearable, yawning sadness. A dull pain that seemed endless and insurmountable.

His phone rang, and he answered.

"Sal?" It was Tina Silver, who had kept on working when Salvatore headed home. He felt a flicker of . . . not happiness, no . . . but distraction from misery.

"Tina, what's up?"

Out of the corner of his eye, he saw Joe slink toward his iPad. Joe was old enough to know when he'd been rejected, and Salvatore was lanced with shame. Allie, still at the table, cast her eyes down at her crossed hands, waiting for him to be finished so they could further discuss beans.

"Robert Fontenot," said Tina.

"Yes?"

"He's a match," said Tina.

"Oh," said Salvatore. In the basketball team photo he'd found of the kid they called Bobcat, the boy was tall and gangly. He'd looked very young in the photo, but had apparently had intercourse with Lucy Masterson.

"Xavier Brownson is not a match. Still no DNA from Hilary Bensen's boy, Charlie Bailey."

Allie began waving to her father, making a motion to hang up the phone.

Salvatore turned away from his daughter, holding a finger over the ear not pressed to his phone. "OK, Tina. I'll call you from the car."

"*Da*-ddy," sang Allie.

"Sorry, honey," said Salvatore. "I'm going to have to go back in to work."

"No," said Allie, bursting into tears. "No, you don't!"

"You're an asshole," said Joe.

Both grandmothers had offered to take the kids for the summer. Salvatore had thought staying together was best, but now he felt he may have been wrong. Something was the matter with him: he was not worthy of his kids' love. The realization made him feel even worse.

"Joe . . ." said Salvatore. His son looked up, wanting a reprimand, wanting any attention.

"Don't call me an asshole," he said.

"Don't go, Dad," said Joe quietly. "Please."

"This is my job. You know that," said Salvatore without conviction. He sounded like a robot in his own ears. "I'm sorry," he said. He was—he was so sorry.

Salvatore texted Peach, not meeting his children's eyes. Joe stood, threw his iPad onto the floor, and ran outside. Allie was sobbing theatrically. Peach arrived within minutes.

"I really appreciate this," said Salvatore. "Joe's in the side yard, I think."

"Oh, Sal," said Peach. "I'm glad to help. I know you're having a hard time."

Salvatore wanted to disagree, but Peach was right. He *was* having a hard time.

As he put the car in gear to drive away, Salvatore looked out the window and saw his son, holding a football, watching him leave. He remembered a gang member tell him once, "Fear turns to rage in the end, man. It always does."

He raised his arm to wave at Joe, but Joe turned away.

THE FONTENOT HOME, DEFYING the neighborhood trend toward modern, was what Jacquie had called "an architectural sampler": it seemed there had once been a reasonable, traditional home, but the Fontenots had added Roman columns flanking a front door that looked to be larger than a normal front door, wings on either side of the house that each boasted giant dormers with strange balconies to nowhere and even a turret on top with—Salvatore squinted—yes, it was a widow's walk, which overlooked not ocean but an expanse of paved driveway. The McMansion even held a four-bay garage. Salvatore could only *imagine* what the backyard looked like (he guessed a tiki bar and pool with naked cherubs "peeing" into the water). For once, he was not jealous of a Barton Hills home.

A balloon sign reading "Annette is an American! GO USA!" seemed to herald a big party in progress. The street was packed with cars and an impressive stereo system blasted Dale Watson tunes. Salvatore loved Dale Watson.

He approached the front door, lifted a large brass knocker shaped like an alligator, jaws open, teeth glinting. A harried-looking woman with a clipboard opened the door. "Welcome!" she said, her attempt at cheerfulness failing pretty badly.

"Here's your party pack! Be sure to wave the mini–American flag during the fireworks champagne toast. Go, America!"

Salvatore clutched his party bag and saw that the speakers weren't playing a recording of Dale Watson but that Dale Watson *himself* was singing by a pool filled with floats shaped like the state of Texas. The enormous backyard was full of party guests, everyone wearing red, white, and blue. Salvatore tugged at his Thrift Town tie. "Are you Annette Fontenot?" he asked.

"No, I'm Mandee, the event planner," said the woman. "Annette's over there, in the red sequins. Enjoy the party!"

What Salvatore wouldn't give to enjoy *anything*. To grab a mini–crab cake or head over to the giant table of beef where it looked like . . . yes, it was Aaron Franklin himself slicing brisket. To crack open a cold Shiner bock and dance to Dale Watson. He sighed. "Is Robert Fontenot here?" he asked Mandee.

She smiled and held her hands up. "No idea," she said.

Salvatore walked past her into the party. He scanned the guests, looking for Robert. There were a few teenagers splashing in the pool, so he moved in that direction. He took a second to pause by Dale Watson, to listen to a song he loved, "Tupelo, Mississippi and a 57 Fairlane" (his second-favorite Watson tune, after "Louie's Lee's Liquor Lounge"). When a woman who might have been an actual Dallas Cowboys cheerleader offered him a pig in a blanket with "Annette Dipping Sauce," he took it—why the hell not? It was absolutely delicious.

By the pool, he asked a young woman in a bikini if she knew where he could find Robert. "Bobcat?" she asked.

"Yes," said Salvatore.

"Maybe in the gaming grotto?"

The goddamn gaming grotto. Salvatore wanted to be rich.

He thought of his sweet son and Joe's old iPad. He thought about how much Joe wanted a pair of Air Force 1 sneakers.

Salvatore wanted to go home. But when home, he wanted only to escape. There seemed to be no relief.

"Hello, friends and family! And friends who are our family!" A voice rang out over the speaker system. Salvatore turned and saw a short man in snug jeans, alligator boots, and a Stetson standing next to Dale Watson on the stage. "Welcome to the Annette is an American party!"

People cheered and a spotlight lit up a nervous-looking woman in a red dress, her Dolly Parton–blond hair held back with sapphire combs. She wore ivory-colored boots with American flag inlays. "Thank you for coming to my party," she said nervously. Annette Fontenot looked tired.

The short man (Robert's father?) held up a glass of champagne. "Cheers to my wife, the love of my life! Congratulations, Annette!"

Salvatore glanced up as a fireworks show began. Watson and his band launched into "The Star-Spangled Banner" and deafening cracks preceded an American flag in the sky, followed by a fireworks Texas flag, followed by what may have been a woman's face, followed by the letter "A."

Where was Robert? Salvatore wandered among the guests, each exclaiming as the fireworks display grew louder and more elaborate. He felt dizzy as champagne corks popped and people jumped into the pool and the party grew rowdier. Watson and his band kept rocking on the stage.

Under a live oak strung with lights, he spotted Annette again. She was being hugged by two women. One wore a short silk dress, her dark hair in an elaborate topknot. The third woman was Liza Bailey. Salvatore couldn't believe it— she was definitely the woman from the Damnations show.

They were talking, heads bent low, champagne glasses catching the light.

He walked toward the women. Liza turned and saw him. He may have been mistaken, but he was fairly sure she recognized him. She squinted as he approached. "Do I know you?" she asked.

How he wanted to say *Yes*.

Instead, Salvatore did his job. "I'm looking for Robert Fontenot," he said, flashing his badge. He watched the three mothers' faces as their elation changed to fear. Above them, fireworks cracked open the sky.

7

Whitney

AFTER THE BROWNSON SIBLING pinching incident, the flight from Texas to New Zealand had been uneventful. (Air New Zealand had added the direct flight in recent years, as "High Net Worth Individuals," or "HNWIs," moved to Austin. From Auckland, many HNWIs took private helicopters or jets to their New Zealand compounds.)

Upon landing at Auckland Airport, Whitney and her family made their way sleepily through customs and into a van provided by the resort. When they arrived at Castaway Bay, they headed straight for their "Family Suite." Jules and Whitney would share the master bedroom, and Roma and Xavier would sleep in an adjoining bedroom's two twin beds. Whitney changed into clean pajamas and fell dead asleep, waking with a jolt when her piercing phone alarm rang.

The resort had provided manuka honey soap and shampoo, but Whitney always brought her own toiletries. She dressed as quietly as possible in a sapphire-blue pantsuit and low sandals (she'd heard the ultra luxury properties she was going to visit prided themselves on seeming "rustic," which usually meant she'd have a hard time walking in heels. Whitney's clients wanted to feel as if they were ranch owners in the Wild West, while Whitney's grandmother had considered never seeing or walking upon dirt the height of glamour).

She finished applying her Dior Rouge lipstick and almost tripped on a pile of blankets by the king bed, crouching down to find Xavier fast asleep. She shook him. "What are you doing on the floor, honey?" said Whitney.

He rolled away. "I'm not staying with her," he murmured.

Whitney sighed. "At least get in the bed with Daddy," she said. Xavier rolled back toward Whitney. She ran her fingers along his cheekbone. "My little cinnamon bun," she said, smiling. He opened his eyes and smiled, too. She rose, and he dragged his blankets into the king bed and fell back asleep.

Something was going to have to give. The situation with Xavier and Roma was untenable. Whitney was a problem solver, so her brain whirred with possible solutions as she made her way to the lobby, where a handsome Irish guy in a golf shirt and white chinos was waiting for her. "Mrs. Brownson?" he said.

"Yes, hello," said Whitney.

"Colum Murphy," said the man, holding out a hand and grinning.

Whitney took his hand.

"Quick coffee?" said Colum.

"You read my mind," said Whitney, perching on one of the clear Lucite stools and taking a look around the lobby. "This is lovely," she said.

"Wait till you see Miro Miro," said Colum. Whitney and Jules planned to trade off during this trip, one of them checking out remote properties their Austin HNWIs might want to purchase while the other stayed with the kids at the lakefront resort.

"Miro Miro, the most amazing property in the world," said Whitney, raising an eyebrow. "So they say."

Colum shrugged. "They're right," he said. "The Kiwis used to complain about being far away from everything," he said, "but nowadays that's the selling point."

"So true," said Whitney.

"You don't need a bunker here," said Colum. "Far enough from the White House to live above land."

"The White House?" said Whitney. She'd heard most of the doomsday scenarios, but getting away from the White House in specific was a new one.

"Metaphorically," said Colum in a low voice.

"I don't know what you mean," said Whitney.

"You can make your own rules here," said Colum, "no matter *who* gets elected."

Whitney nodded. Was he talking about money laundering? Her clients did hate the federal government, that was for sure. *Far enough away from the White House to live above land,* she thought. That was a good one: menacing yet vague.

After a coffee (and one for the road) Whitney and Colum drove in Colum's Mercedes to the heliport and boarded a Miro Miro helicopter. Whitney had been in helicopters before, but whether it was Colum's lime aftershave, jet lag, or the gorgeous New Zealand coastline spreading below her, she felt elated. The entire country was the length of Maine to Florida, with a population of around five million people. But from the sky, it looked like an uninhabited paradise.

They rose above the harbor and headed north. As they flew up the coast, Whitney gazed at the forests and fields, the glimmering sea. The weather was simply perfect: mid-seventies, with watery sunlight. (In truth, Whitney preferred the almost harsh, egg-yolky Texas sun, but she couldn't afford an escape compound anyway. Not yet.)

The aircraft landed on a putting green. Whitney disembarked, scanning the distant ocean and blue mountains, the sandy, pine-forested terrain. Waves roared in her ears. Miro Miro (named for an almost extinct Northland bird) was three thousand acres of dunes and forest with seven miles of coastline. Only 150 modern homes would be built here. It almost felt like the moon, but glamorous.

"It's something, eh?" said Colum.

"I just got here," said Whitney, "and I don't ever want to leave."

"Yeah," said Colum.

The golf club cost in the high six figures to join, but anyone (who'd been recommended by their "home club") could play. The caveat? You could play only once in your life, unless you became a Miro Miro member. Whitney toured the clubhouse (with Miro Miro's millennial credo framed on the wall: NO ASSHOLES ALLOWED), and visited a few homes under construction. They were designed simply, elegantly. With brass fixtures, restaurant-quality kitchens, and deep marble tubs, the so-called cottages were exquisite.

Whitney loved the pizza oven on wheels, the fire pit made of swamp kauri logs where members could watch the sunset with cans of beer, and the low-key clubhouse, but wasn't sure how her clients would do with the preppy golfer vibe. She had never met a Google employee who wore chinos. They were not young men (or women—there had to be women working at Google, Whitney assumed, but she'd never met one) who ironed or owned a pants steamer. Jules would love Miro Miro, though.

After an exquisite lunch of fresh fish tacos and gazpacho, Whitney and Colum boarded the helicopter back to Auckland, then strolled to Colum's car. He put the convertible top down for the short drive to Whitney's hotel. Colum said he'd pick her up again in the morning, and gave her a kiss on the cheek before driving away.

Whitney felt giddy as she entered the resort. From the lobby, you could peer through enormous wall-to-ceiling windows to the large lake. Whitney scanned the beach for her family and saw only Roma, who appeared to be sitting on top of a young man whose hands were in her hair. Whitney put her shoulders back, all her newfound serenity gone in an instant. Where the hell was Jules?

"Roma!" cried Whitney, going outside.

Her daughter looked up, and met her gaze steadily, not moving from the young man's lap. He looked uncomfortable, trying to stand. Roma flipped her hair over her shoulder and nestled back against the boy's chest.

She was twelve.

Whitney, overcome, marched to their room, where she found Jules and Xavier watching television. "Mom!" said Xavier.

"Hello, darling," said Jules.

"Roma is making out with some man on the beach!" said Whitney.

Jules looked back at the television.

"Jules!" said Whitney.

"All right," he said, standing up reluctantly. "I'll go see . . ."

"Thank you," said Whitney, though she suspected he wouldn't do anything, just stroll to the bar and back and pretend he'd intervened. Neither of them wanted to deal with Roma, who could ruin any vacation, no matter how idyllic. "Thank you, Jules," she repeated.

Luckily, Roma burst into the room before Jules had to do (or pretend to do) anything. He sat back down. "Hi, sweetie," he said.

Roma ran into the bathroom in her string bathing suit, sobbing.

Whitney sighed.

"Whitney, could you purchase our daughter a bathing suit with a bottom half?" said Jules.

"I did not buy her that *thong*!" said Whitney.

Xavier raised his hands and made a goofy grimace, trying (as always) to smooth things over.

Roma slammed out of the bathroom wearing Whitney's robe, her arms across her chest. Mascara leaked from her eyes. "What's the matter?" said Whitney.

"The matter? I'll tell you what's the matter! Because *you* embarrassed me, David said we can't hang out anymore. He said he wasn't *comfortable* hanging out with me. Because of *you*!"

"Sorry, dear," said Whitney. Her head was throbbing, and she went toward the bathroom, hoping she had Tylenol in her cosmetics case.

"And he was from *Australia*!" cried Roma. She began crying again. "I hate him!" she said. "And I hate you!"

Whitney went into the bathroom, closed the door, and sat on the toilet seat rubbing her eyes. A bleak feeling rose in her chest. Something bad was coming, she knew. They should change hotels. They should go home. Mothers talked about the hair on the back of their necks standing up when their kid was about to have a meltdown at a party. When a toddler was about to need a nap. Whitney believed in her mother's intuition.

She pulled out her phone and found another resort closer to the city. She made a reservation for the following day, texted Colum the change in plans, found a restaurant for dinner off-site. Then she splashed water on her face and went back into the bedroom. Roma was asleep in her room, so Whitney told Jules and Xavier about the change in plans. "We'll move hotels first thing in the morning," she said.

No one seemed surprised.

Roma seemed calmer at dinner, picking at her fish and chips. They walked back to the resort and did not argue when Xavier made a bed out of pillows on the floor of the master. Whitney took a Xanax and slept well.

She was so deeply asleep that Jules could barely wake her when the police came.

The boy named David, the Australian, was missing. When his family had reported his empty bed, a sweep of the resort was ordered. His bathing suit and shoes were discovered by the side of the water. It was a tragedy, the other guests whispered, as they watched the flashing lights of police cars.

Whitney agreed that it was. It was a tragedy.

Jules packed their car swiftly. The Brownsons were gone before a resort employee found David's naked body in the lake.

-8-

Annette

THE DETECTIVE WAS KIND. He informed Annette that Bobcat's DNA had matched the semen found in the victim. Detective Revello told Annette he could quietly exit with Robert and not cause a scene. "But you need to bring me to your son. Now," he said.

"I'll find him," said Whitney. Liza looked like a deer caught in headlights, stunned. Her best friends' obvious relief that it wasn't *their* sons being arrested filled Annette with fury.

"No," she said. "Please. Go get Louis. Tell him to get rid of everyone."

"Whatever you need," said Whitney. Liza nodded.

Annette led Revello to Robert's bedroom. Robert had told his mother earlier that he and his friends had stayed up late and that he wasn't in a party mood. She'd said he should feel free to shut his door and relax. Louis wanted his son to be social, as he was, but Annette understood how exhausting talking to others could be.

She opened Robert's door without knocking and saw that

his friends were gone and he was asleep. "Please wait here," she said.

Revello looked reluctant, but nodded.

Annette went to sit on the side of Robert's bed, cradling his face. His beautiful lips, his eyelashes. She wanted her son to be innocent, to be good. But she supposed almost every man behind bars had a mother who wished for the same.

Robert opened his eyes. The room smelled of Axe body spray and socks. Annette stared at him.

"Roberto, mi pequeño . . ." said Annette, calling her son what Maya still called her.

"What is it?" said Robert.

Annette exhaled. She whispered in Spanish, asking Robert to tell her the truth, to tell her everything.

Annette watched his eyes narrow, calculating, but then his face went slack. He was out of ideas. He was out of bravado. He was scared.

"Speak to me," said Annette.

"She was my girlfriend," said Robert, so quietly Annette could scarcely hear. "At least I wanted her to be." He looked straight at her, imploring. "Mom," said Robert. "What am I going to do, Mom?"

"Robert," said Annette, "did you hurt her?"

"No, Mom," said Robert. "I promise, Mom! I wouldn't ever hurt her!" He closed his eyes and curled into a ball, turning away. He began to sob, his shoulders shaking. He said something that sounded like "I can't go to Midland."

"What happened?" said Annette.

Robert didn't answer.

Annette lay next to him and held him, remembering the evening his flag football team lost the championship in a brutal game. "I worked so hard," he'd said then, curled away from her in this very same bed. "I worked so hard and we lost anyway." Annette couldn't read his emotions, couldn't tell if he was grieving or guilty. What was wrong with her that she didn't understand her son?

"It's time, Mrs. Fontenot," said Revello.

Louis, ashen faced, joined the detective at the doorway to Robert's room. "Toby will meet us at the station," he said.

Detective Revello read Robert his rights. Annette watched as her son was handcuffed and led to the staircase.

"Let me go with him!" she cried, but Louis held her back.

-9-

Liza

ONE OF THE REASONS I'm good at being a ghostwriter is that I've been a chameleon for as long as I can remember. I become whatever people want me to be. It's almost effortless now—sussing out what others want or need and then transforming. Who am I, truly? I have no idea.

As a girl in a resort town, I watched the summer tourists. I saw how the teenagers wore their hair long, tucked behind an ear. They wore sweatshirts from boarding schools, Birkenstock sandals. Their teeth were perfect and white, even though they all smoked American Spirit cigarettes.

I saw how my crooked teeth marked me as a townie; I learned to smile with my lips shut. I found a Pomfret boarding school sweatshirt at the restaurant lost and found, waited a few weeks, then wore it constantly. I practiced the heavy-lidded stare that made the girls look stoned even when they weren't stoned, the way they stood with their chests caved in, à la Kate Moss and her "heroin chic." They were wispy, ethereal, whereas my classmates at Falmouth High were loud and brash. The summer girls didn't *need* anything, they didn't *strive*, they didn't shriek or laugh loudly.

I wanted to be one of them.

During the summer after my senior year at Falmouth High School, Patrick noticed me for the first time at a Jetty Beach bonfire, one of the parties where the locals mixed with the rich kids from Boston and New York City. He looked like a teenage John F. Kennedy with his jet-black hair. He drove an old BMW and lived (I knew because I'd followed him home once) in his parents' enormous home on Juniper Point Road.

The first time we made love felt magical to me. Patrick was so *calm*, truly kind, and his home was everything I'd dreamed of. From his wide front porch, you could see the entire ocean. Inside, the home was cluttered with antique furniture made bright by sun streaming in the floor-to-ceiling windows. The kitchen had been renovated—every appliance was top of the line, gleaming steel—but the layout was the same as when a whaler's wife probably stood at the window waiting for her husband to return. Every room was carpeted with thick rugs, and I loved the furniture, reupholstered in expensive fabrics the color of the sea: pale green, deep blue.

Patrick's mother was an amateur art dealer, so the paintings were rotated in and out of the house: sometimes, there would be a Jasper Johns above the low-slung velvet couch in the living room; sometimes, a more classic Cassatt. I knew little about art, but Patrick's mother walked me through new acquisitions every time I came over, educating me. At the time, I thought she was grooming me to be Patrick's bride. Looking back, I think she was just bored.

I was in love, with both Patrick and his lifestyle. I felt for the first time that there might be a safe place in the world for me.

But Patrick's languor, I learned after I'd been sleeping with him for a few weeks, was due to heroin. In late July, Patrick overdosed at a party I wasn't invited to and was sent to a fancy rehab in Vermont. He ran away from the rehab and showed up at our trailer, saying he wanted to marry me. My mother was thrilled, but I could see the writing on the wall: Patrick was high when he arrived, and I knew a future with him would not be the secure life I craved. But what were my options? I said yes.

We were engaged, Patrick living in my trailer with me, my mother, and Darla when I realized I was pregnant. Although (as I've said) many of my memories are absent or blurry, I can still remember with absolute clarity the night I woke next to Patrick and stared at a starless sky. All I'd known was that I needed to escape.

-10-
Salvatore

AS SALVATORE DROVE ROBERT Fontenot to the station, he tried to meet the kid's eyes in the rearview mirror, but Robert stared down at his lap and was silent.

The Fontenots were no idiots: before Salvatore had even finished arresting Robert, their lawyer informed APD that Robert would plead the fifth. They would surely post bail as soon as it was set, which would likely be the next morning. Salvatore knew the prosecutor would want more than just the DNA match to have a prayer of convicting. No jury would send a kid to jail for having sex; no prosecutor would even take it that far.

As he waited for processing, Salvatore thought through the case. Robert Fontenot had had sex with Lucy Masterson. It could have been consensual or rape. Where had the opiates come from? What sequence of events led to her death? Did the basketball prodigy from Barton Hills hold a woman underwater until she drowned? If so, *why*? And what did his buddies know? Salvatore needed more evidence that Robert had been involved in Lucy's death—he had to get one of the other lifeguards to talk.

THE GARDNER BETTS JUVENILE Justice Center was clean and organized but bleak. Armed guards nodded as they admitted Salvatore, checked with the sheriff, led him to Robert Fontenot's cell.

On the bottom bunk, another juvenile offender stared into space, seemingly comatose. Robert lay on the top bunk curled up like an infant, his knees hugged to his chest. Salvatore could see only his neat haircut and his back, which read GARDNER BETTS INMATE.

"Robert?" he said. The cellmate sat up, met Salvatore's gaze.

"He OK?" said Salvatore.

"How would I know?" said the other kid, lying back down and closing his eyes.

Robert didn't move. Salvatore called his name again. Finally, he rolled over but did not rise. "I'm not supposed to talk to you," he said.

Someone began to scream in the cellblock. Another cry joined the first. There was banging, yelling, a soundtrack of mayhem. It was so loud. Salvatore was sweating: either the air-conditioning was broken or the temperature was set way too high.

"I didn't kill her," said Robert.

"That's what they all say," Robert's cellmate said.

"I believed her," said Robert. His eyes were glassy. Salvatore wondered if he was having a panic attack, or maybe detoxing? "I believed her. She said . . . she said she loved me," said Robert.

For a moment, it seemed as if things quieted in the facility.

The screams ceased; the breathing, the singing, the obsceni-ties went quiet. "She loves me," said Robert. "She promised me. She said she'd stop."

"Oh, man," said the kid on the bottom bunk. "He's crazy, right?"

Salvatore's stomach eased for a moment. If Robert *was* insane, he could get the boy out of here.

"Please help me," said Robert.

-11-

Whitney

WHITNEY DECIDED IT WAS time. Her plan had gone wrong; this was clear. She could not bear the thought of Bobcat in jail. The sweet boy! He had reached for Whitney's hand when they walked to elementary school, taking her fingers easily, as if she were another mother.

Could Bobcat's girlfriend be the same woman Whitney had texted?

Was it Whitney's fault that Bobcat was in jail?

What had happened on the greenbelt?

Whitney grabbed her Kate Spade case from the medicine cabinet. She was tempted to make sure the phone inside it would still turn on, but she didn't want the location services pinging nearby cell towers. She had to assume there was an APD tech department who could pull the damning messages even if the phone was dead. Whitney didn't understand any of this stuff! She was not a career criminal, just an over-wrought mother trying to keep her children safe—both of them. She might be condemned, but this was the only plan she'd had. Things could not continue. And so—as risky and absurd as her actions may have been—she had acted. But she had never thought of the girl on the other end of the transaction. She had thought only of her own babies. And now here she was, driving on Manchaca in the middle of the night.

Detective Revello's house was south of Stassney in an area Whitney called "up and coming" on her website. Whitney found the address she'd obtained by paying a few bucks online. Revello lived in one of a row of identical brick ranchers, maybe worth three hundred, three-fifty at most.

Whitney parked a few blocks away and pulled her sweatshirt hood over her head. As she walked, she removed the phone from the Kate Spade case, approaching Revello's house from the side. She tossed the phone onto his worn welcome mat, hoping he didn't have a video doorbell and pretty sure she was out of its line of sight if he did.

This was insane.

She was desperate.

Whitney saw now that she had been deluded, thinking she could fix things. But she couldn't wait until her son was dead! She was almost out of hope now.

She drove home, reactivating her security system despite her knowledge that the greatest threat was already inside her house.

Whitney thought of Bobcat in a jail cell and felt nauseous. Whatever happened to him over the night was her fault. Whatever Annette was feeling now was Whitney's fault.

She was a monster.

Was she a monster?

Whitney rubbed La Mer into her face, trying to avoid her own gaze.

Cellphone Transcript Record
512-XXX-XXXX

MEX
Is this Kobe?

Kobe Nadkarni
Who's this?

MEX
It's Joe

Kobe Nadkarni
Why does it say
MEX?

MEX
Scored a new
phone. Found it on
my doorstep, boi

MEX
Yeah loading in

Kobe Nadkarni
Noice. Can u play?

Kobe Nadkarni
Join my party

Lola
Where should I send the money?

MEX
?

Lola
Venmo?

MEX
One sec

MEX
Do you have V-Bucks?

Lola
??

Lola
Venmo or PayPal?

Lola
??

MEX
Venmo @SalvatoreRevello

Lola
OK

Lola
Did u get it?

MEX
Yes

Lola
OK when can we meet?

Lola
tonite???

Lola
Please

Lola
7-11?

Lola
??

Lola
??

Kobe Nadkarni
You ready? Let's go

MEX
One sec. People are sending
me $$ for no reason!

Kobe Nadkarni
Wut?

MEX
Rando wants to send me money.
I gave my dad's Venmo

Kobe Nadkarni
Yur Dad gonna flip.

MEX
Yeah

Lola
7-11?

Lola
Now?

MEX
Can you play?

Kobe Nadkarni
Not rn

MEX
When?

Kobe Nadkarni
Tmrw b4 school

> **MEX**
> OK

Domino
I said OK for the 40.
Venmo pls?

> **MEX**
> @SalvatoreRevello

Domino
Got it?

Domino
??

> **MEX**
> Dude I am copping new
> Air Force 1s tomorrow.

Kobe Nadkarni
Bruh

> **MEX**
> People be sending me $$

Kobe Nadkarni
Joe, did you steal this
phone or wut?

> **MEX**
> I'm a gangsta

-13-
Salvatore

SALVATORE'S PHONE BEEPED AND he glanced down: it was a payment of eighty dollars into his Venmo account, from someone named Lola. Salvatore frowned, assuming it was a mistake, turning the phone over.

He no longer smoked, and he'd already had the two beers he felt was an OK amount of beers for a weekday night. He'd be forgiven for sinking deeper into drinking—he was still a heartbroken widower, after all—but it was such a tired cliché. Salvatore's father had been a medium-level drunk. A "functioning alcoholic." While he was home in body, his Budweiser habit allowed him to disappear every night. Salvatore got the appeal, he truly did, but he didn't want to be that sort of dad, especially without a wife to remember cat costumes and teacher conferences. Being a medium-level drunk dad required a present mom, and Salvatore didn't have the luxury.

So he held an empty beer bottle and sat in his yard and watched the moon.

Salvatore had always thought that if he lived his life correctly, happiness would come. And maybe that was where he'd fucked up. He'd spent his life scared that he'd take a step wrong.

Now he saw: the happiness was the barreling forward.

That was it. The movement, the drive. He thought of Liza Bailey, of being young, of waking up next to a woman he'd met just hours before, touching hot skin.

Was it too late? Could he still gather strength, just throw himself at something, if only to feel that velocity again? What was there to lose, when you gave up on figuring it out . . . or worse, when you saw that there *was* no figuring it out?

It was the velocity.

His phone beeped again. What the hell? It was a forty-dollar payment from someone named Domino.

Salvatore stood and went inside, walked by Joe's room and noticed the light on. He turned the knob and saw his son hunched over a glowing object. "Joe?" he said.

Joe dropped the object—it was a phone that Joe had plugged into his wall—and looked up, panicked. "I just found it! I just found it on our doorstep," said Joe.

"Found what?" said Salvatore.

Joe held up a shiny iPhone. "People sent money," he said, starting to cry. "I just wanted the Air Force 1s."

Salvatore took the phone from his son. He wanted to leave, examine the call log. But he had seen what happened when parents, in the name of "protecting" their kids, stopped connecting with them. Sometimes, keeping a kid's head above water depended on having uncomfortable conversations, hearing things you didn't want to hear.

"What happened?" he said, fighting an urge to look at the phone and not Joe. "Start from the beginning."

"I heard a car," said Joe. Salvatore wanted to ask for the

details of the car, but stayed silent. "I went to the door, and found the phone."

"OK," said Salvatore.

"I . . . I don't know. It didn't have a code. I just texted my friend Kobe."

"Your friend Kobe has a phone?"

"Dad," said Joe. "Everyone but me has a phone."

Salvatore nodded, trying not to let his judgment show. "Then what happened?" he said.

"People just sent money," said Joe. "I shouldn't have responded."

"Can you show me?" said Salvatore.

"Yeah," said Joe. Salvatore sat next to his son, both of them leaning back against Star Wars pillows. Joe wore athletic shorts; Salvatore should have put him in pajamas. Did Joe even *have* pajamas that fit him anymore?

Joe hooked his bare foot around Salvatore's calf. "Do you know how to turn on an iPhone, Dad?" he said kindly.

Of course he did. But he needed to let Joe drive. "Show me," he said.

"OK," said Joe, navigating to messages and handing over the phone.

Joe had written to some friends trying to impress them, but for the most part, the phone was empty. It was so empty, it seemed someone had wiped it. But there were three text streams between the phone's owner and people who wanted to buy "candy." One of the people buying "candy" was named Lucy Masterson. She'd bought twenty tablets of "candy," paying with Venmo, meeting at the Barton Hills 7-Eleven ("by the Redbox") two hours before an untraceable caller dialed 911 to report the discovery of her dead body.

Salvatore hit "Contacts," dialed the one named MOM.

He gazed at his son. A panicked voice answered the call.

"Hello?" said a woman. "Hello?" said the voice. "Roma? Roma? Is that you?"

"Who is this?" asked Salvatore.

"This is Whitney Brownson. Who the hell is *this*?"

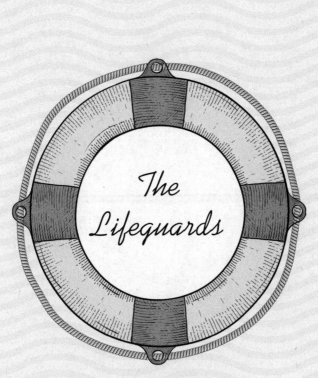

The Lifeguards

THE DAY LUCY DIES

AFTERNOON

-1-
Xavier

XAVIER WAKES IN A hospital bed, his mother and sister at his side. "Oh my God," says his mother. "He's awake. He's awake!" She leans close to him, touches his face.

"It was her," Xavier manages.

"Shhh," says his mother.

"Are you fucking kidding me?" says Roma. "He eats something and gets food poisoning and it's *my fault*?" She stands, crosses her arms over her chest.

"Be quiet," says Whitney.

"This is insane! Why do you hate me, Xavier?"

"Shhh," says his mother. A doctor, a young woman in a white coat, comes into the room and looks relieved. Roma winks at her brother. She seems cheerful, amped up.

"He's going to be OK," says the doctor.

"Oh, thank God," says Roma, transforming her face into the face of a concerned, loving twin. "That was so stressful for Mom and me," she adds.

Xavier closes his eyes. He imagines taking Bobcat up on his offer of borrowing his father's gun. Just to warn Roma, to wait until she is asleep and press it to her temple. She would wake up and see that he is not scared of her. That she has to leave him alone. He tries to tell himself he could do it. For just an instant, he imagines his life without her, how light and beautiful every morning would feel.

"Oh my God, he's *crying*," says Roma. "Mom, look, he's crying like a baby!"

Xavier imagines pulling the trigger of Bobcat's gun, imagines it being over—all the fear, the attempts to win her, the poisoning, the pain. Roma is a part of him, always, but something inside her is twisted. Bobcat's dad's pistol would be cold in his palm. It would be so easy, just one pull of the trigger, one shot.

-2-

Bobcat

ROBERT DRIVES TO LUCY'S apartment, the gun in his glove compartment. He's still shaking from what his father made him do.

(His father, a coward.)

Xavier has sent a text: TURTLE ISLAND, 8PM, BRING IT PLEASE. I'M READY.

Xavier is even polite when he's texting about killing someone. Not that Robert thinks Xavier will do it. They all know Roma's a psycho, but there has to be a better way. Sure, drunk on the greenbelt, Robert had talked about his dad's pistol, about how Xavier could end all his misery with one shot. And who would suspect Xavier, the perfect twin? All they'd have to do is maybe write a fake suicide note for Roma, or . . . who knows? Make it look like a burglary, or like she was hiking and got attacked. But Robert didn't mean it and neither did Xavier. They like to talk a big game but they're not murderers.

(Though in *Call of Duty* it feels fantastic to kill.)

(But that's not real.)

(Still, he likes it, maybe too much.)

His father also talks a big game, but he gets off on making Robert shoot a coyote. Pathetic. Robert almost refused, but he knows how close he is to being sent to his grandparents' house in Midland. He's "one more thing" close. If he even gets a B, he'll be packed off to the middle of nowhere.

(Fuck.)

(His grandpa is worse than his dad.)

(None of them even know what a motherboard is.)

The coyote's burial was the worst part. But Robert took a long shower and scrubbed off all the dirt, the stink of death. His father asked where he thought he was going as Robert left. Too many triumphant whiskeys in to even notice Robert had the gun.

He should probably lock the car but he forgets. All he can think about is Lucy, her body, her low laughter.

(He actually loves her.)

(He actually does.)

(He knows it.)

If she wanted to get married, have a baby, seriously, he would say yes. Probably not legal, but whatever. She doesn't want that, doesn't seem to want much, actually. He just shows up when he can, and if she's home, they're good. She is often not home, and does not answer his texts.

(It bothers him; he loves it.)

But now Lucy answers his knock. She's wearing sweats and a Willie Nelson T-shirt. "Hey," she says, reaching her hand out and putting a finger through his belt loop.

"Hey," says Robert. He is immediately ready.

"Want some popcorn?" she says, pulling him toward her.

"No," he manages, pressing her to him, *my God, my God.*

Afterward, he says, "I love you."

She rolls away from him. "You don't," she says.

He wishes, when she is gone, that he had insisted.

Charlie

CHARLIE IS SITTING ACROSS from his father at Kerbey Lane Cafe. His mom once told him that she worked here while she was pregnant with him. So far, Patrick ("Call me Dad!") seems OK enough. Definitely on something, jittery and shifty-eyed, and maybe that was why his mom left? Has his dad been a druggie for *fifteen years*?

"So," says Charlie, after they have ordered pancakes.

"Call me Dad," repeats Patrick. His face has a lot of lines, running out from his bright eyes and across his forehead. Charlie stares at him and tries to understand his mother. "By the way," says Patrick, sliding a business card across the table. "This is your aunt Darla. She asked me to give this to you. She said to call her if you ever need anything." Charlie looks down at the card: DARLA KING, MASS. BAIL ENFORCEMENT.

"What?" he says. His mother has a sister?

"Not much of a market for bounty hunters anymore," said Patrick. "She also sells essential oils."

"Thanks," says Charlie. He feels bewildered as he imagines a whole family tree opening its branches above him, unfurling its roots below. Patrick begins drumming his fingers on the table, looking around the restaurant but not at Charlie.

"Um, so is there anything you want to know about me?" says Charlie.

"She never told me where she was," says Patrick. "I told myself . . . I didn't let myself think about you."

"I guess my mom didn't . . ."

"No," says Patrick. "She didn't. She left and there was no way to find her."

"Did you even try?" says Charlie, knowing he's fishing for something but unable to stop himself. "Did you try to find us?"

"Of course I did!" says Patrick. But instead of elaborating, he holds up his coffee cup and taps it with his fork. A waitress turns and gives him a withering look, which he either doesn't see or ignores. He mouths *More coffee?*

"Be right with you, *sir,*" says the waitress.

"How did you try to find me?" says Charlie.

Patrick looks at him blankly. "I'm going to run to the men's," he says, standing up.

Charlie feels himself sinking. His wrath toward his mother, which has sustained him for a long time, begins to ebb, exposing a bedrock of need. He's been so angry at her for keeping him in the dark. He's imagined many scenarios:

His father is so wonderful she can't bear to share Charlie.

His father is actually dead and she won't give him the details out of some kind of misguided guilt.

His father is famous.

His father is a felon.

But it looks like his father is just a junkie.

Patrick walks back toward the table. Their waitress returns with coffee and their pancakes. Patrick sits, meets Charlie's gaze sideways. "You were saying how hard you looked for me," says Charlie.

"I sure did," says his father.

Charlie uses the side of his fork to cut into his blueberry pancakes, then spears a large mouthful. "Tell me more?" he says.

"I have a quick errand," says Patrick. "But I'll be back."

"What?" says Charlie.

"It's a work emergency," says Patrick. Charlie wants to hate him—he does, in fact, hate him—but his father's desperation corrodes any anger into pity.

"So you're an addict," he says.

"I want to get better," says Patrick. "I *will* get better. I want—" He looks at Charlie. His eyes are pools of need. "I'm sorry," he says. Patrick stands up. He takes a deep breath. "I don't want to be . . ." he says. He pauses. "I thought coming here, that maybe I would somehow . . ."

"Just go," says Charlie. "I've got Mom."

Patrick looks stricken. But he takes the chance Charlie's given him to break away. He turns back a few times, as if he has something to say, but his addiction is more powerful than any remnants of love, and he exits the café.

Charlie sits at the table for a minute. He takes a bite, then another. He cleans his plate, then starts on his father's pancakes. He opens up TikTok.

MY DAD IS A JUNKIE, he says.

I DON'T EVEN NEED A SOUNDTRACK FOR THIS ONE.

I FOUND MY DAD, AND HE'S A JUNKIE.

THAT'S WHY MY MOM NEVER . . .

He stops recording, just posts. He finishes his father's sausage and home fries. The waitress returns. "You all right, sweetheart?" she says.

Charlie nods. He *is* all right. He has his mom, and his friends, and his city, Austin, where he is beloved, where Zilker Park waits for him, day or night, where he can enter the greenbelt along secret trails and see his best friends. He feels sorry for the man named Patrick, and he feels sorry for himself, but he's OK.

On his ride home, Charlie thinks about the "rager" happening that night in Barton Hills. He pulls into his driveway. What a waste the whole day has been. His Oak Glen house is small and falling apart. His mom is trying so hard. Charlie texts her: CAN WE GET FREEBIRDS BURRITOS FOR DINNER?

She responds in seconds. YES! EXTRA GUACAMOLE?

He smiles. RICE KRISPIE TREATS?

DON'T PUSH IT, she writes, though he knows she'll splurge on the Saran-wrapped, buttery dessert squares they have by the Freebirds cash register.

He types quickly: I LOVE YOU.

She sends back exploding hearts: Mom is getting advanced.

His phone rings: Amir. "Baby. Hey."

"Hey," says Charlie.

"I saw your TikTok."

"Yeah."

"Are you OK?"

"Yeah."

"Can I come get you after work?"

"Let's just meet at the 7-Eleven, OK?"

There's a brief pause, and Amir assents. "I want to tell you something," he adds.

"What?" says Charlie.

"I'm sorry about your dad," says Amir.

"That's what you wanted to tell me?"

Amir laughs. "No," he says. "I'm nervous to say it first."

"What is it?" says Charlie, flirting, a smile lifting his lips. A sun grows inside Charlie's stomach. He feels its heat and light spreading out to his fingers and toes, to his brain. Amir loves him, he thinks. And he loves Amir.

"I'll tell you tonight," says Amir.

The
Sixth Day
of Summer

2019

KXAN Morning News

YOUR REAL NEWS—FIRST!

Good morning. I'm Denise Simon coming to you *live* from the Barton Hills neighborhood, where police have arrested a suspect in the murder of Lucy Masterson, a young woman whose lifeless body was found on a South Austin hiking trail just six days ago.

Denise, what can you tell us about the arrest?

Good morning, Scott. I'm standing in front of the home here on Down Cove where an underage suspect was arrested last night. It's a very large home, as you can see. Zillow estimates the property value at four million one hundred thousand dollars. It has a pool.

Well, I would hope so! Wow. Four million dollars. In South Austin.

It is a lot. I was surprised myself. Zillow lists some of the features of the house . . . let me see . . . it has a million-gallon, whole-house water filtration system—whatever that is—a natural gas outdoor grill, high-end built-in appliances including wine fridge, a Luma video security system, outdoor speakers on upstairs and downstairs patios and in the atrium, and multiple outdoor living spaces including a ground-level, custom viewing deck overlooking the greenbelt.

I'd like to live in that house!

Wouldn't we all? But anyway, the arrest was made right here at the four-thousand-square-foot home, apparently during a party.

A party?

As you can see, Scott, there are still remnants of a balloon sign. It appears to say, "Go USA."

Go USA?

Yes, Scott, that's what the balloon sign says.

OK . . .

Witnesses say the suspect was arrested and taken into custody inside his home.

That's a big home, all right.

Yes. And as you can see, it's surrounded by news crews. Police Chief José Ramirez is holding a press conference at nine A.M. and we will know more then about why this young man was arrested. I'm coming to you *live*.

Wow, what a story.

Yes, Scott, it's hard to believe.

And they arrested him in the middle of a party, wow.

Yes.

Well, let's get over to Stacey here, who's going to tell us about the weather. Another summer scorcher, Stacey?

You've got that right, Scott! Get out your sunglasses and get yourself to Barton Springs, because we are headed over 100 degrees for the fifth day in a row. This is going to be a June to remember!

-2-

Barton Hills Mamas

TESLALUVR

A kid from the neighborhood was arrested last night! Apparently, a basketball star! Does anyone know more?

CARLA G

Oh my God—what?????

VICKI B

Yes. I live next door. His name is Robert Fontenot but they call him Bobcat. There are reporters everywhere. They had some huge party last night and I could NOT even get the kids to bed. They didn't even invite us! I heard Aaron Franklin was there. Bobcat once sat down on my front lawn and played with my son. I thought it was cute at the time but now it seems very suspicious. The mom is *quite* the bombshell though half the time she looks like she just rolled out of bed. She works at Hola Amigos! Though obviously doesn't need to.

I can't believe I'm in the middle of this drama!

BOYMAMA

I have been on the wait list at Hola, Amigos for two years!

NYCMOM

Same here! The dude who runs that place is *hot*.

OAKLANDMAMA

Do you think a Barton Hills kid could have murdered someone?

MAMATOCHLOE

Their house is a monstrosity. Just FYI. I feel like the dad must have designed it himself. NO coherence. Appalling.

VICKI B

Dad is white and blasts Travis Scott from his truck. Need I say more?

MAMATOCHLOE

No! Ugh.

-3-

Whitney

WHITNEY WAS PUTTING ON her earrings when she heard someone press the buzzer at their front gate. She affixed the gold backings on her diamonds, peered into the surveillance camera, allowed the sedan entry. When she opened her front door, Detective Revello was walking up her driveway.

"Detective," said Whitney. She felt dizzy, put her hands on her knees, then righted herself.

"Are you all right?" said Detective Revello.

"I'm sorry," said Whitney, trying not to faint. "Xavier has a lawyer, and any questioning you have will have to be conducted through him. Do you need the number?"

"I'm not here for Xavier," said the detective. Whitney took a deep breath, her heart hammering.

He looked at her, his deep blue eyes calm and wise. Could he hear the thudding, the blood rushing in her ears? Here it was. Here it was. She tried to imagine him saying the words. He shook his head once, slowly.

She gazed into his eyes, thinking, *Please.*

In a barking command, Revello said, "Go ahead."

From either side of him, two officers emerged. Was Whitney dreaming? They walked past her, into her house. Whitney said, "What the hell do you think you're—"

But they were handcuffing Roma, who was standing in the hallway in pink pajamas. "You have the right to remain silent," said a female officer, as Roma began to scream. "Anything you say can and will be used against you."

"Mommy! No! Mommy!" shrieked Roma.

"We're arresting your daughter for drug trafficking and possibly homicide," said Salvatore.

"I'm calling our lawyer," said Whitney.

"Feel free," said Revello.

Roma had collapsed, shrieking. "I'm handcuffed!" she cried. "Mommy, stop them!"

Whitney picked up her phone from the counter. She dialed a nonsense number, pretended to be doing something to help her daughter. But she had already done everything she could to help her daughter.

This plan was the final plan, her last resort.

Pretending to wait for someone to answer, Whitney watched as the officers pulled Roma to her feet. Roma looked at Whitney, shaking her head. "I didn't do anything, Mommy!" she cried. "At least let me get dressed!"

Xavier entered the hallway in his lifeguard shorts and T-shirt. "Mom, what's happening?" he said, alarmed.

"Go back to your room," she said.

The officers walked Roma to a squad car, helped her inside. She continued to cry and scream at her mother. "Why aren't you stopping them, Mommy!" she screamed. "Mommy! Why aren't you doing anything? Why are you standing there and letting them—" The officers closed the car doors, cutting off Roma's voice.

Detective Revello watched Whitney. "You seem very . . ." he said.

"What?"

"You seem very calm," said the detective. He turned and walked toward his car. Whitney put down her phone. When Detective Revello drove away, Whitney stood in the doorway of her home.

There was silence.

Finally, finally, there was silence.

4

EVIDENCE FILE 202
THE STATE OF TEXAS VERSUS ROMA BROWNSON

TEXT STREAM RECOVERED BY APD TECHNICAL FORENSIC DEPARTMENT

Conversation between Lucy Masterson and Roma Brownson (MEX), dated May 31, 2019:

Lucy Masterson
Hi I saw yr post and I would like some candy.

MEX
How much and what?

Lucy Masterson
All 80mg u have

MEX
I will leave candy in white bag by dumpster at 7-11 Barton Hills 7pm Venmo @romamex $80 per. I have ten

Lucy Masterson
Thank you.

MEX
Got Venmo thx

-5-

Annette

ANNETTE WAS STARING AT her home bar and trying to decide if any of the glittering bottles held a liquid that would fix her. She heard Louis's phone ring in the bathroom, heard him turn off the shower and answer.

"Oh my God!" cried Louis, and Annette ran upstairs screaming, "What? What is it?" She grabbed his arm, breathing in sharply. Louis was dripping wet, holding his cell to his ear in one hand and his towel around his waist with the other.

"Is he OK?" said Annette, thinking of Robert in jail. "What's happened?" she repeated desperately.

Louis dropped the phone and the towel and embraced his wife. He was shaking, crying for the first time Annette had ever seen. "He's OK," Louis was saying. "He's OK, he's OK."

Annette began to cry.

"He's OK, baby. He's OK. They—"

He gathered himself and took a deep breath. Noticing his nakedness, Louis took his monogrammed robe from where it hung on the back of the bathroom door and put it on. He rubbed his eyes. "They just arrested Roma Brownson," he said.

"What?"

"It's not Robert. It was never Robert."

"I don't understand," said Annette.

Louis said, "Fuck." He turned to Annette. "Roma Brownson. Did you ever . . . could you imagine . . ."

Annette shook her head, speechless. "Can we . . . can I . . . can we go get Robert?" she said.

Louis said, as if unaware he was speaking audibly, "I thought he'd killed her."

"Louis!" said Annette.

"You don't know what it's like," said Louis. "Someone says they're going to leave you? You go . . . you can go crazy. You can do anything."

Annette wanted her husband to erase what he had just said; she wanted to go back in time, to not have heard him. "What does that mean, *you can do anything?*" she said.

"I'm just saying, you can't hold a man responsible for—" Louis stopped himself.

"For what?" said Annette.

"We're animals, in the end, Annette. All of us. I know you don't want to believe that, honey, but it's true."

Annette stared at him.

"You know your precious *coyote?*" said Louis. And though Annette had not answered, he went on. "Coyotes are *dangerous,*" said Louis. "They can attack, Annette! Who even knows! And so I protected you. I protect my family. You do what you have to do. That's what being a man is, Annette. But you get to pretend life is unicorns and rainbows. Because I protect you, and allow you to live in a fucking bubble with your spoiled friends. All of you, you get to pretend you're safe."

"The coyote?" said Annette.

"Actually, Annette, Robert handled it."

"Oh, Louis."

"I'm getting dressed," said Louis. "Toby's on the way." He went toward his walk-in closet, where the maid had hung all his ironed shirts, each hanger spaced exactly one inch from the next.

"You made our son kill the coyote?" said Annette. Louis didn't answer. "Why would you do that?" she said. "How, Louis?"

"How *what?*" he said.

"You told me you got rid of the gun."

"Grow up," said Louis. "You can believe what I tell you and be secure, or you can be an adult in the real world. That's your call."

Annette watched her husband dress, feeling painfully awake. Her skin hurt, understanding how much she had *wanted* to be oblivious, how much pleasure she had gained by allowing herself to trust whatever Louis told her.

What had she done to her son? Maybe Robert thought she condoned Louis's actions—his sexism, his firearm, his insecure concept of manhood. Maybe Robert thought she was too dumb to understand, or too weak to stand up to Louis.

Was she?

Austin American-Statesman

GREENBELT MURDER IS A "CRAIGSLIST DRUG DEAL" GONE WRONG

At a news conference this morning, Austin Police Chief José Ramirez announced that the so-called Greenbelt Murder Case is connected to a "Craigslist Drug Deal."

"We have reason to believe that the victim, Lucy Masterson, bought prescription hydrocodone pills from an online drug dealer in the hours before her death on the Barton Creek Greenbelt," said Ramirez. "More details to come, but the Austin Police detectives are following every lead. In the meantime, please keep an eye on your children's mobile devices. These opioid dealers are a scourge on our fine city, and we will stop them. I repeat: we will stop them. But we need your help."

Ramirez announced the formation of a tip line specifically for any suspicious behavior related to opioid abuse in the public schools or online drug trafficking with so-called Craigslist Drug Dealers. The tip line is listed below and all callers will remain anonymous.

The body of Lucy Masterson was found in the early-morning hours of June first on the Barton Hills Greenbelt. A teenager from the neighborhood was arrested last night but—in a whiplash change of course—a different Barton Hills teenager, as yet unnamed, was arrested this morning.

Many Austinites are unaware of the trail system that runs through the city, culminating at Barton Springs and Auditorium Shores. "It seems sketchy down there," says Leanne Gorowski, who operates Austin Duck tours. "I'm happy to pay my three dollars for a swim at Barton Springs, but to go down around those trails? Bunch of potheads and homeless people, if you ask me. Anybody with three dollars in their pocket would stay near pavement."

At the Gus Fruh swimming hole, packed with families on a recent Saturday, a local mother disagrees. "My three-year-old twins, Florence and Harriet, and I come swimming here every day," says Rachel Mishansha. "It's the jewel of the city, and one reason we moved from Brooklyn." She adds, "You think the greenbelt is sketchy? Try Cabrini-Green. This place is paradise." When asked if the body found on the greenbelt made her feel unsafe, Mishansha says, "Look. There is danger everywhere. I keep an eye on my kids, and it's 106 degrees, and we're going swimming. It's safer here than in a real city! By which I mean a bigger city. A city where you can get real Chinese food. You know what I mean?"

-7-

Liza

I WANDERED THROUGH MY house. Whitney and the lawyer had been calling me nonstop until I turned off my phone. Did we need to run? Was Bobcat still in jail? I didn't want to leave Oak Glen, but even if Charlie's DNA didn't match (and of course it wouldn't . . . there was *absolutely no way* the boys had attacked a woman, held her down and . . . no. It was unfathomable), there was a possibility that Charlie's face—and mine—could end up in the papers.

Our photo in the national news . . . it could reach Cape Cod. The thought of my sad past—the gray skies, the desperation, my broken mom—filled me with fear. I would not allow the black cloud to reach us. I would make sure Charlie never felt the awful sense of doom, the belief that there was nothing better, no way out.

There was always a way out. Besides, doing *something*, anything, always felt better than staying still. When I stopped moving, the pain caught up with me, old emotions, new worries. I preferred to stay in motion.

I had a Ziploc bag with a few photographs of my old life

including one I'd taken of Patrick at a beach bonfire, the flames lighting up his face. I'd thought then that he looked like a J.Crew model in his fisherman's-knit cable sweater and chino shorts; I stuck the photo in between the pages of the Bible from Charlie's First Communion, jammed them both in the bottom of a duffel.

I added clothes and the copy of *Joy of Cooking* I'd been marking up since I'd moved to Austin. All my underwear, my bathing suits, nice clogs. I went into the kitchen and opened my spice drawer. It stuck a bit and needed a strong tug.

I gazed blearily at my rows of beautiful spices—deep orange turmeric, red peppercorns, priceless strands of saffron, my trademark chicken rub. I was exhausted.

There was only so far I could get before I needed new license plates. Would the police put out some sort of statewide search for a mother and a kid who was in the wrong place at the wrong time? I knew my brain was scattered, frazzled, delusional.

But it felt as if I could see the truth clearly: Barton Hills was not the place where I would own my home and be safe. I had to go somewhere else, find someplace new where I could stay, where I could finally rest.

I was so worried for Annette and sweet Bobcat. But what could I do? As soon as the detective had flashed his badge I had panicked. Worse: I knew him! I'd had sex with Detective Revello a million years ago. Wonderful sex! As he stood before me saying he was going to arrest a kid I thought of as my son, I had watched his lips, remembered kissing him. I was a mess. I was full of desire and fear. My life had exploded so quickly.

My most valuable item was impossible to move: a Big Green Egg barbecue smoker. Charlie had won the grand prize at his elementary school carnival in third grade: a giant green ceramic cooker worth thousands of dollars. It had taken three dads to transport the thing in Louis's F-150 truck, and Charlie and I had screamed with delight when it arrived, watching the DVD immediately and learning how to use it together. We fired it up twice a month or so now, along with its accoutrements (called, cringingly, Eggcessories: a meat thermometer with a remote sensor you clipped to your belt, pizza stone, wok, vegetable basket, meat "claws" for brisket, matching aprons, and two BGE branded folding chairs). We'd even attended the Big Green Egg Fest when Charlie was thirteen, joining meat smokers from around Texas for the weekend. Had I hoped I'd find a boyfriend among all those portly guys in aprons? I had.

"WHAT ARE YOU DOING?" said Charlie, appearing at the kitchen door.

"I'm . . ." I said. "I'm just organizing things."

"You're packing. I'm not blind, Mom."

"Charlie," I said, opening my palms.

His eyes bored into me. After the incident at the pool the day before, we'd barely spoken. "Listen, Mom, I know you're scared," said Charlie. "I'm scared, too."

"I'm not scared," I said, moving toward him to hold him and give him comfort, the way no one had ever done for me. "Everything's OK," I said. Becoming the mother I'd always yearned for, I said, "I've got you . . . and we're safe."

Charlie slipped from my arms, shaking his head, backing away from me. "It's like you just can't stop lying, even when I need you!" he said. "We are NOT SAFE, Mom!"

"Charlie," I said. "You need to calm down. We need . . ."

"What I *need*," said my son, "is reality. I *need* to tell you the truth, and I need you to listen to me!"

"Charlie—"

"My dad came here, OK?" said Charlie. He started to cry. "I get it. I know why you left. He's a junkie, Mom! He's a fucking waste! I get it! Why didn't you just tell me? You let me think . . . you let me believe . . ."

"Your father?" I said. "Patrick? He was here?"

Charlie ran into his room and slammed the door.

I sank down, lost.

I wrapped my empty arms around myself.

-8-

Salvatore

IT WAS AN OPEN and shut case, and Salvatore knew he wouldn't get many of those in his career. The teenage girl had been selling drugs she probably stole from her parents and her friends' parents—that part of the equation was still to be determined. Maybe she was hooked in to a bigger dealer, which would be a lucky strike for him. Regardless, busting a so-called Craigslist drug dealer was a big deal. A career-defining deal.

Finally, he could stop worrying that everyone thought he was broken.

They had not released her name, but some internet sleuth had figured it out—photos of Roma (culled from her own social media) were burning up the internet like wildfire: her long hair, the short shorts, her wounded yet haughty expression. She was the epitome of a rich child gone wrong. "Affluenza" in pink pajamas.

And her parents! Whitney and "The Lion" Brownson were semifamous real estate moguls focused on gentrifying the city, exploiting people's fears to sell multimillion-dollar "doomsday bunkers" and homes with giant, remote-controlled gates. The Brownsons had helped usher in the "new Austin," a soulless megacity of overpriced real estate and chain restaurants, and they'd actively profited off the changes.

The public was out for blood, and Roma Brownson was a flesh-and-blood teenager in custody. Her lawyer would get her out on bail within hours, unless the judge believed she was a flight risk. She *was* a flight risk, of course: the Brownsons could easily spring their daughter and flee. A cursory Web search showed Salvatore that the Brownson Team, in fact, specialized in foreign properties; a whole section of their website was devoted to New Zealand and countries known for money laundering: the Cayman Islands, Liechtenstein, and the Isle of Man.

The Isle of Man!

For at least a few hours, though, Roma was in police custody. Salvatore opened the door to the interrogation room. It was 10:00 A.M. on the dot; they'd moved Roma from her cell twenty minutes early to give her some time to fidget, get nervous. "Good morning, Roma," said Salvatore. "Can I get you anything? Coffee?"

He'd interviewed many teenagers in his career, mostly abused and/or abandoned kids who'd turned to crime to save themselves. They were usually terrified, whether they were masking their nerves with bravado or sobbing openly. They were *kids*, the same as his own children, no matter what they'd been through. Salvatore was expecting Roma Brownson to be the same; he'd assumed this situation would be horrible for her, but might change her fundamentally into a better person. Kids were kids, and malleable. There was always a chance to help them.

But as soon as Roma Brownson looked up, Salvatore knew he had been wrong.

She looked at him steadily, her expression ice-cold. Salvatore felt a shiver in his low back—he remembered a sociopath he'd prosecuted years before named Carl Kress. Carl's gaze had been the same. There was something wrong with this girl, something fundamental.

"No," said Roma. "I don't want your sad coffee, but thanks."

"OK," said Salvatore, sitting down opposite the girl, trying to arrange his face so that she wouldn't see how her demeanor chilled him.

Roma crossed her arms over a thin chest. She wore scrubs and hospital socks, the same as all the juveniles at Gardner Betts.

"Let's start with the evening of May thirty-first," said Salvatore. He pulled out a pen, wrote the date on top of a steno pad he kept in the interrogation room.

"I was *home*," said Roma. "Someone took my phone. This is a setup. The only question is *who*. Who is setting me up? That's your mystery right there. But I have faith in you, Detective. I know you can figure this out."

Salvatore sat back in his seat, the metal edge of the chair hitting his back at a bad angle. He winced. "You were home," he said, "when your brother and his friends found Lucy Masterson's body?"

"Yes," said Roma.

"Had you ever met Lucy Masterson?"

"I'd heard Bobcat was boning an *older woman*," said Roma. "But I'd never met her, no."

"What is your relationship with Robert Fontenot?"

Roma rolled her eyes. "Oh my God," she said. "He's not my type. He's a weirdo. I mean nice, but more like a computer than a person. Have you seen *Rain Man*?"

"And Charlie Bailey?" Salvatore moved the conversation forward, not engaging.

"What did Charlie say about me?"

"How do you and your brother get along?"

"I wish he were dead."

Salvatore remained calm. He'd heard a lot worse. "Why's that?" he asked.

"Because my parents love him more than they love me," said Roma. "I'd kill him if I could. But you can't lock me up for that, now, can you? For wanting to kill someone? For dreaming about a world without my perfect little brother?"

Salvatore changed tack. "Have you ever taken drugs?"

Roma shrugged. "Of course," she said. "But never Oxy. That's what she died of, right? We've all watched the Snapchat ads, Detective. We know about Big Pharma and the Sacklers and not getting addicted to opioids."

Salvatore recalculated, putting aside the fact that Roma was fifteen, feeling as if she might be capable of anything.

Had she been to his house, planted the phone?

Why would she incriminate herself?

Had her brother planted the phone, knowing Roma had it out for him?

Had she been in contact with Salvatore's children?

The thought of Roma contacting Joe made Salvatore's heart race. "What do you think happened to Lucy Masterson?" he asked.

"Clearly, she was an addict," said Roma. "I think she OD'd."

"Did you sell her the drugs?"

Roma's lip curled. "Why would I sell drugs? My parents buy me whatever I want."

Salvatore looked at her. "Because you wanted Bobcat to yourself?" he ventured.

"Please," said Roma.

"Who do you think sold her drugs?" said Salvatore.

"Charlie's the only one who doesn't have money," said

Roma. "I don't know—maybe he took my phone. He has a sad old phone with a cracked screen."

"Anything else? I'd really appreciate your insight here, Roma."

"I see what you're doing," said Roma.

"What am I doing?"

"You're trying to appeal to me, win me over by asking my opinion."

Salvatore laced his fingers across his belly. "Or," he said, "I really don't know what happened to Lucy Masterson. And you might have insight I don't have, so I'm using you to get it."

"What if I'm using you right back?" said Roma, a smile playing at the corners of her lips that made Salvatore's stomach turn.

"So you think Charlie took your phone and sold drugs to Lucy . . . then took her swimming and watched her sink? Or tried to save her but failed?"

"Yeah," said Roma. "I guess. All I know is that Charlie needs money, and none of the rest of us do."

"OK," said Salvatore, standing. "Thank you."

"Can I go now?" said Roma.

Salvatore turned before leaving her alone in the room. "Oh, no," he said. "You're not going anywhere."

"You'll be sorry," said Roma.

"Thank you for your time," said Salvatore, closing the door behind him, happy to be out of her presence.

Someone had planted the phone, Salvatore knew. But the evidence was clear and simple: Roma Brownson had sold drugs to Lucy Masterson, who had died of an overdose.

All Salvatore had to do was nothing and the case would be solved.

Whitney

WHITNEY TOOK THE QUIZ when Roma was five years old. She found it in a magazine. She was halfway through a strong cup of coffee and the nanny had just arrived to play with the twins. She grabbed a pencil from the mug on her desk and curled up on the couch.

IS YOUR CHILD A FUTURE PSYCHOPATH?

1. Is your child cruel to animals?

Many future serial killers express their anger using animals. Look at the below photo of Jeffrey Dahmer—who went on to receive fifteen life sentences—as a little boy with his kitten. He has his hand around the kitten's neck!

Jesus. Whitney averted her eyes from Dahmer's freaky childhood grin but checked YES. Roma had thrown the family cat in the pool the week before, and (according to the former nanny, who had quit) shoved it away from the side every time it tried to get out. Roma, said the former nanny, had watched the cat drown.

2. Does your child love fire?

Pyromania is another bad sign. Like cruelty to animals, making fires is a way for a budding psychopath to express anger and defiance.

Whitney bit her lip and checked YES. Roma had been stealing matches and setting fires outdoors for a long time, and the week before, she'd lit her twin brother's stuffed frog on fire and tossed it into Xavier's "big boy bed." Luckily, the nanny who'd quit two nannies ago had smelled the fire and grabbed Xavier before the fire reached him.

3. Does your child wet the bed?

Many children who are later identified as having "callous and unemotional traits" wet the bed for longer than is considered normal. The humiliation of being a bed wetter, as well as parents' well-meaning attempts to make the child stop, can lead to explosive anger and the inability to handle it in a healthy way.

Oh, dear. Whitney placed a neat "X" in the YES column. She and Jules had done *everything* to try to stop Roma's bedwetting: promising her candy, buying a mattress that set off a gentle alarm when wet, restricting liquids after a half glass of water at dinner. But nothing worked. Roma almost seemed proud every morning as she announced, "My bed wet! Bad girl!"

4. Does your child enjoy breaking rules?

Every child breaks a rule or two, of course! But a worrisome trait to notice is if your child violates rules and gets joy and adrenaline from doing so. Future psychopaths can only feel when they do something bad and get away with it. Normal life doesn't provide them with enough serotonin and happiness. So watch out for a child who seems happiest when they have stolen another kid's toy, or deliberately done something you have told them specifically NOT to do!

Whitney thought of the dog gate Roma had left open, allowing their pup into the street; the bills Roma had hidden, driving her father nuts; the times she'd opened the front door and toddled out, despite the rule that she was not allowed outside by herself.

Whitney checked YES.

5. Does your child lie without remorse?

All kids lie! They lie to get out of trouble and to avoid punishment. But when your child lies for NO REASON, this is a concern. Children with callous and unemotional traits can lie with confidence, and they lie because they get pleasure from tricking others.

Whitney penciled YES, remembering the time a neighbor called to express her sympathy for Roma's beloved grandfather dying of cancer. (Roma's fabrication.) Whitney once stood *right next to her daughter* as Roma described a nonexistent pony named Sam. And she could never forget Xavier running to her in abject terror, believing Roma's lie that she and Jules had adopted him and were considering "sending him back." Whitney could still see Roma's lopsided grin as she watched her mother try to convince her son that he was her son.

6. Does your child bully others?

Children who humiliate and harm others for thrills should be watched carefully and evaluated by a psychiatrist. Sometimes, bullies have been

mistreated themselves. Children who cried out as infants and were ignored might turn into children who bully others. They might want
power or attention . . . or to be like their violent parents, whom they
idolize.

Whitney checked YES, though she resented the implica-
tion that she might be to blame for Roma's penchant for bul-
lying other kids.

7. Is your child insensitive?

Future psychopaths don't seem as fearful as normal children. They
don't sense stress in the same way, and seem to lack compassion.

Whitney finished her coffee and put down the mug. Roma
seemed completely driven by amusing herself. She had told
Whitney the day before that she wanted to kill Xavier.

NOW, SO MANY YEARS after taking the quiz on her daughter's
behalf, Whitney had finally outwitted Roma. For years, Whitney and Jules had hoped Roma could be cured. Whitney took
her daughter to therapists and psychiatrists; she had even
checked her in to a psychiatric hospital against her will, but
Jules had checked her out a day later, claiming a mentally ill
child would ruin them. ("No one," said Jules, "wants to think
about their realtor having a daughter with mental problems.
We can handle this at home.")

At home, Roma walked around at night, terrifying her
brother. Any pets were soon "missing." Every day when Roma
went to school, Whitney waited for bad news—a hurt child,
or worse. Whitney grew more and more fraught, desperate,
but Jules could not be convinced to send Roma away. He in-

formed his wife that he would sign his daughter out of any facility Whitney "trapped" her inside.

One night, Whitney prayed for help. In the morning, she woke with a plan. She started her research that day, watching a *20/20* episode about how teens buy drugs online, scanning Craigslist and learning the lingo ("No LE" for "no law enforcement" . . . as if a cop would read "No LE" and stay away).

On the first night of summer, Whitney advertised pills she had left over from an old Pilates injury: "Candy 80mg. $80 each. No LE." She put Roma's cell number as the contact, then took her daughter's phone and changed the passwords. A stranger named Lucy Masterson had responded within minutes. Whitney had donned Roma's clothes, left the pills in a paper bag by the dumpster at the 7-Eleven.

When she got Lucy's Venmo payment, Whitney turned off Roma's phone and hid it in her Kate Spade makeup case. It was a one-time event. Her plan was to report the texts to the police in the morning . . . and the police would take Roma. At least for a few days, maybe longer. While she was gone, Whitney could make a plan for Xavier, try to convince Jules it was finally time to get Roma help.

Before it had all gone wrong, in the revolting 7-Eleven bathroom, Whitney changed back into her own clothes. She'd scrubbed her hands with the cheap soap and shivered, over-whelmed with hope.

Whitney exited the 7-Eleven, certain that no one had seen her. Until she looked across the parking lot.

Charlie Bailey.

She didn't know if Charlie had seen her. He'd seemed pretty wrapped up with the hoodlum he was kissing. But Whitney didn't know.

And she needed to execute this plan, make sure Roma

stayed safe behind bars as long as possible. What if Charlie told the police—or *his mother*—that he'd seen Whitney that night, wearing Roma's clothes. If Whitney ended up in jail, Xavier would have no one to protect him.

Whitney had planned only to have Roma put away for selling drugs! How was she to know that her sole customer would wander from the 7-Eleven to the greenbelt, overdose, and fall to her death where the Three Musketeers were swimming? How was she to know the random person who had responded to her "candy for sale" post would be sleeping with Bobcat?

She could handle this.

It was one last thread.

Whitney needed to make sure Charlie Bailey stayed silent.

-10-

Annette

THE METAL DOOR OPENED, and Annette's son emerged from the Gardner Betts Juvenile Justice Center, flanked by two officers. He looked diminished. "I'm so sorry, Mom," said Robert.

She shook her head, overwhelmed. He thought he could fix everything with an apology, as his father had taught him.

"Sorry for what, honey?" said Annette.

Robert looked at her, seeking. He was a boy who had fallen in love. Annette wanted to protect his heart, to show him another way.

"I don't know," he said.

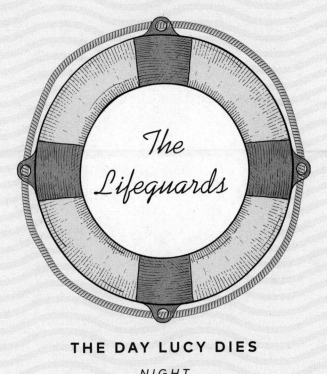

The Lifeguards

THE DAY LUCY DIES

NIGHT

Charlie

THEY BUY SNACKS AT the 7-Eleven, and in the car, Amir kisses Charlie. His mouth tastes of Takis: cheese flavoring, some corn derivative, fake lime. Charlie can't help himself: he puts his hand on Amir and Amir is hard. "Not here," he says.

"Where?" says Charlie, moving his hand up and down slowly, keeping his lips pressed to Amir's.

"Fuck, man," says Amir, laughing.

"I can't wait," says Charlie, moving to Amir's chest, unbuttoning his shirt. His father is almost forgotten, and the stupid kid he'd been, just hours before, paying for a strange man's plane ticket, getting through half a cup of coffee before this man—who looked just like him, if he had been strung out on heroin for decades—ditched. Charlie is an idiot, but kissing Amir makes it all OK.

"I can't wait either," says Amir, straining against Charlie's hand. "But we should wait. We're at the 7-Eleven. There's your friend, Roma, right there!"

Charlie looks up and sees a figure in an Austin High sweatshirt placing a wrapped package by the dumpster. When she stands, though, Charlie sees that although the woman wears Roma's favorite hat and her clothing, it's Roma's mother, Whitney. "Shit!" he says, laughing.

Amir puts his hand on Charlie's hand, smiles at Charlie. Whitney walks into the 7-Eleven, seemingly unaware that she is being watched. "Wouldn't think that rich bitch would shop at the 7-Eleven," says Amir.

Charlie laughs. "It's not Roma, it's her mom," he says.

"What?" says Amir. "Why she dressing up like a teenager?"

"Maybe a TikTok thing; who cares?" says Charlie.

"Speaking of . . ." says Amir.

"Fuck," says Charlie. He'd forgotten to take down the mournful video he'd made.

"What happened?" said Amir.

Charlie takes his hand off Amir's dick. "I guess I don't have a dad," he says. "There's not much more to say about it, really." This is his story now, and it sucks. "My dad's a drug addict," he says. "Maybe that's why my mom took off in the first place. I don't know."

"I'm sorry," says Amir.

Charlie rests his head on Amir's chest. It is what it is, and he's glad to know the truth, anyway. Wondering took a lot more energy. He lifts his head. Amir kisses him.

Charlie looks up and sees Whitney again, but this time she's dressed in her own clothes, some purple dress, fancy leopard-skin boots. Did she change clothes in the 7-Eleven?

Whitney's walking right past the car. Charlie doesn't think she's seen them but he can't be sure. As she waits to cross Barton Skyway, the heart-shaped locket she always wears on her right wrist glints in the sun. She turns, then, and looks straight at him.

-2-
Xavier

THEIR MOMS ARE GETTING bombed at his house, so Xavier texts his friends to meet at Frog Island. It's their secret name for some deep water where, as toddlers, they found tiny tadpoles.

The first night of summer! Xavier feels fine despite his psycho sister's attempts to poison him. He stops by Thunder-Cloud Subs, grabs a Texas Tuna and a lemonade, and walks along Barton Skyway to the secret turnoff. From Winifred, he makes his way to the unmarked greenbelt entrance. It takes about twenty minutes to reach Frog Island, and then the Cliffs, where his friends are already waiting for him. Bobcat is still in his uniform.

"You're not supposed to wear your lifeguard uniform when you're not at work," says Xavier.

"Cannonball!" says Bobcat. He jumps, and Xavier watches him grab his knees midair, land in the water with a giant splash.

Charlie follows. "School's out!" he cries. Xavier goes for it. The water feels perfect. They shove each other, pushing heads underwater, swimming in circles and whooping. But then Xavier, floating on his back, sees a woman on the Cliffs. She's wearing a yellow sundress and staring at them. "Hello?" he calls.

The other boys look up.

"Oh my God," says Bobcat.

-3-

Bobcat

ROBERT WONDERS IF HE is dreaming when he sees Lucy on the Cliffs. He'd brought her here once, a few weeks before. Why is she here now? "Lucy?" he calls.

"You know her?" says Charlie.

And then she jumps, or falls. Her dress flutters around her as she goes down, and she hits the water hard. The boys are silent, waiting for her to emerge. Robert imagines her bells of laughter, how she held on to him as they made love right here, then searched for tadpoles.

Lucy does not rise.

"Where is she?" said Charlie.

"What the fuck is happening?" says Xavier.

"Seriously!" says Charlie. "Where is she?"

Robert dives under. His friends follow suit. It is Xavier who lifts her body after a few moments, but she seems unconscious. He propels her to the muddy bank, where they perform CPR. Lucy is unresponsive.

"Fuck!" says Charlie, rummaging through his clothes and

all his crazy elbow pads and gear. "My phone doesn't have reception!"

"Is she dead?" says Xavier. "Is she dead?"

"Lucy!" yells Robert, shot through with terror.

"We need to call 911!" says Charlie. "My phone doesn't work! We need to call 911!"

"What's wrong with her?" says Xavier. "Is she dead?"

"My dad's going to send me away," says Robert. "We have to say we don't know her!"

"We *don't* know her," says Xavier.

"Promise me," says Robert. "We don't know her. We just found her."

His friends stare at him. In the center of their triangle is Lucy. She is dead. Robert touches her face with the back of his hand.

"Jesus Christ," says Xavier.

"Please," says Robert. "Please. Promise me?"

They are his best friends. They are the Three Musketeers. They promise. And then they run to the trailhead, get their bikes, and ride.

The
Seventh Day
of Summer

2019

Whitney

WHEN SHE OPENED HER eyes on the morning after Roma's arrest, Whitney realized she felt rested. Somehow, miracle of miracles, she had slept. She felt amazing, lush, heavy with relief. There was so much to be done, from calling Roma's lawyer to managing the PR disaster sure to come, but for a few, blissful minutes, Whitney turned on her side and curled back into herself. She clutched her sister's gold heart locket in her palm.

She went to check on Xavier. Before taking the key from around her neck, Whitney decided, on a whim, to try his door. The knob turned in her hand, unlocked. She pushed the door open, there he was: her beautiful boy, sleeping late.

Whitney picked up Xavier's phone, entered his passcode. It was hard to see without her reading glasses.

She sent the text to Charlie.

Biting her lip, she deleted the message so her son would never know what she had done. Then Whitney placed the phone quietly back on Xavier's bedside table.

-2-

Annette

ANNETTE'S MOTHER ARRIVED AS Annette was lying next to
Robert in his bed, scratching his back even though he was
already asleep. Annette saw her mother's face on her front-
door surveillance app and rushed to the door. "Who is it?"
called Louis.

Annette did not answer, just slipped outside.

"What's going on?" said Maya.

"Not here," said Annette. Louis could watch everything.
Annette placed her phone in the mailbox and took her mother's hand.

At El Borrego de Oro, Maya ordered chilaquiles with
beans. When Annette said, "Just coffee for me," Maya raised
an eyebrow but said nothing. She had driven straight from
Laredo to get to Austin as soon as Annette called and said she
was in trouble. Now, Annette told her mother the story from
the beginning: the arrest, the coyote, Robert's release.

"I thought once I got my papers . . ." she said.

Her mother sighed. She looked old and tired. "Only God
can keep us safe," said Maya.

"Do you believe that? Really?" said Annette.

"Yes," said Maya. "And so do you."

"Oh," said Annette. "Well, that's good." She stared out at the lot in front of the café, where every parking space but theirs was filled with a truck.

"God will protect you and Robert."

"OK, Mom, I get it," said Annette, picking up her fork and taking a bite of her mother's breakfast.

"But being an American?" said Maya.

"Yes?" said Annette.

"It means you can leave," said Maya.

Annette met her mother's penetrating gaze. "Where would I go?" she said, tears filling her eyes.

"Wherever you want," said Maya.

Liza

I HAD FINISHED JAMMING whatever I could fit into the Mazda 5 and went to rouse Charlie. My initial plan was to drive to San Antonio, about an hour and a half away, and get on one of the buses to Mexico. I'd considered a rural town high in the mountains called Real de Catorce, but then I remembered a woman for whom I'd ghostwritten a cookbook called *Love from Oaxaca: Paulina's Perfect Mole Sauces & Stews*. I'd visited Paulina and fallen in love with Oaxaca. Charlie and I could make a life in that small Mexican city, I imagined: He could join the children kicking a soccer ball around one of the picturesque town squares. Of course the kids I remembered were elementary school age and Charlie didn't speak Spanish, but it was a start. I knew the first-class buses were very nice, with movies and food, but the cheaper tickets might not require a passport . . . and if they did, I hoped the written ledger would never find its way to Detective Revello.

Detective Revello! The more hours I went without sleep, the more I remembered the night we'd shared. I'd snuck out of his West Campus condo at dawn—I wasn't ready for a lover. I thought anything that diverted me from Charlie was dangerous. There would be time for me, I thought. Now I wondered what my life would have been like if I had kissed Salvatore instead, curled around him that morning.

It didn't matter anymore.

But I thought about it anyway.

I stepped into Charlie's room. "Honey?" I said, approaching his bed.

There was a pile of blankets, and as I got close, my heart began to race. "Charlie?" I said.

I touched the blankets. The bed was empty.

"Charlie?" I cried. I moved around the house, looking everywhere. I called his phone, but it went straight to voicemail.

-4-

Salvatore

SALVATORE GAVE HIS NANNY the day off and picked up Joe and Allie himself. He spotted Joe outside school, staring at his non-snazzy sneakers. Kid after kid ran to a car driven by a mom. Salvatore ached to text Mae Mae and flee.

Salvatore typed, SORRY FOR LAST MIN TEXT BUT CAN YOU STILL GET KIDS? I NEED TO

Joe looked up before Salvatore could finish the text. He grinned and began waving. "Dad!" he cried. "Dad! I'm over here!"

Salvatore held the phone in his hand. He could still send the text, pull away, go to a bar, go for a hike, go to work, go hire someone to hold him, buy some running shoes, run until he collapsed.

But it was time to accept Jacquie's death, to embrace the memories of his life with her, and move forward. What remained was his son, his girl, and the memory of Liza Bailey's kiss, the person he'd been once, ready for love. Could he be that man again? Life wore you out either way. Loneliness left you empty, and love pierced you with the worst pain and the best joy.

Joe yelled, "Dad!"

Salvatore had a choice.

-5-

Liza

I TEXTED WHITNEY AND Annette in vain, telling them Charlie was AWOL and I was scared. Despite our hundreds of wine-soaked nights, our promises and conversations, afternoons spent caring for each other's children, it was becoming clear that when it mattered, we'd immediately reverted to protecting our blood. Was all the quiet I'd thought was a safe weave of community watchfulness—of *love*—nothing more than expensive houses with personal alarm systems to alert the owners of an outsider coming too close?

I sat on my front step, feeling completely alone. I remembered my childhood neighborhood—trashy, sure, but I was never lonely. I missed the chaos of Bluebird Acres, the way everyone knew our business. Oak Glen was barren in the blinding sunlight. None of the new houses had front porches, just high gates and backyards hidden from view. I had always felt safe in this quiet corner of the city, but now I felt isolated and scared, wishing someone would wander by and ask me how I was doing.

When Mack was sick, I had waited for help. When my

mom was too drunk to make dinner, I had waited. But no one had come to help me then. And, it seemed, no one was coming now.

In the middle of the hot afternoon, I remembered the "Big Mother" app I'd installed on Charlie's phone after reading about the start-up in the *Austin American-Statesman*. How could I have forgotten? I opened the app, and watched as it pinpointed Charlie's location. I squinted, confused. Charlie was . . . on the greenbelt?

I donned flip-flops. A breeze rustled the leaves of my oak trees, and I felt panic rise in my throat. Following the glowing orb on my phone, I began to run from my house toward the place where, not long ago, a crew of EMTs had carried the body of a woman named Lucy out on a stretcher inside a body bag.

It was so hot.

The paved road ended and I stepped over a metal divider and into the greenbelt. The ground was muddy, overgrown bushes almost hiding a small trail. But I knew the path was there. I walked along it, breathing in the pungent scent of stone and water and dirt. As always, I was struck by the presence of such a wild place so close to the city. But instead of feeling thankful, I was terrified. Anything could happen down here. I knew it. I peered at my phone, praying I would not lose cell service.

I followed directions, approaching the Cliffs, but then my path toward Charlie veered off the trail, descending a steep embankment. I was still at least twenty feet above shallow pools of water and rock bed. I stumbled, almost falling headfirst off the rim, and vowed to step carefully. I was dizzy and overheated. When had I last eaten anything? I couldn't remember.

I made my way along a narrow precipice high above the

creek bed. One wrong footfall and I would tumble off the outcropping. As I walked carefully—so carefully—my eyes grew blurry with unshed tears. The trail followed the cliff line and then turned. I saw a crevice in the rock, felt my way around the edge and leaned into a dark space.

Adrenaline made my heart thump wildly. I tried to make sense of the app, which was now having trouble connecting. From what I could tell, the dot showed that Charlie was *inside* the rock.

Impossible.

I pushed deeper, wedging myself into a crevice, breathing hard with exertion. I forced my body between two boulders, gasping, feeling woozy, as if I might pass out. The stone was cool on my flushed face. My eyes adjusted and I looked around. I was standing, it seemed, in a cavern. White and light brown stalactites and stalagmites glowed with refracted light. I looked around in awe.

Secret Cave.

For years, I had heard stories about Secret Cave, a place where speakeasies had held parties during Prohibition, where teenagers hosted raves, where children disappeared and never returned. I had never believed it was real.

Yet here I was.

I started to cry, overwhelmed. I didn't know where I was going. I didn't want to be here.

No one is coming.

No one is coming to help you.

No one.

I wanted to sit down. I felt like that girl again, desperate for anyone to take over, to hold me. But I did not sit. I moved forward as fast as I was able. The cave narrowed and grew darker. I lost track of the turns, at one point dropping to my hands and knees to pull myself along a passageway. Water ran around me; I could hear it. I emerged into a large space that smelled of cool moss. It was completely black.

I was sobbing now, murmuring words like *please* and *help me*. I used my phone's flashlight to look around. At the very back of the cave wall, I saw a narrow line. I approached, and found a hinge.

It was a door.

-6-

Annette

ANNETTE CALLED INTO ROBERT'S bedroom and asked him to come with her to the 7-Eleven. "What?" he said.

"Ice," said Annette. "We need some ice. And lottery tickets." Her father had always bought Annette and her siblings lottery tickets when they went to the filling station, and Annette had carried on the tradition. None of them had ever won a cent.

Robert shrugged, and they set off in his truck. Annette drove. They did not say goodbye. "How are you?" she asked, when they had fastened their seatbelts.

Robert looked at his hands and shrugged.

Annette wanted to end this uncomfortable moment. But she forced herself to wait. Robert mumbled something. Annette put her hand on his shoulder. He spoke again. "There's something wrong with me," he said.

"No," said Annette. "There's nothing wrong with you."

"Then why didn't Lucy stop taking drugs?" said Robert. He turned to Annette. "She said she would stop. She promised. I told her I loved her. I thought that's what I was supposed to do. I just feel like my brain is different, or something. I don't know how to be normal. I'm trying, but it's like I'm in a play, like I have to act all the time."

"We can talk to a doctor about all of this," said Annette. "Brains are different. Yours is perfect, but there's no reason to feel so confused."

He nodded. "Do you ever feel that way, Mom?" he said. "Like you're pretending to be normal? Like you have to watch everyone all the time and copy them to fit in?"

"I feel that way all the time." As Annette said it, she realized it was true.

"I thought I could make her stop taking pills," said Robert. "But she took them anyway. It's my fault."

"It's not your fault," said Annette. She thought of her kind father, his hard work, his respect for others. And she wanted to be near him. In Laredo, Annette could relax. She could drop the false version of herself she'd been so carefully upholding. She could surround herself with people who built her up.

"Mom," said Robert, as she breezed past the 7-Eleven, heading for the highway.

"Yes, amor?"

"Do you feel different now that you're a citizen?"

Annette smiled. "No," she said. "Actually, I'm just the same."

"Where are we going?"

Annette didn't answer, wasn't sure how to answer. Where were they going? She said, "Laredo."

"OK . . ." said Robert. "What, for the weekend?"

"Your grandmother will be so happy to see you," said Annette, deflecting.

"What about Dad?" said Robert.

"And your uncles, too," said Annette. "They love you so much, Roberto."

"Roberto," scoffed Robert, mocking her.

Annette felt tears in her eyes. His caustic, mean tone was the same as his father's. Cutting, hurtful, ready to pretend it was "a joke" if you got upset. It was not abuse like a fist, but it hurt anyway, kept Annette in line.

"Yes, Roberto," said Annette. Her voice was little more than a whisper. She was scared that her son, like her husband, would shame her. Instead, though, Robert grinned.

"OK," he said. And then, as he'd always asked when they went to Laredo, he said, "Can we get paletas?"

"Of course," said Annette. "Of course, little one."

She hit the gas, passed car after car, and drove south, toward home.

-7-

Liza

"CHARLIE!" I CALLED. THERE was no answer. The door deep in the cave had no handle. *Was* it a door? Could it be?

I began to pound on the rock. Claustrophobia and panic made my blood hot. "Charlie!" I screamed. I heard a clicking and a bright light made me wince. A hand grabbed me. I reared back and pain shot through my wrist, my bones in a vise. I was yanked through what seemed to be a man-made entranceway.

I held my free hand to my eyes, momentarily blinded, adrenaline flooding my veins. As my vision cleared, I saw Whitney. Her fingernails dug painfully into my skin. The room was cool, clammy after the stultifying outdoor temperatures. I saw Charlie sitting at a desk. He was pale and looked terrified.

"Charlie?"

Whitney slammed the door. Her expression was furious. I looked around, taking in deep leather couches, sconces, and mahogany-inlaid walls. "Where are we?" I said. "What's happening?" The room was lit by skylights and a window showing . . . the Eiffel Tower in Paris?

THE EIFFEL TOWER FROM DIFFERENT ANGLES—FOREVER!

I remembered Whitney describing the Parisian vista, laughing as I sipped a "mom marg" at the Packers' pool in what felt like another world.

An aboveground world.

A real world, with real light.

I peered at what I'd thought were skylights and saw that their color was flat, the view blue with no variation or clouds. The hue was a bit off, too bright, without the yolky yellow tinge of Texas sky.

"Is this the Packers' doomsday bunker?" I said.

Whitney continued to grip my wrist. "Yes," she said. It must have been the fluorescent lighting: I could see the bones of her skull under her skin. Her face was sharp and nightmarish. Was she sick? I blinked to try to dispel the vision.

"What are you doing here?" I said.

When I think back, I can see that these were the last moments I could still cling to the belief that Whitney was the person I'd wanted her to be: generous, larger than life, queen of a mythical place I'd always dreamed of belonging. A "summer girl" grown up. She was the foundation of my "Liza" persona. I thought that without her, I was nothing, a fraud.

"Mom," said Charlie, his tone low and grave. "You need to listen to me, Mom."

"I had to talk to Charlie somewhere private," said Whitney, cutting him off. "I'm in trouble, Liza. I'm in real trouble."

"What's going on?" I said, bewildered. Why would Whitney contact my son if she were in trouble?

"I saw her," said Charlie quietly, speaking only to me.

"What?" I said.

"Liza, listen—" said Whitney.

"Mom," said Charlie, his eyes aflame. "I saw her at the 7-Eleven. She was in the parking lot. It wasn't Roma selling drugs that night. It was Whitney."

My gaze skittered between them, taking in this extraordinary statement. Whitney met my astonished glance and shook her head almost imperceptibly, her eyebrows raising and her lips in a bit of a benevolent smirk: *Kids say the darndest things.*

I half-returned her smirk.

We remained in this strange space for a moment, as if things were the way they had always been between us. Whitney had not let go. I tried to pull free, but her nails cut deeper. I must have conveyed pain, because Whitney became authoritative.

"Charlie's wrong," she said, releasing me, placing her hands out, as if smoothing an invisible blanket.

"I'm not wrong," said Charlie.

"Whitney selling drugs?" I said. "Honey, that doesn't make sense." Whitney nodded, her shoulders relaxing.

"I know what I saw," said Charlie ferociously. "And I know you won't believe me."

My son's words hung in the air. He watched my face, his jaw tensing. He made a disdainful noise—a sharp, disappointed exhale. Hopelessness washed over his features.

"Why would Whitney be selling drugs?" I pleaded, my own voice childlike in my ears.

"I wouldn't lie to you, Liza," said Whitney, grabbing my wrist again. I felt a flicker of fear, a cold knowledge seeping into me, the understanding that Whitney was unhinged, that she might do me real harm.

And worse: she might hurt Charlie.

A dull pain throbbed in my stomach. It was a familiar feeling, one I'd learned to accept as the price of being Whitney's friend. The ache was the cost of ignoring my heart to

remain inside a fantasy. Have you ever stood still while someone lied to you? If so, you know the sickening feeling. Your
brain wants to make the situation less disturbing, and oh, how
you want to convince yourself the liar is telling the truth.

I wanted to continue believing in Whitney *so much*.

But the ache grew in my gut as I looked at her, the room
almost dissolving around us, only Whitney's eyes still penetrating and clear.

My real family had been screwed up and poor, riddled
with addiction and bad decisions. I had thought escaping
them, making a different life for my son, was an obvious win.
But suddenly, in this dungeon meant to keep a family safe
indefinitely—trapped together underground—I was stabbed
with regret.

"Whitney, you're hurting me," I said.

She pulled me toward her forcefully, encircling me in her
skinny arms. Her grip was too tight. She smelled of lilies. I
remembered resting my head on my mother's chest, the smell
of her: cigarettes, the tang of last night's alcohol in her sweat,
and the Werther's caramels she loved.

What if I couldn't escape who I was?

What if, even though they were poor and screwed up, my
blood family was the only family I could have?

What if, instead of devoting myself to making a new life
entirely, I had tried to stay?

In Whitney's feverish embrace, I was pierced with yearning. I missed my mom.

Get out.

My heart spoke to me clearly.

For the first time in a very long time, I overrode my desire
to be someone I was not, and I listened.

Get Charlie and get out.

Over Whitney's shoulder, I scanned the room, noted the

fake windows. I took in the staircase, where I knew a door led to the Packers' outdoor pool. I saw a patio, which was lit with natural light—or a near-perfect facsimile.

When Whitney's hold on me loosened, I took a tentative step toward the staircase.

She reacted immediately, grabbing a remote from the desk and pushing a button. Metal walls descended, blocking the patio and the windows.

"What the *hell?*" said Charlie.

"Whitney!" I said.

She looked crazed, her eyes moving quickly between Charlie and me. "I didn't know what else to do," she muttered, her voice almost robotic. "She tried to kill him. She's going to keep trying." Her face changed before me, growing older, exposing her private desperation. She looked haggard, exhausted, and suddenly *real*.

Charlie was staring at her, his mouth slightly open.

"I pretended Roma sold drugs. I was just going to report her to the police. I thought it would give me . . . I don't know . . . a few weeks. She poisoned Xavier. She's going to kill him, Liza. She's going to kill him."

"Whitney—"

"You'd do the same, right?" said Whitney, raising her deadened gaze to me. "If someone were trying to hurt Charlie, you'd do anything . . . wouldn't you?"

-8-

Annette

ANNETTE HEADED TOWARD LAREDO, but her son said, "Stop."

"We're going to see Grammy and Pops," said Annette.

Robert held up his phone, showing her a message from Xavier:

MEET ME AT SECRET CAVE ASAP? I NEED YOU.

"Mom, I need to go back," said Robert.

"No," said Annette.

"Xavier says he needs me," said Robert, and Annette felt a twinge.

The highway rolled out before them, blinding in the afternoon sun, filled with trucks and car exhaust and the hovering fumes of gasoline. It was her way out.

She paused, approaching a U-turn.

Cellphone Transcript Record
512-XXX-XXX

XAVIER
Meet me at Secret Cave ASAP?
I need you.

CHARLIE
What's up?

CHARLIE
Xavier?

CHARLIE
Omw

BOBCAT
Did you mean to text me too?

BOBCAT
Xav?

BOBCAT
Omw

-10-
Liza

"I WAS THE ONLY one," said Whitney. "I was the only one who could stop her."

"Oh, Whitney," I said. I knew that Whitney was telling the truth, maybe for the first time in a long time. I understood how terrible it felt to have no plan—to accept that life was an uncontrollable chaos—and how powerful the belief that you were in control of your children's lives could be. How you could desire the illusion of control so much that to keep it intact, you would become someone you didn't even recognize.

"It's the same as what you did," said Whitney, her voice crackling with anger, gaining strength. "You made up a story about Patrick, and then you lived in that story—you made me *help* you."

Charlie looked directly at me. "We don't have to pretend anymore, Mom," he said. "Not about Dad, not about anything. I'm OK. I'm good. Look at me, Mom. We're OK."

My son. I had taught him to be scared. I had believed I could buy his way to safety, keep all my sad secrets from him.

But everything I'd built—the patchwork of employment straining to rip, a house with a fancy address but duct-taped pipes, rich and feckless friends—it was worthless. None of these people or things belonged to me.

Only Charlie, who was mine.

As I looked at his face, I began to see my sister. My *blood* sister, the one I had left in Cape Cod. Charlie's cheekbones were the same as Darla's, his red hair her shade, and his expression—defiant yet hopeful—reminded me powerfully of her.

My sister, so small, looking up at me, starting to realize her life was tough, but still clinging to a belief that I would be the barrier between her and the ugliness beyond. She'd grip my hand when we left our trailer, assuming I could hold her.

But I had let her go.

I had run.

Where were my mother and Darla now? Could I find them and begin to mend what I had ripped apart?

Charlie waited, watching me, to see if I would let him down again.

"Please," said Whitney. "Charlie, if you can just stay quiet, just do nothing . . ."

"Mom," said Charlie in a low but audible voice.

I turned to him.

"Choose me, Mom," said Charlie.

Whitney's demeanor changed as she slipped her regal persona back on like a royal costume. She breathed through her nose, raised her chin. "I wish you were a real friend," she said.

"Whitney, I *am* a real friend—" I said. I reached down and gripped a chair for balance, the leather sickeningly soft and warm beneath my palm. My other hand landed on the desk, fingering the edge of a decorative sculpture, a two-foot-tall brass replica of the Eiffel Tower.

Whitney stared at me for a long moment. And then she said, "Goodbye."

Charlie turned to me. I knew the walls of this bunker were made to withstand a nuclear explosion. Whitney would leave us down here, because she would always take care of herself. I had thought Whitney, Annette, and I had been as close as sisters, but every one of us had chosen fear over love.

Including me.

It was simple to paint Whitney as evil—and I understood Charlie's view of her—but as a mother, I understood why Whitney had tried to fix things. It was what we did—it was how we bore the terror—we pretended we could keep our beloved ones safe. I was sorry that I hadn't been a good enough friend to see how Whitney was struggling. I'd wanted to believe she was perfect. I'd wanted to think she was in control.

Because if Whitney couldn't save me, no one could.

No one is coming to help you.

No one is coming.

It was up to me to save myself.

And so I did.

-11-

Salvatore

SALVATORE PARKED IN FRONT of Liza Bailey's home. He was feeling light, which was absolutely the wrong emotion for the situation. His weird good cheer made no sense.

It felt like hope.

Liza opened her door. There would be a time to tell her he had never forgotten her. That the memory of her filmy dress and the way she peeled her beer label off with her fingernails had stayed with him, the promise of possibility, of joy. But now was not the time.

Liza's son, Charlie, sat on a worn-out couch, his face weary. Salvatore refused coffee, sat on a chair across from the boy. The living room was filled with sunlight. The other lifeguards, Robert and Xavier, flanked Charlie on the couch, their expressions alert.

"Charlie," said Salvatore.

Charlie didn't meet Salvatore's gaze. He looked, instead, at Xavier, who nodded, giving him permission, it seemed.

"What happened on the night Lucy Masterson died?" said Salvatore.

Charlie turned to his mother. "Tell him the truth," said Liza.

Charlie inhaled. His friends pressed their shoulders to his, shoring him up. These boys' unity gave them a calm and powerful strength.

"I'm listening, son," said Salvatore.

"I was at the 7-Eleven," Charlie began.

ON THE FIRST SATURDAY of summer, when my doorbell rings, I find both Xavier and Bobcat on the front step. "Boys!" I say, opening my arms. They both hug me perfunctorily and I inhale their wonderful, feral smell.

Bobcat is even taller than the last time I saw him, his muscles ridiculously defined. "Hi, sweetheart," I say. "Are you back for the summer?"

"Just for the weekend," he says. He adds, "My mom's at her boyfriend's *trailer*," wincing theatrically.

"Don't you like Hank?" I say, laughing. Bobcat shrugs but looks happy. Annette and I have had many conversations about *should she, would she,* and *when,* though she's been sparing with the details now that she and her former boss have finally given in to the white-hot attraction they fought for so long.

All she's said, texting late one night, is: WORTH. THE. WAIT.

"Um, is Charlie here?" says Xavier. He has cut his hair very short, exposing the ears Whitney always told me he was ashamed of. I guess she was wrong.

"We're here for Charlie," Xavier reminds me politely.

"Sorry," I say. I call Charlie, and add, "Come on in, boys."

They do not come inside. I can tell the boys are itching to go.

Salvatore's house—now our house, too—is spacious and unfashionable. Our street is as lowbrow-sounding as it gets: Slaughter Lane. But we are happy in this big brick rancher, with a La-Z-Boy couch and an ugly kitchen big enough for recipe testing. Some of Salvatore's friends made the basement into a teen paradise for Charlie and lugged our Big Green Egg smoker to Salvatore's backyard. I bought a new king-sized mattress for our bedroom on layaway. Salvatore has nightmares and thrashes around, but when I hold him tight, he quiets.

As it turns out, our long-ago magic still casts a spell. We like to play old Damnations CDs and slow-dance in our backyard while my famous brisket cooks slowly on the BGE. When I press my ear to Salvatore's chest and hear his heart, I feel forgiven.

Someday, I will tell him everything. Only my son knows me truly, and that is enough.

Charlie had said, "Choose me, Mom."

I chose him. I chose myself.

And isn't that the definition of self-defense?

"We're headed to the greenbelt," says Charlie, emerging from the basement in a bathing suit and soccer slides, a towel around his neck, pushing past me.

"Have fun," I say.

He turns at the last minute. "Mom," he says. "You want to come?"

"Yes!" cries Sal's son, Joe. He wants more than anything to be accepted by Charlie and friends, to be a cool teenager.

"Please, Liza!" says Allie. "I'll go put on my bathing suit! IT HAS A UNICORN!"

"Are you sure?" I ask my son.

Charlie doesn't lie. When he nods, I run to grab my pool bag.

WE PARK AT XAVIER'S house and make our way to the secret entrance. The boys lead us carefully along the trail.

"This is awesome!" says Joe.

"Come on," says sweet Charlie to Salvatore's kids. He takes Joe and Allie—holding their hands—down to the water: the cliffs are too high for them and they scuttle to the muddy bank below.

The Cliffs are dangerous for sure—Life Flight helicopters hover above this spot every few weeks or so in the summer, searching for confused hikers or someone who fell off and hit rock. There's a sad and beautiful marker for a nurse who wasn't properly attached to the harness system and fell a hundred feet to her death while trying to save a lost soul.

And of course, this is where Lucy died. I don't even notice that the boys have been gathering wildflowers along the trail—their arms swinging in large arcs into the greenery—until they place them on a stone near the cliff edge.

If they can reclaim the joy of this place, I think—shuddering a bit at the thought of the Secret Cave, the doomsday bunker, and the brass sculpture—so can I.

Xavier and Bobcat launch themselves off the Cliffs. You have to know what you're doing here, and they do. They soar in free fall and land just right, breaking the surface of the water. Despite everything that's happened, they seem to feel invincible, which was what we moms had hoped for all along.

They are sixteen, it is summer, and life is glorious. From below, all the children watch me, calling encouragement.

I think of Whitney and Annette, remembering the endless days we'd spent here with our babies, then our toddlers, our growing twelve-year-olds.

I visit Whitney with a thermos of her favorite cinnamon coffee. She was once my best friend, after all.

I hesitate. It's a long way down. I stare at the water. "Is it cold?" I call.

"Freezing!" responds my son.

"Is it safe?" I ask.

"Probably?" says Charlie.

"Go, Liza," yells Bobcat.

"You can do it," says Allie.

I look at Xavier and Bobcat, at Joe and Allie. All the bright faces I love, turned up toward me to see what I will do. The kids' smiles are wide and untroubled. I lean forward and then back. I take a breath to calm my racing heart, and it doesn't work.

"Don't worry!" says Charlie. "We're lifeguards!"

I had wanted more than anything to find someone I could count on, and all along he had been right beside me. Charlie's eyes are as blue as his father's. He is strong, unbroken, big-hearted. I have done what was needed to get him here . . . at least here, to sixteen.

I jump.

Acknowledgments

I AM THANKFUL TO be surrounded by a family of beautiful friends with whom I am raising my kids. You know who you are. Thank you.

I am also honored to be supported and inspired by my brilliant editor and treasured friend, Kara Cesare, and the entire team at Ballantine/Random House, including Kara Welch, Kim Hovey, Jennifer Hershey, Allison Lord, Emma Thomasch, Taylor Noel, Jesse Shuman, Benjamin Dreyer, and Gina Centrello.

Thank you to my agent, Michelle Tessler at Tessler Literary Agency, to whom this book is dedicated, and to the wonderful Mary Pender at UTA.

I am also grateful for Dominic Riley, Hannah Finlayson, Sarah Harden, Reese Witherspoon, and the Hello Sunshine team; the world of bookstagrammers and readers; and the friends and writers who read my pages.

I could not have written this (or any) book without the wisdom of Beth Howells, Vendela Vida, Andrew Sean Greer, Elin Hildebrand, Allison Lynn, Jodi Picoult, Owen Egerton,

Christina Baker Kline, Paula McLain, Jardine Libaire, Meg Wolitzer, Mary Helen Specht, Dalia Azim, and Leah Stewart. Major thanks to the incredible Julia Romero and her editorial guidance. Many thanks to Ben Carter and Gil Green for the use of their gorgeous artwork.

Thanks to my mom and sisters, Brendan and Peter Westley, the Chappell and Roux and Meckel and Toan families for supporting and loving me.

Last but never least, thank you to my hilarious, smart, kind Ash (who inspires me every day to be as strong and brave as he is), Harrison (whose grace and hilarious texts make my days bright), Nora (my shining star), and the craziest schnauzers in Texas. My heart, always, is for the man who inspires me every day to fight for what matters and nap when you can—my love, Tip Meckel.

The Lifeguards

AMANDA EYRE WARD

Random
House
Book Club

Because
Stories Are
Better Shared ™

A BOOK CLUB GUIDE

A Note from the Author

Dear Readers,

Thank you for choosing my latest novel, *The Lifeguards*. I can't wait to hear what you think of the ending (more below) and how you choose to celebrate the book and female friendships. I hope you'll mix up a pitcher of margaritas and put out some chips and queso dip.

The idea for the novel came to me when I called my fifteen-year-old son one summer afternoon and he told me he was jumping the cliffs in the greenbelt near our home. I hadn't known there were cliffs, I didn't know who he was with, and I realized with a shock that he was no longer my baby. Even worse: *I* was no longer a teenager tasting freedom. I had become a mom worrying at home. So while the book is a murder mystery, it's also about motherhood and friendship.

These emotions led me to examine my "mom friendships," and how they'd been formed and were changing. Who were we all, now that we'd morphed into moms and our boys were growing apart from us? What if we were forced to choose between our love for each other and protecting our families?

The *Lifeguards* is my love letter to Austin, and I had a magical time researching this novel and immersing myself in my city. I interviewed police officers, ate breakfast tacos and BBQ, mapped out hiking trails, had vulnerable conversations with my friends, and visited glamorous open houses and design showrooms. (I even researched "doomsday bunkers"!) And the ending! Let's just say I wrote it a few different ways. I hope I can visit online book clubs and share all the possibilities I mapped out as I discovered who Liza, Annette, and Whitney truly were . . . and who they were meant to be.

Please be in touch! Email me through my web site. I can't wait to hear your thoughts about my novel, the ending, and your favorite margarita and queso dip recipes!

Yours,
Amanda

Questions and Topics for Discussion

1. Between Whitney, Annette, and Liza, which character did you most relate to or empathize with? Did your perception of the character change at all as you read and, if so, how?

2. Parenthood is a significant theme throughout the book. Discuss each mother's relationship with her son. How are their relationships different? Similar? Why do you think the author chose mothers as her main characters?

3. Discuss the themes of protection and sacrifice. How did you feel each character navigated these issues?

4. Which scene in the book stuck with you the most?

5. What did you think about the detective's storyline? Why do you think his story was included?

6. How do money, class, and privilege play into this story?

7. *The Lifeguards* is written with alternating points of view. What did you think of this structural choice? Did it create more suspense for you?

8. The author specifically chose Austin as the setting. How did you feel that played into the plot? If you imagine you

were to write a novel about where you live, what characteristics would you give your own setting?

9. Talk about the various real-life elements (message boards, texts, flyers, news bulletins) that the author incorporated. How did they influence your experience of this story?

10. Discuss the ending of the novel. Were you surprised to learn the truth?

A Q&A with Amanda Eyre Ward

The Lifeguards is a murder mystery, but it's also about mother-hood and friendship. How has being a mother inspired your storytelling?

Before I had children, I (like many young people, and especially novelists) thought about how to be a good person, what my purpose might be in the world, where I am meant to fit in, and with whom. After I had children, I found myself in full "mama bear" mode, wanting to protect my kids. That was my first thought in the morning and my last thought at night—are they OK? How can I keep them safe? For this novel, I wanted to explore the question *What if you are forced to choose between keeping your kids safe and being a good person?* In other words, how far would a mother go to protect her children? Would she be willing to do anything?

An unexpected and fascinating element of *The Lifeguards* that grounded the reader in the story and in the Barton Hills neighborhood was your use of other media interwoven into the story—flyers, news bulletins, chat boards, etc. What inspired these methods of communication?

I love reading my neighborhood emails every morning. It's always so fascinating to see what people are concerned with and posting about—a window into my neighbor's private lives. So when I decided that the Barton Hills neighborhood and Austin, Texas, would be characters in *The Lifeguards*, I had to find a way to give them voices, and using listservs and other media was a way to do this. As a reader, I love books that allow me to piece together a mystery. I have a few books on my desk that I constantly refer to as I teach myself to write. One of these is Gilly Macmillan's *What She Knew*, which uses diaries, letters, and police reports to tell a riveting story.

You mentioned in your author letter that you wrote the ending a few different ways. What was the writing and revision process like as you worked towards the final ending? How did you know when you had found the ending that fit the way you wanted?

When I begin writing a novel, I open a pack of multicolored index cards and sketch images on the cards, or jot down phrases. I try to make a plan to somehow translate the dreamy fragments in my mind into a world and eventually a story on the page. I work in a "cottage" in my backyard—I use quotation marks because it's really a tool shed, albeit one we've painted and I've filled with books and a blue velvet couch. So every day, in pajamas in my "cottage," I sip coffee and pull an index card from one of my bulletin boards. (I have two bulletin boards and three whiteboards, not to mention piles of books, a coffeepot, and dog treats to lure my mini schnauzers to keep me company.)

I write pages based on whatever card I've chosen that day, hoping to create an elegant, interesting story. Sometimes I just get stuck. Around the middle of act two of *The Lifeguards*,

I couldn't write from the cards I'd selected. They just seemed . . . wrong, especially the climax scene I'd envisioned. I went for walks, talked to writer friends and my editor and agent, lay in bubble baths, and tried to figure out where I'd gone off-track. I typed and deleted and wrote again. I went to a motel room (my favorite trick) and completed a functional draft. (This became the first version of the novel.) But then, in a dream, I saw the true ending of the book. I woke up, re-wrote the end, and sent it to my editor who called and agreed: *The Lifeguards* was finally—finally!—finished. I love how it all falls apart and then comes back together.

What was the most unexpected part of the writing process of *The Lifeguards* for you?

I started writing *The Lifeguards* before Reese Witherspoon had chosen my novel *The Jetsetters* for her book club and before I had ever heard of the coronavirus. By the time I emerged from the happy Hello Sunshine whirlwind, my sons and daughter were quarantining at home. Instead of quiet mornings writing, I found myself struggling with Zoom math classes and stumbling upon my boys making morning ramen in the kitchen. So returning to my novel became an escape. Being able to unravel a mystery—and return my characters to safety—was an antidote to the fear of the unknown that overwhelmed me during the pandemic. By the time I could hug my mom again in 2021, the book was done. Writing *The Lifeguards*, being able to escape to a safe and sunny Austin every day, hiking alone in the greenbelt and imagining the days when it would be filled with friends again, was an unexpected haven.

If you enjoyed *The Lifeguards*, read on for a
preview of Amanda Eyre Ward's new novel,
THE PEACOCKS, coming soon
from Ballantine Books.

Save the Date

FOR THE WEDDING OF

Sylvia Peacock & Basil Rampling

JULY 31
MUMBERTON CASTLE

FORMAL INVITATION TO FOLLOW

Prologue

IN THE MUMBERTON CASTLE Bridal Suite, Sylvie Peacock lay awake. She climbed down from the four-poster bed, parting velvet curtains, and walked toward the window. Moonlit treetops were a silvery ocean. The dawn songs of goldcrest and thrush would begin soon, but in the deep of the night: only silence. What was she doing in a crumbling castle in England? How had fate—or lust, or the last glowing embers of hope—led her here, of all places, preparing to marry again?

Was thirty-five too old to reimagine her life?

Suddenly, Sylvie missed the elementary school library where she worked, missed the thrum of a second-grade class choosing their weekly books, the smell of peanut butter and paper. Another chance at love was intoxicating, but now Sylvie just wanted to go home to her dog and her bungalow on Hibiscus Street.

She moved toward an ornate armoire and touched her wedding dress, which she had picked out with the help of her best friend, Florence. They had spent a humid morning hitting the bridal boutiques—Grace Loves Lace, Ever After Miami—before ordering Cuban sandwiches and strong coffee at their favorite café and finding the perfect dress on eBay: a long, swishy affair with a big bow in the back, a goddamned *bustle*, and pockets. Sylvie liked to tuck a tiny notebook and pencil in her pocket in case someone recommended a book that she'd want to read later.

Sylvie's first wedding dress had been short and breezy. She'd worn gold sandals, holding a bouquet of daisies. Her first husband, Alexander, had called her his mountain girl even as they married in a bayside ceremony in Peacock Park. A word about peacocks: Sylvie had no problem with them! But if your last name is Peacock, every holiday is an occasion for friends to send cards festooned with the fowl—peacock mugs, peacock feather handicrafts, etcetera. Sylvie's eldest sister had looked it up once: Their name came from the Middle English *pecock pacok pocok* or Old English *peacock*. "In 1940, Farmer and Teacher were the top reported jobs for men and women in the USA named Peacock. Less common occupations for Americans named Peacock were Truck Driver and Clerk," Vicky had read over a long-distance call.

Their father had been a Montana cop.

None of these facts meant that the Peacock girls had an affinity for the bird, with its creepy, cat-in-anguish cries. But when Alexander came home thrilled about Miami's Peacock Park, Sylvie had acquiesced. Two beautiful birds had walked by their wedding, one spreading its plumage. It was cool, she had to admit, and at the time Sylvie considered it a good omen. Now, she couldn't stand the sight of peafowl of any sort.

Sylvie's first husband, a native Floridian, had directed the elementary school choir at Coconut Grove Elementary. Sylvie was still surprised every morning not to find him in the Music Room although he had been dead for ten years. Under his tutelage, the kids had sung David Bowie and the Beatles.

The new choir director taught the kids a Taylor Swift medley and Katie Perry's "Firework." When Sylvie heard choir practice down the hall, she would stop whatever she was doing (securing book flaps with library tape, ordering more spine stickers) and let the sweet voices wash over her. She would think, in answer to the Katy Perry lyrics: *Yes. Sometimes I do feel like a plastic bag. Drifting through the wind. Wanting to start again.*

SYLVIE FINGERED THE EYELET lace of her gown, rough against her fingertips. Her mother's veil—which had been cleaned and wrapped in tissue after her sister, Allison's wedding—hung at the ready.

Sylvie would not sleep, not tonight.

If she called her sisters, Allison and Vicky, would they come to her? They had been strangers for so long, locked into the people they'd once had to be. And yet, who else could understand the riot of uncertainty inside her: shards of childhood loneliness; longing for her father's cigar-and-soap smell; a heart that would not—despite all evidence—give up on love?

When they were children, the Peacock sisters would meet in the rocks behind their house at night to escape their mother, Donna. Sylvie was the smallest but insisted she did not need help climbing Skull Rock. She would glance back periodically, to make sure her sisters were watching, protecting her from anything, from everything.

At the top, the three girls made a nest of tangled limbs. Sylvie sat in Allison's warm lap as Allison stroked Sylvie's strawberry-colored hair. Vicky's head rested on Sylvie's shoulder.

It seemed they were the only people in the world—they had each other, and joy, an endless Montana summer. They pointed out stars and told stories about how they would fall in love and marry and always, always live in Bitterroot Valley.

NOW, SO MANY YEARS later, Sylvie missed her sisters although they were asleep nearby where she stood, shivering, in a satin "Bride to Be" robe. She had just a few hours to choose between the terror of hope and fear's familiar comforts.

Sylvie had believed her sisters would always be beside her, watching out for her. She'd counted on their arms around her if she'd needed a hug. She didn't know who or how to ask for help, even as it dawned on her, as she exited her suite, that she had made a grave misstep; she was falling.

Six Months Earlier . . .

ONE

Sylvie

IT WAS NOT ABOUT the money.

Everyone would think—her mothers and sisters would surely think—that it was about the money. And, OK, Sylvie knew she would *not mind* being rich. Honestly, what little girl didn't dream of being a princess and/or a rock star and/or seriously wealthy?

Sylvie was going to be seriously wealthy. But her love for Basil Rampling was not about the money. She'd fallen for him when she thought he was just a bookworm with a sexy accent.

The first time Sylvie saw Basil's name, he had posted a poem on the "Checkoutmyshelves" app, a sort of "Instagram" for book lovers. Every time one of her contacts posted a new book cover, Sylvie's phone made a trilling sound that gave her a weird, warm pleasure. Sylvie rarely hit the double-heart icon that signaled the book lover should get in touch, but Basil had intrigued her from the start.

The poem he'd posted was called "Recess" by Darren Sardelli:

Recess! Oh, Recess!
We love you! You rule!
You keep us away
from the teachers in school.
Your swings are refreshing.
Your slides are the best.
You give us a break
from a really hard test.

Sylvie recognized it immediately—it was from *Galaxy Pizza and Meteor Pie,* one of the books checked out most often from her Coconut Grove Elementary School library. Published in 2009 by Laugh-A-Lot Press, the book was out of print, and Sylvie had taped the library copy together a few times already.

She was inside her cluttered office, preparing to help supervise the lunchroom, when she saw Basil's post. On a whim, she double-hearted it, then left her phone on her desk and went to the cafeteria, wearing her apron with the scissors in the pocket so that she could cut open kids' chocolate milk and applesauce pouches.

After lunch duty, Sylvie returned to her desk, unwrapped her egg salad sandwich, and peeked at "Checkoutmyshelves." Basil had double-hearted her back and sent a note, responding to her latest post, a stack of her favorite detective novels:

Tana French is the best! How does she do it?

Have you rad Louise Penny?

Ha, meant to say "read," but she is so "rad."

Peeking around, as if she might get caught feeling so delighted, Sylvie typed back: *I love Penny! Have you read Ruth Ware?*

His response was almost immediate: *Yes . . . but the wig at the end of "The Woman in Cabin 10" was a bit much for me. Prefer Tana French & the Dublin squad.*

Sylvie agreed absolutely. She scrolled through his account. He often tagged the Miami Public Library, posting covers of books of bird paintings, cookbooks, literary fiction (Ann Patchett and Alice Munro), books about travel (Pico Iyer's *The Lady and the Monk, Four Seasons in Kyoto* and Paul Theroux' *Dark Star Safari*), and many, many thrillers.

They messaged back-and-forth all afternoon, Sylvie taking breaks to do her job, reading to her kids in the kiva and then helping them find books, checking them out with her special wand and its satisfying beep.

In her library, all children were equal. Not all the students spoke English at home, but this didn't matter when they exclaimed over bright pictures of pirates (J 904.7), dinosaurs (J 567.9), or Halloween crafts (J 745.594). Some parents remembered library day each week—sliding the plastic-clad books into monogrammed backpacks—and some children looked at Sylvie with genuine fear when they'd forgotten. She had a loose policy and usually hit "override" when a kid was blocked due to overdue fines. Her library's treasures were meant to be held, brought home, paged through, loved . . . maybe even lost.

Every year she had to pay for missing hardcovers, spending a glorious day going wild at Books & Books. She couldn't think of a better use of her tiny salary.

SYLVIE WAS FIVE-THREE, AND wore her long, auburn hair twisted up and held with a clip, chopsticks, or—in a pinch—a pencil. She had pale blue eyes, almost-invisible lashes, and unruly brows. Her nose was long and thin, elegant, and her chin was a little bit pointy. Sylvie could do with a department-store makeup consult or a YouTube tutorial. She kept meaning to make time to investigate eyeshadow and lip liner, but ended up reading instead. Long walks with her dog, a rescue greyhound named Willie, kept her from the ravages of the Whitman's chocolate samplers she loved and bought herself at Publix.

Late in the day, as the fledgling Coconut Grove Band was assembling in the library, Sylvie put a mug of water in the microwave to heat up and opened her cabinet, choosing a hibiscus-and-orange tea called "Passion." Although it was 70 degrees outside in January, Sylvie's office was cold and she pulled on a sage-green sweater that her oldest sister, Vicky, had sent the previous Christmas. Sylvie sat down at her messy desk to play with her phone a bit before she was due to lead the "Math Pentathlon" after-school club.

Basil had sent a long note, telling her he was a wildlife photographer, originally from Northern England. His full name was Basil Rampling, and Sylvie immediately envisioned *Sylvie Rampling* in calligraphy letters in her mind. This was a childhood habit and completely ridiculous—humiliating, even.

That said, Sylvie Rampling *did* have a nice ring to it.

Basil was leaving Miami in the morning to head to the Santa Ana bird sanctuary on the south Texas coast (it was golden-cheeked warbler season). Shooting a feature for *Audubon*, he would be gone for three weeks.

Although Basil was the first man Sylvie had wanted to talk to in a while, she felt a bit relieved that he was headed out of town—it took the pressure off. As the days went by, they messaged about books, then began to open up to each other about other things—his divorce and sadness about his young daughter, Penelope, moving with her mother to New York; Sylvie's widowhood. The poem "Recess" was Penelope's favorite, as it turned out. It was remarkable how quickly Sylvie and Basil grew close—she began calling him in the evening as she walked Willie, eager to hear about his day photographing birds on the swampy, magical Gulf coast. His accent was entrancing. When he said he'd like to fly home and have her over to his place for dinner, it didn't even seem creepy.

Sylvie went to Annie's Vintage and chose a robin's-egg-blue sundress for her first date with Basil. He lived on Indian Creek Island, a posh address. An armed guard stopped Sylvie before she was allowed to enter the island, making sure she was on his list. Following Basil's directions, she drove past enormous modern mansions, then reached a metal gate. Basil had told her about the gate; she punched in a code and drove down a dirt road. Every inch of this land was worth a fortune.

She was a bit unnerved, trying to reconcile Basil's home address with the man she'd come to know—a man who loved to sleep outside, nestled in the "Cat's Meow" sleeping bag he'd bought himself as a U Miami undergrad after moving from an area so far north it was almost Scotland.

Sylvie drove for ten or so minutes, turning a bend and reaching a jaw-dropping expanse of waterfront property. There was a small dock with a canoe, a hammock slung between two live oak trees, and a smallish ranch home. Basil came outside as she parked. "Sylvie! You're here!" he said, picking her up by the waist and spinning her. She laughed, swooning with happiness; when he placed her down, he kissed her. His lips were warm and lingering. Sylvie felt dizzy with desire, but this pleasure was immediately cut with guilt.

Alexander!

"Whoa," said Sylvie.

"I know," said Basil. He was, like Sylvie, thirty-five years old. He was tall, his exposed forearms milk-colored. He had breakfast-tea-colored eyes, thick eyelashes, and dark hair that needed a trim. His skin was pinkish from the sun. This was a man, Sylvie noted, who would need sunscreen, 50+, for all occasions, especially in Miami. His kiss shot through her. It was chemical: she wanted more.

Basil led her inside his home. The front room had white-washed walls, terracotta tile floors, a wooden table covered with a simple yellow cloth. Large windows framed a pink evening sky. Sylvie breathed in the smells of cumin and chicken.

"Full disclosure," said Basil, holding up his hands. "My housekeeper made these enchiladas. She was worried I'd disappoint you with spaghetti and canned red sauce."

Housekeeper? Sylvie wasn't sure what to make of this. She has once hired Merry Maids but felt so guilty afterward that she'd overpaid them and never called again.

"Well, I can make one thing," said Sylvie, "and it's chocolate chip cookies."

Basil nodded thoughtfully. "That's a good one thing," he said. "Have you tried Mexican vanilla?"

"No."

"There's a fellow who parks his truck outside the entrance to the bird sanctuary," said Basil. "He sells stuffed animals—birds mainly, embroidered cotton dresses, tequila, vanilla, and cigarettes. You can buy one cigarette for a peso."

"I once found a pack of American Spirits in my sister's backpack," mused Sylvie. "Allison used to be pretty wild."

"Allison's the middle one?" said Basil. They had talked about their families on their long phone calls; Sylvie was glad Basil remembered.

"Yes: Vicky's the oldest, then Allison, then me," said Sylvie, smiling. "I tried to run the show even though I was the baby. I threw away her cigarettes and gave her a big lecture. Not that she listened to me!"

"I always wanted brothers and sisters. Or even one brother

or one sister . . . ," said Basil. His words trailed off as if he re-membered something painful. He had told Sylvie about a lonely childhood living in a decrepit castle where his father was the caretaker—drafty, haunted rooms, long winter months, a fireplace that sometimes stopped working, and beans-on-toast. The castle had a hawk and owl center (they spelled it "centre"). When Basil's mother died, young Basil had believed her soul lived on in a hideous Hooded Vulture named Penny. "They look like chickens, but frightening. Truly hideous, truly," said Basil. Sylvie loved how he said dark things in a way that made her laugh. Was this a British trait?

Basil spent afternoons with Penny—talking to her, feeding her, flying her around the castle grounds. Basil's past sounded like a harrowing movie to Sylvie, and every time he men-tioned it, she wanted to hug him.

Sylvie tried to lighten the mood. "I'd like a cotton dress, and I'd like vanilla. And, OK, tequila."

Basil laughed, and Sylvie felt relieved that she'd been able to pull him from dead-mouse-filled memories.

She explored his home as he tossed a green salad with sliced apples, cherries, and goat cheese. The living room had two low-slung leather couches, a woven rug, and an Eames chair. Sylvie paused—she'd long coveted an Eames—even on Craigslist, they went for thousands. On the mantle was a pho-tograph of a little girl seated between two standard poodles: Basil's daughter, Penelope.

"My ex-wife even got the *dogs*," said Basil, mournfully.

"I'm sorry," said Sylvie.

"Isn't Penelope something? Of course, she's bigger now."

Sylvie nodded. She could not find words, so reached for his hand.

———

WHILE SHE HAD BEEN snooping around, Basil had set a picnic table in the yard. Sylvie gazed over the water as she ate, and they fell into an easy banter. Basil returned to what she'd said before, about how being the "baby of the family" had defined her, asking her to explain. "I guess," she said, placing her fork down on her empty plate, "Maybe since our mom was . . . kind of . . . *mean*, it was up to us sisters to take care of each other. I never felt like I could rest or take a break. Because they might need me."

"Do you still feel that way?" said Basil.

"Yes," said Sylvie. "It doesn't make any sense—we don't even talk to each other that much, but yes, I still feel that way."

They watched the bay in silence. "Do they take care of you?" asked Basil.

Sylvie didn't answer. In truth, they did not. Sylvie took care of herself.

AND NOW SHE WAS going to marry Basil. She would move into the tiny cabin on waterfront acreage worth a zillion dollars. They could read together every evening, and the housekeeper would leave warm, delicious food in the oven, and Sylvie could kiss Basil anytime, anywhere, and forever. It was truly not about money.

(Was it about sex and more sex and oceanfront sex? Possibly so.)

Sylvie dialed her sister's landline. Allison had a cell she always lost and rarely used and a wall phone with a rotary dial and a curly cord and a satisfyingly heavy earpiece. Sylvie decided news of a marriage should come through the wall phone. She bit her lip as Allison's phone began to ring. One, two, three, four rings. After ring number five, Sylvie gave up.

Next was Vicky, who lived in Brooklyn. Vicky was always too busy to talk and prefaced even her calls *to* Sylvie with "I don't have time to talk but. . . ." Vicky never answered and didn't answer now. When her assertive, somewhat bossy message came on—*Leave a message for Victoria Peacock after the tone*—Sylvie cut the line.

Deflated, Sylvie didn't try her mother, Donna. She knew from experience that Donna was just going to make her feel crappy.

Impulsively, Sylvie composed a text message about her engagement. "I deserve this," she told herself as she stared at the words. Her heart hammered in her ribcage.

What about Alexander? said the voice in her mind.

"Alexander is dead," she told herself. She added, to her sisters, to her mother, to herself, "I am not a gold digger. I am a librarian."

Her thumb hovered over the "Send" button.

PHOTO: © CORY RYAN

AMANDA EYRE WARD IS the *New York Times* bestselling author of seven novels including *The Jetsetters*, a Reese's Book Club x Hello Sunshine pick. She lives in Austin, Texas, with her family.

amandaward.com
Twitter: @amandaeyreward
Instagram: @amandaeyreward

Find Amanda Eyre Ward on Facebook